The Wrecking Squad

The Wrecking Squad Book 1

Nick Snape

Copyright © 2025 by Nick Snape

This is a work of fiction. Names, characters, places, and incidents either are the product of the author's imagination or are used fictitiously. Any resemblance to actual persons, living or dead, events, or locales is entirely coincidental.

All rights reserved. No part of this book may be reproduced or used in any manner without written permission of the copyright owner except for the use of quotations in a book review. For more information please use:nick@nicksnape.com

First Edition

First edition March 2025

Book Cover by Getcovers.com

www.nicksnape.com

(No generative artificial intelligence (AI) was used in the production of this work. The author expressly prohibits the use of this publication as training data for AI technologies or large language models (LLMs) for generative purposes. The author reserves all rights to license uses of this work for generative AI training and the development of LLMs.)

Also by Nick Snape

Weapons of Choice Series
Hostile Contact

Return Protocol

Zuri's War

Finn's War

Alien Rebirth

Invasive Species

Legion Earth

Nemesis Earth

The Wrecking Squad Series
The Wrecking Squad

Butcher's Folly

Warmonger's Wrath

The Scorching Standalones
The World in My Hands

Just Press Play

Warriors of Spirit and Bone
A Dragon of the Veil

A City of Ashes

A Queen in Blood

PRAISE FOR THE AUTHOR

'*A masterful voice in modern sci-fi*' **SPR**

'*Nick Snape's creative storytelling, rich world-building, and engaging characters make this book an unforgettable journey.*' **Literary Titan**

'*Stunning series. Very highly recommended.*' **Goodreads**

'*Sci-fi with pace, heart and unafraid to tackle deeper questions of what it means to be human.*' **Amazon Customer**

'*Wildly creative*' **Self-Publishing Review**

For Martin
For being the voice across the void

Chapter 1

"This is Karal Mining Control. Come back RCKN5QD." The comms crackled. Rebekah glanced over to Savvo, who deliberately stared ahead and tried not to catch her eye. "You listening Wrecking Squad? We got some work to do." The flicker of a smile at the corner of his mouth betrayed her co-pilot, and Rebekah looked to the roof of the *Sunstar*'s small cockpit in exasperation.

She turned the comms relay on. "Crew. If you insist on giving us an inane handle, Trent-fuckwit-Pike, then it's Wrecking *Crew*."

"Hey, I just work with what I have. VERT gave you the ID Code. Can't blame the messenger."

Rebekah growled, allowing every nuance to echo across comms and into the spatial void between Pike's ears. The man couldn't give a shit as he doled out his orders from Karal's Mining Control HQ that rotated amid the Minx asteroid family. Now mined clean, they had drilled out the core of three of the largest and spun them up to provide a modicum of gravity for those who worked this section of the asteroid field. Not that Pike ever left his little piece of paradise. He, his team and VERT, the Karal oversight computer, pulled the strings of their mining web from the comfort of

M1, while the miners and the repair crews frequented the tunnels of the imaginatively named Minx 2 and 3 asteroids.

Rebekah sighed, ignoring Savvo's lopsided grin. "What's the job, Pike? We're beat after a fourteen-day run. Every mining bot on ZY1 needed some form of repair. We were working 18-hour straight days."

"I know, Bek. And your report says you're towing the autoship *Zenati* in for overhaul. But you're the only crew in the air, so to speak, and we got us a little problem. Be worth your while. I know you'd like the money." Pike's tone set Rebekah's thoughts up and running. He never spoke of money, just contracts. Savvo turned to face her, one eyebrow raised quizzically.

Rebekah quietened the comms. "Go and run a sweep of the local frequencies. See what the chat is," she said, flicking her head towards the auxiliary comm unit. A second thought crept in. "And the twins ... whatever they can find. I smell something *expensive*."

"On it," said Savvo, unbuckling. His boots clamped to the floor, the click and thud of each step on the metalled deck disappearing along the corridor as he left.

She clicked the comms back on, trying to suppress the hope of a good score. "Go on, Pike. Hit me with it. You never mention money, so this has to be something special."

"Hah. Piqued your interest, did I Bek?" She winced, ignoring the hated nickname. "Autoship *Hatton* is hauling its payload our way from D5. It's been a little misaligned for a week, and every time my engineers get it back on track, the navcom glitches again within a few hours. Your burn is currently in that direction, and well ... you're the nearest."

"Not a problem if it's a few days. Any longer and we're talking about an issue." Rebekah glanced back as Savvo re-entered, his face troubled. She ignored him for now.

"Days? No, you don't understand. We thought we had it sorted, but now it has realigned again. It's only a few hours out. Kind of need something done now, or it'll miss its berth on M4's docking station." Pike sounded strained, a tension Rebekah had not heard once in the three years the crew had worked for Karal.

She clicked off the comms, eyeing Savvo, who seemed agitated. "Spit it out. I'm flying blind here and we could miss out on a huge score. Hours, he says."

Savvo scrunched up his lips, giving a little shake of his head. "Twins are scanning now. The chat is full of wild shit. They've been tracking the *Hatton* for over a week. Skinflint bastards wouldn't send out a repair team when it was far out, and now they're panicking 'cos everything they've tried has gone to crap. Get this, they've evacuated M4. Got them all hanging in space."

"Damn," said Rebekah, her mind playing over the consequences. And the cost. "I want to know what the payload's worth. Now." Savvo grinned, tutting as he clanked out the door and headed midships for the twin's cabin.

"Okay, Pike. Send me the nav-plan, the expected route and current pathway. I need mass, speed, acceleration rate and all the changes you've tried. And then I'll think on it." She waited, trying to suppress a grin. The glow of the console gave a healthy amber sheen to her skin, but it was her brown eyes that shone right now.

"There ain't no time to think, Bek. This needs doing now. I tell you what, how about I scrub ten percent off the remaining loan you took against your ship?" Her mind reeled a little. Ten percent.

"Twenty percent. And that's a starting figure to be revised once I have the data..." she trailed off – the slate Savvo had dropped on the console containing enough zeroes to give her palpitations. Sweat broke out on her brow. "Screw that, Pike. The *Hatton* is carrying platinum, rhodium ... shit, all the PGMs. Fifty percent. And that goes up depending on the assessed danger level to my crew using the Karal Calc. Get me?"

"I ..." The comms went briefly silent. "VERT authorises the deal. Verbal contract confirmed by Trent Pike, status Mining Command, ID Code classified."

"Contract confirmed. Rebekah Khan, captain of the *Sunstar* under Karal ID Code RCKN5QD." Rebekah tried to keep the joy from her voice, but it was a struggle. Savvo tapped her on the shoulder and pointed to the data that flooded his console screen.

"We will drop the *Zenati*, Pike. She has enough fuel to bring about a slow to dead stop in a few hours. Well within recovery range. Be in touch once we have a burn plan." Rebekah clicked off the comms after his confirmation and spun her pilot's chair to take in Savvo's grin.

"Fifty bloody percent? I can't ... I can't believe it," he said. Unable to keep still, his fingers drummed on the console as he scanned the previous data. "Really?"

"It'll be more once we get a risk to crew assessment. There's no way this is going to be easy. Pike is in a panic. Lose a payload like that into the black, they'll have to send out chasers to recover it. Their costs will spiral." She paused, wiping her brow before running fingers through her close-cropped hair. "Crew meet in five minutes. Get the data out to everyone."

"Twins?" replied Savvo, as he pulled his eyes away from the data stream.

"Time to earn their keep."

Rebekah placed the slate precisely on the galley table, with her coffee flask at the top and to the right, where it always sat. The crew filed in one by one, though she kept her eyes on the data streaming through the slate as the navcom made its calculations.

Hendricks sat opposite, the engineer in her early forties and the eldest of the crew. Her gnarled fingers betrayed a steady hand and temperament.

Well, mostly. Arin sat next to her, red hair and alabaster skin a testament to his heritage, or as he put it, the latent gene that popped up in his family whenever they were missing a black sheep. He was Hendricks' right hand, and she kept him on a leash. The younger man was the risk taker every crew needed when shit was going down in the madness of space – but only when allowed.

Rebekah glanced up and smiled at them both as they nursed their divergent tastes in coffee. One white and packed with sugar, the other as black as space. "We good?" she said.

Hendricks grimaced. "The engines are as sweet as a nut. Purring," she replied.

"A-okay," added Arin with a wink.

Rebekah shook her head. The wry smile the mismatched pair always sparked in her breaking out. Savvo walked into the galley, stepping his large frame aside as the twins followed in his wake. Whip thin, skin achingly pale and their hair shockingly white. The girls sat on the two chairs Rebekah had locked down on the deck for them. This was a rare visit, but they had followed orders, which was a good sign. Perhaps the call for the sensor sweep had garnered their interest – or what it had discovered.

Her crew. Every one of them needing each other.

"We are in a short time frame. So here goes. We have a chance to pay off half the loan on the ship. Maybe more if we can up the Karal Calc. From the moment we encounter the *Hatton*, you will be recording. Understand? From then on, Heki and Tremil, you are to remain in quarters and only use the internal comms coded HT2."

"HT?" said Arin. "Don't tell me – hammer and tongs, right?" Both twins raised an eyebrow at Arin, the glint of their eyes combined with a sour expression causing instant quiet in the sub-engineer.

"Stow it, Arin. Are we clear?" The twins nodded. "Good. We are on a steady burn and curving to match the *Hatton*'s flight path. If they'd contacted us a day ago, this would be a simple catch and snatch. Right now, we need to work on a navcom hack from the *Sunstar*, with a backup override plan for the autoship's auxiliary thrusters. Should both those fail, we blow their engines and plant the emergency autodrive."

"There's no way they'll stop it on their own," said Hendricks, and she took a sip of sugar-filled coffee before continuing. "Not in time."

"No. We program the drive to bring it back into the asteroid field. Or at worse, slow it down so the chasers can fetch it. We can't let the opportunity pass. This goes right, the payday is massive. If we manage to keep the *Hatton* inside their claimed space, we save Karal a fortune," said Rebekah.

"And if not, and the other companies get wind, we'll have negated the usual terms and get nothing but an hourly bloody fee and fuel costs," added Savvo, who leant, arms crossed, against the back wall.

"Exactly. Okay, HT, I want you both on the navcom interface. Acquire standard recovery crew access for us, and I sent you data on the navigation glitch. I want an analysis of that and any suggested patch you can devise. Hendricks, you're on the override of the thrusters, and Savvo, prep the autodrives and any additional fuel requirements. You have forty-five minutes before I need whispers on your plans. That's a go, people." Rebekah stood, only for Arin to raise his hand. Her eyes rolled, but she had to admit he was right, though she'd planned to have that conversation a little more privately.

"And me?"

"I need you to prep ZZ3 and the required drive disengagement explosives."

"Woah, hang on there, Captain. What do you mean?" Arin stood; fists balled. She knew his usual signs. Tough.

"If we have to, ZZ3 will blow the engines. Simple." She never let her eyes drop from his, and waited him out.

"But ..."

"Do your job right, and ZZ3 will come through it. Otherwise, ..." Savvo said, and mimed an explosion, ready to take Arin's heat as a second-in-command should.

Arin stared, but the fight went out of his eyes. "To you, it's just a robot," he muttered, walking away. Hendricks slapped him on the shoulders, looking back to wink towards Rebekah and Savvo.

"Is it possible to love a bot too much?" said Savvo as he followed them out, heading for the recovery bay and its collection of salvage equipment.

"I'd say he crossed that line a long time ago," replied Rebekah, just loud enough that Savvo heard and gave a thumbs up over his shoulder in reply. She entered the cockpit, switching on the screen to bring up the latest image of the autoship. "Just hope we haven't."

Chapter 2

The *Sunstar*'s engines tuned down, the burn steadily reducing. Rebekah drew the ship closer to the *Hatton* as their pace aligned, pleased to see that despite all the supposed issues it had suffered, the autoship remained stable in its flight. At its centre sat a huge cargo bay which, by all the data, was packed with enough PMG assets to give a good-sized planetary economy a run for its money. There was no debris, no signs of impact. Whatever was wrong, a quick visual survey run through the *Sunstar*'s computer matched everything Pike had sent them.

It was beginning to gnaw at her.

"We are in the pipe," she said over the internal comms. "HT, you're up. Report by HT2 only. Hendricks and Arin, I want your progress reports in five minutes. Get us in."

She couldn't just wait for her crew. She never could, despite their time together on the asteroid belt, and all the years before that. Rebekah ran through every option, filing away tangents into those portions of her brain where a wired implant, her chip, supplemented memory.

"Options, options," she said, staring into the distance when the incessant click of magboots echoed along the corridor.

Savvo report in. "I've got *Spot* ready. Remotes are working great. Placement of the autodrive will change by the second, and the closer we get ..."

"The less likely we can fulfil the contract. Yeah, I know." The click of the internal comms drew her attention.

"Captain." One of the HT twins' voices – no one could tell which – filled her ears. The monotone drone remained consistent whenever they were on comms, with little emotion to give a clue beyond the words. Face to face, there was a richer depth to them both, though it was still well below human standards. Not a surprise, but she had to change her tack – almost as if communicating with the ship's computer. "We have navcom access at recovery crew level."

"And?" She caught herself, pushing away the frustration. "Can you make the relevant changes?"

"We have inputted the expected pathway. This has been accepted, and subsequently the changes made. But these have not been actioned." There was no clue in the voice as to why, or whether, they had a plan to do something about that.

"Can you dig any further?" she nudged.

"Not at the current access level."

"But you could ... you know, go deeper?" Rebekah pushed, cautious because it was the first time she'd asked anything of the twins beyond normal procedure.

"Absolutely, if we have the order, Captain."

"Could you hide your tracks?" Rebekah mouthed a prayer to any god that professed luck as their major foundation.

"Yes. Is that an order, too?" came back the monotone. She couldn't decide if they were looking for permission, or simply ensuring they adhered to the procedure expected of 'crew'.

"Yes, on both counts. Dig, find out why the changes are not actioned, countermand that issue if you can, and tell me all about it. And fast, HT.

Otherwise I'm sending ZZ3 to that ship and things get real dangerous real quick." The comms clicked off.

"Hendricks?"

"Locked out," came the terse reply. "No access allowed. I think Pike's team has triggered the failsafe. Screwed. Maybe I could do more if I was on that tin can."

"Not happening, Hendricks. Too long out of a suit. What about the auxiliary thrusters?"

"Same. Need to be hands on. Are you going to need them on the current trajectory? What about Savvo?"

Savvo clicked in, "I have a twenty-minute window to push the *Hatton* towards a slow stop. That's closing in on impossible. With the thrusters, make that forty. Otherwise, we're looking at guiding it away and Plan B, trying to keep the bloody thing inside Karal space."

Decision time.

Fifty percent.

Shit. With what she was thinking, maybe half that again in Calc.

"Arin. You and ZZ3 are up." She could feel the tension over the comms. The judgement from Hendricks and Savvo. That's why she was captain. She could face the hard decisions. "I can't order you, Arin, but..."

The comms clicked over. "Oh yes. I'm in. Arin is on duty! Suiting up, El Capitaine. This is going to be a rush."

Hendricks slapped the buckle home, bashing each and every joint of the spacesuit with far more gusto than Arin appreciated.

"Ow, ow, ow, old timer. I'd quite like to be in one piece when I set off, never mind when I get back." Arin grinned, his face flushed with excitement, but there was a warmth in his gaze towards the engineer. He placed a hand on her shoulder and tilted his neck, the suit mirroring his movement. "Now you keep my coffee warm and my Danish ready, you understand? Stop your worrying."

"No risks," she spat back, her lips tight. "You hear me? This ain't no film. Procedure. To–the–fucking–letter. Get me?"

Arin saluted. "Yes ma'am."

She slapped his helmet, tutting. Arin only grinned in response and tapped a button on his wrist. Behind the engineer, a figure creaked, its large body rising from the deck and unfurling like a fabled gorilla from its nest – only one twice the normal size, and four times as strong. The eyes glowed an eerie red. The mouth Arin had painted on, however, smiled back with a wide, toothless grin.

"Ready ZZ3?" Arin said.

"Affirmative, oh great leader," came back the mechanical voice.

"Great leader?" said Hendricks, shaking her head. "For fuck's sake." She wrapped the explosive pack around the lumbering robot's midriff, and Arin ordered the bot to lower itself to the deck so she could attach the shoulder straps. Hendricks left and cycled the bay airlock, her face stoic as she waited for the door to close. Arin winked, but she refused to acknowledge it.

ZZ3 stepped forward, and Arin felt the bot's second set of arms clamp about his suit and lock into place. "In three, two, one ... punch it."

The bay doors opened, and ZZ3 engaged thrusters. Man and machine exiting in unison. A second set of thrusters kicked in, and the bot steered towards the autoship in the distance.

"Running secondary systems check," announced Arin. "As per procedure outlined on she-who-must-be-obeyed's list of priorities. I am in the green. Come back, *Sunstar*."

"I have you, Arin. All green from here. Savvo has the *Sunspot* ready to launch."

"Affir-ma-tive," replied Arin. "In the pipe, eh ZZ3?"

"Yes, oh great leader. We are on target. ETA five minutes. Four minutes until pinion launch if required," replied the bot.

Arin kept his focus ahead, and as they closed in on the autoship, checked his feed several times for any anomalies. All scans matched, confirming no debris was being thrown about, which was a space crew's worst nightmare. Within a hundred metres, ZZ3 prepped the pinion gun, and Arin knew the bot would engage it should any concerns get flagged.

The ship seemed almost peaceful, serene. The glint of its metal hull welcome as he neared. An alert sounded, flashing yellow. In the vagaries of space, something was affecting their trajectory and ZZ3 fired. The powerful projectile whipped outwards and struck near the centre of the designated ten-metre circle on the autoship's hull. The proximity systems kicked in, and the pinion clamped on like a limpet with a thin cord trailing back to ZZ3.

"Secured," said the bot, and they reeled their way towards the ship. Once clamped on, the bot's systems aligned to the ship's, and the airlock opened. Arin detached, and with a gentle pat on ZZ3's arm, guided himself into the airlock. Only then did he look back, a worried frown upon his face. The engines were a volatile element ZZ3 had to deal with. The autoships were designed to run themselves, and had numerous fail-safes built in should things go wrong. That included the ability to blow the engines clear of the ship, but after a few incidents when this had occurred due to software glitches, the recovery crews now carried the explosives. A rare event, and the *Sunstar*'s – and ZZ3's – first.

"Take care. That's an order," Arin said, and spun about to head inwards. The airlock was currently redundant. Present only should a crew need to board and undertake long-term repairs without a suit.

He eye-clicked, and his HUD threw up an internal schematic of the *Hatton*. With a second click, a lovely green line identified his route to the auxiliary control room.

"I'm in," he said over comms. "Headed towards the control room."

"*Sunspot* is away," cut in Savvo. "Let's get this done and you bloody out of there, Arin."

Arin clanked on; his magboots' click only detectable through the haptic sensors of his suit. Reassuring, nonetheless. Floating about an out-of-control tin can that was about to have its engines blown, was not something he wanted to experience. Especially for a second time.

He locked the memory of the dropship crash away. "Focus, dickhead." He checked the HUD and took left and right turns down the ultra-tight corridor. No point in wasting space. On a third turn, the corridor was filled with an inert repair bot, its many limbs flat against its wide hull.

"Shit." He ran a scan, the suit judging he had about three centimetres clearance in the midriff. He sidled in, compressing the suit a little to add extra leeway. Halfway through and the bot flinched, a tremor running along the nearest robotic limb.

"Fuck, no," Arin said, and rocked back left, the way he'd come, then hurled himself to the right as he released his boots. He sailed through the gap, and came to a sudden stop. The helmet alarms hit yellow, then red. The HUD flashed a specific warning about his ankle, one the pain agreed with as something squeezed.

"Divert power," he murmured, and eye-clicked the relevant switch. The suit expanded around his lower leg, relieving the pressure.

"Arin," came Rebekah's voice. "That is not green, I see."

"Fucking repair bot," he gasped, and looked back. The bot had hold of his ankle, and two more limbs twitched, one glowing with internal heat. "And a bloody soldering iron—"

"What?"

Arin didn't reply. The tip of the snaking limb rapidly changed to white hot and whipped out towards him. Instinctively, he raised an arm, blocking the appendage. The tip seared into the forearm of his suit. Red turned full scarlet, warnings of suit failure filling the heads-up display.

"Rebekah ..." he said, but he needed help now. "ZZ3 protocol 'save your glorious leader', action code Arin. Now."

"Confirmed," came the robotic reply, but Arin couldn't wait. Without leverage, he was screwed. With the first eye-click, he engaged his boots to maximum, swivelling enough so they clamped down with a jar to his knees and feet. The pressure on his ankle eased, but didn't release. With no time to check, his left arm rammed into the offending soldering limb. His flat palm met resistance, and a second eye-click powered a surge to his shoulder and elbow motors. The wrench hurt like hell, but the limb snapped away, and he shoved it into the corridor wall. Blaring filled his suit as it began to depressurise.

"Fucking choices," he shouted. He released his right boot and slammed it down onto the extended limb gripping his ankle. A second heel plant and something gave. The grip relaxed, and he pulled his left boot away.

The suit's self-repair kicked in, and the hole began to seal. With no time to check on the likelihood of success, he turned away, throwing himself along the corridor before the soldering limb attacked again. It whipped past his visor, charring the wall and melting a scar along the clean surface. A strike to his hip followed, sending him into a flat spin. No alarm sounded, and he took a breath as he whirled. There, in the ramped corridor, was the upper half of ZZ3. The hulking machine had left its lower limbs somewhere, and dragged itself at pace through the tight corridors. Two massive hands held the offending limbs in a vice-like grip, and the bot shoved the soldering limb into the repair robot's hull. Arin imagined an electronic scream as the bot shook violently, flame flaring inside as gases and melted electronics mixed. With a yank, ZZ3 tore the limbs free, peering down the corridor as the repair bot died.

"Thanks, ZZ3," said Arin, and grasped a handhold before engaging his boots. He clamped to the deck, the sudden violence hitting home as he blinked towards his saviour. "Not a bad job."

"HUD Interface states, with scrubbing, you have only thirty minutes of air available," came the reply. ZZ3 extended its arm, releasing an emergency oxygen cannister that floated gently his way.

Arin caught it and nodded towards the robot as if it was crew.

Of course it was crew.

One of the team. The squad. And not a sacrificial lamb to the god of money if he could help it.

"Clear my path back and return to the objective, ZZ3."

"Yes, glorious leader."

"Too right. Back in the green, Captain. You see the feed? That's got to be worth a bit of Calc," said Arin, checking his HUD for Rebekah's reaction. The slight visual lag left him with her concerned face. It somehow warmed him to know she had his back, as always.

"I'd rather you were alive, dickhead. But yeah," Rebekah said. "When this is done, I want to know what makes a repair bot malfunction like that."

"Me too."

Chapter 3

"HT?" Rebekah said, aware she was addressing the twins as one over the comms and filing that away for later. "Where we at?"

"Sorry?" came the terse reply. "How is that relevant?"

She mentally kicked herself. "The navcom? Are you any closer to resolving the issue?"

"No. We have isolated the command structure and the offending algorithm. But it is self-perpetuating. There is a trigger program rebuilding it every time we act, buried deep within the architecture of the system. Or …" Rebekah blinked. If it had been Savvo, even Arin, she would have sworn they were delaying for dramatic effect. But not one of the twins. "… perhaps an external module."

"Sabotage?" Rebekah said out loud.

"So it would seem."

She thought for a moment. "Download any evidence which hints that way and … from the repair bot, too? If there's any remote connection left after ZZ3 dismantled it, see if you can scrape any data."

"Repair bot?" came the monotone reply as Rebekah sent the visual recording. "Ah. That would appear to be against its protocols. We will see."

Rebekah sat back, eyeing Arin's feed as he entered the auxiliary systems compartment. Again, a sparse, functional space, with barely the room to move about. He clamped to the floor in front of the console, thick fingers flying over the big keyboard that had been specifically designed for access in a spacesuit. Something caught Rebekah's eye about five centimetres to the side of the board, and she adjusted Arin's camera angle, zooming in. Odd.

"Arin," she whispered, then said it louder. "Arin, come back. Speak to me."

"Nearly in, Captain," he said. "You looking over my shoulder? I mean, it's kind of creepy."

"Stow it. What's that to the left of the console?" she said, a slight frown on her face.

"Where ... ah." She watched as Arin moved in closer, lowering his head. A little apprehension fluttered in her stomach as he reached out, but it was the only way. She flicked to the right screen, bringing up his HUD data. His suit probe absorbed a portion of the matter piled beside the keyboard. Piled. In space, nothing should be in a pile unless it had magnetic or possibly electrostatic properties.

"Damn ...," she mouthed. "You recognise that signature?"

"No ... wait. You mean ... shit, Rebekah." Arin stepped away from the console, his heart rate escalating. The eye-click showed he was running a full suit scan. She felt powerless, unable to even count the seconds. If it came back he was infected, their options were limited to two with the resources at hand. Abandonment, or manipulate ZZ3 somehow. She flinched as the data swamped her screen.

"I'm clear," Arin said.

Rebekah choked in relief. "Step away," she said. "Go now. You get any of those little nanite bastards on your suit, I'll have to leave you. You know that."

Arin's feed swept the keyboard, and to her horror, fell upon the spot where the pile had been. Nothing remained. Not even a telltale smudge where the probe had touched it.

"But the ship?" he said, though he followed orders, backing away from the console. "The fifty percent."

"Fifty percent of dead. They're banned, Arin. For good reason. There are war criminals out there who baulk at their use." She swore. "We need to do this a different way. We restart the visual feed, scrub what just happened and deal with the data analysis later. Edit point one." She eased out a breath to calm her heart. What did they used to call this? Catch-22. If Karal realised her crew not only knew about nanites, but also recognised them, they were in deep trouble. Yet, if they carried on regardless, who knows what the little shits were programmed to do? She'd seen them eat away a spacesuit, while the wearer waited for their death. And the *Sligo*? She shuddered. Two hundred dead as they dismembered the life support.

"Edit point two," Arin said. His feed went still as he paused, Rebekah waiting on his first words. "Captain? You seeing this? There's interference on the feed." Arin slapped the camera, illustrating the lie.

"Lost you there a second, Arin. How's it looking?"

"Console's locked. I can't get in. You listening in, Hendricks?"

"I am," Hendricks replied, the tone steady and very unlike her usual drawl. Rebekah recognised tension when she heard it. It was her job. "If that console's locked, and the navcom is screwed then we should blow both to prevent any more thruster adjustments. That leaves us with the main engines. ZZ3 needs to remove those ASAP."

"And then I work my magic," added Savvo. "We're on this, Captain."

"So, we're talking Plan B, containment to Karal space. Get going Arin. You have … ten minutes on my mark … Mark."

Arin shifted his utility belt and selected the back pouch. He removed a small package, smiling to himself while ensuring his hands were clear of the camera feed. Karal-issue explosives were powerful, designed to deal various yields in a set of eight different directions. Electronically adjusted and triggered, and completely useless if a nanite took a fancy to it.

He rubbed a thumb over the chem explosive, his own design, and stared at the console with trepidation. A simple act to place it and set the fuse. But he needed to be close. He pushed in a simple magnet, and sidled up, shoving the explosive towards the lower part of the controls while ensuring his feed looked elsewhere. He calmed his thoughts, erasing every sensation but the gentle float of the pack until it neared the metal casing. Arin imagined the soft clunk as it attached, and set his HUD timer as he spun and headed down the corridor, upping the servos on his suit.

He bypassed the crushed repair bot, breathing hard with the effort it took to move at pace within the confines of a suit. Yeah, the servo-motors helped, but his muscle memory had long forgotten the different type of movements required when pounding from maglock to maglock on the deck. He briefly considered flying, but that was inherently dangerous.

Taking the four turns his HUD indicated, he reached the bridge door. The suit linked, and to his relief, it slid open. "I'm in," he said, receiving an affirmative from Rebekah. He glanced at the countdown, twisting his neck nervously before entering.

"Switching over to ... analysis," said Rebekah in his ear. "I'll monitor your data feed as we can't trust the navcom."

It was what she left unsaid that mattered. In the background, Rebekah would be analysing whatever his suit detected in the room. She had his back.

He visually scanned the bridge. Or as near to a bridge as an autoship got. The external access consoles for each element of the ship were all jammed in tight. He could see none of the powder residue, but the odd telltale smudge here and there was enough to set his senses reeling.

"I have a heart spike, Arin. I can't detect any reason for it," said Rebekah, making him aware the atmosphere was clear of any threat. "You okay?"

"Do you know the last time I had to run in one of these, Captain?" He let out a few extra breaths for effect.

"Diet and extra training for you," she replied.

"After we celebrate getting Pike off our back. I mean fifty percent, that repair bot's got to be worth at least another … say twenty percent in Calc. I felt really threatened, you know. I'm sure I pissed myself. Without ZZ3 …" He flinched, realising he had revealed the personal safety protocol he'd added to the robot over the feed. He walked over to the navcom as he spoke, "I'd have had a soldering iron probe up where the sun don't shine."

Rebekah was letting him ramble. He took that as a sign his tinkering would be forgiven, and withdrew a second explosive without looking. He worked by touch, keeping the feed steady. Once ready, he glanced to the countdown. Four minutes, easy. He let the explosive go, and it clamped to the side of the navcom. Satisfied, he turned to leave as the door shut. A single flash of red above it set a stone in his stomach. It wasn't that it closed, more the emergency seal that followed.

The ship shook.

"Rebekah …"

"What the hell? Arin … Arin. HT have stated the navcom just made a huge adjustment. As soon as you opened the door."

"Eh?"

"It's a straight path. An alteration of five degrees in the flight plan and the bastard thing is headed straight for Karal H-bloody-Q."

"Space is too bloody big for coincidences," said Arin, using one of Hendricks' favourite phrases. It was all rapidly going to hell in a handcart. That was another.

"Engine release in five, four, ..." said ZZ3.

"Rebekah, the door seal has activated."

"Three, two, ..." continued ZZ3.

Vibrations rippled through the deck, the haptic sensors in his boot playing merry hell with Arin's apprehension.

"One ... There she blows ..." said ZZ3 with finality. "Mission complete, oh great leader."

"Say again, Arin. I had ZZ3's comms on override."

"The door is sealed."

"That's what it's supposed to do. Oh." She had obviously checked her feed. "But with you on the outside. Shit. ZZ3 ... Arin."

"Again? On the way ... oh glorious leader."

Arin checked his countdown. "I have two minutes until the charge blows. Then this room will be full of ... deadly debris. Yes? If Savvo delays beyond that, what happens?"

Rebekah's comms clicked in. "I built in some slack before the navcom change. We had four minutes. Miss that, we miss the window, and all we can do is delay its progress into the black. But now? We're calculating. But we need you safe, what about the charge?"

Arin turned about, blinking as he watched the navcom ripple. No, not a ripple. More a swarm. "I don't have four minutes. You seeing this?" The nanites were surrounding the explosive, so small they were near impossible to see with the naked eye on their own. But they weren't alone, far from it. He scanned the rest of the consoles; it didn't help his mood.

"Shiiit," said Rebekah.

"Not helping."

The door bent inwards, a bulge that was soon joined by a second and third. Arin desperately wanted to get out of the way of what came next, but there was no chance he was stepping any further into that room. A fourth blow and the doorway gave, a crack through which red eyes gleamed. The fifth had him dropping to the deck, the metal door flying overhead to crash into the navcom before spiralling on. Arin could only think how many nanites it would have sent pissed off and weightless into the room.

He ran, squeezing past ZZ3 who stepped aside.

"Run," he shouted, imagining the lummox of a robot staring at him and wondering what all the fuss was about. He'd personally scrubbed any memories of nanites from the bot's memory, just to be sure. "ZZ3, run."

On reaching the final corner, a giant hand scooped him up. Constrained by a second limb, Arin sensed his suit clamp to the bot. With legs dangling, he suddenly sped up, and erupted from the open airlock as the explosion rolled down the corridor. Despite the desperation of the exit, his mind apportioned the danger. ZZ3 would deal with tracking its disengaged lower half floating ahead of them, and their trajectory that meant missing the *Sunstar* and running out of air. His job was to scan for any errant nanites that may have come along for the ride. And pray.

"They're clear," Rebekah said, eyes running over the data feed muddled by local interference. None more so than from the massive engines that had spiralled off into the black somewhere, spilling enough electromagnetic radiation to have shorted any unshielded ship.

"Am I safe to fire up, Captain?" said Savvo.

"We need to correct, Savvo. The course adjustment ..."

"Played into our hands. The first bit of luck. The new angle means I can steer her to a stop near M4. Or at least, use P45 and the debris field as a brake. They're just bits of rock."

Rebekah checked the autodrive's feed, and satisfied it was far enough away, sent the affirmative. "Activate."

She sat back, rubbing her brow clear of the sweat that had emerged there. Wiping her hand on the usual towel, she placed it back where it belonged before taking a slow drink of water from the flask at her side. "Arin. I got nothing here. Talk to me. Please."

There was a long pause filled with the rapidly disappearing drive's static.

"Our great and glorious leader has taken a sedative," came ZZ3's reply. "After confusing one of my circuits with something he didn't like. I tried to explain, but he felt it was for the best."

Rebekah grinned, closing her eyes a second. "Can you tight beam the data scan ZZ3? Just so I can be sure. Savvo will send *Spot* to bring you in."

"Yes, Captain."

Chapter 4

"You hearing that, Pike?" Rebekah opened the comms, ensuring the cheers from her crew filled Pike's ears. "Now that is the sweet sound of success. Except for Arin, who right now is counting our Calc with a little glee in his heart." She watched the *Hatton* glide to a slow stop against the tethered probe. It sat forty clicks out from the welcoming outer scaffold of M4 docking station, gleaming in the distant light from the sun. It spoke of relief, the potential of a debt-free future – and an undercurrent of dread that sat icily around her heart.

"I'm seeing it too, Bek," he replied. "Got to say, I didn't think you had a hope in hell in bringing it home. Every faith you'd keep it in our space, but that's some result."

Rebekah detected the relief in Pike's voice, setting her wondering what would have happened if they'd failed. Karal were a good company overall and looked after their workers on the belt better than most, yet the rumours were that might be changing without a big payload soon. Could this be why the *Hatton* had been sabotaged? But there were cheaper ways to do it, and more likely out on the asteroid belt too. A small rock with enough velocity for instance.

"We'll download the feed when we get chance. Got a lot of radiation from the autodrive when we blew it into the ether, so it'll need a scrub. I'll get on it as soon as we dock." She waited for the usual gripes and got none back.

"Roger that. Your quarters have been upgraded on my word. District 2, Level 4, one week. Don't get so drunk you forget where I housed you. Enjoy the grav. Out."

Rebekah whistled. "Level 4? Shiiit, we got eighty percent standard grav."

She brought the *Sunstar* into the recovery dock of M4, letting the tower's auto system take her the last click and settled into the bay provided. Only two other ships sat on this side of the asteroid waiting for a refuel and restock, or for their crew to finish R&R. Karal ensured each of their different teams got their standard grav requirements, rotating them into quarters that had been relinquished by those going back out to repair the mining bots or to recover equipment that succumbed to the harsh environment. But District 2, that was reserved for those who worked in the lower echelons of management, their only sight of the belt through a screen.

"Crew meet," she sent over the internal comms. "Have I got some banging news for you all." With the docking register complete, Rebekah slipped off her mic and undid her restraints. With a slow stretch, she unlocked the chair and spun about to head off towards the galley. She could already smell the combo of coffee and herbal teas along the corridor. A sign they were eager to get done and off the ship.

She entered, accepting the coffee flask from Savvo and giving the welcome liquid a swirl before a first taste. Once on Minx 2, she planned on spending a few of her hard-earned creds on something a mite stronger.

"Okay, arses on seats. Done with the back slapping?" she said, eyes roaming over each of the crew. The twins were absent as she had expected.

"Good. We need a little dose of reality before we board the shuttle for M2, right?"

"You mean the ..." Arin caught himself, and swept the galley, nodding as he caught sight of the four red LEDs shining from the corner cameras. "... nanites?" He raised an eyebrow. Combining it with a deliberately annoying wink.

"Yes, I mean the nanites. Anyone got any thoughts?" she continued. Everyone shifted in their seats.

"Well," started Savvo, leaning against the galley cupboards, "only the same as you."

"Which is?"

"That it's a jenky way of sabotaging a ship and a repair bot. I mean, this close to the black, they could just have hit the *Hatton* with a bloody rock," he said, eyes flitting up to meet hers. "It stinks of money."

Hendricks shuffled in her seat, making as if to say something, then clamming up.

Rebekah tilted her head towards the older engineer. "I need your insight, Dricks. We're flying a little blind here."

She coughed, then stood up and began to walk and talk like she always did when something bothered her. "I can only see two reasons for using those little bastards. The first is once the job is done, no one can trace them back. Just a residue, and even that will dissipate as soon as it hits any form of atmosphere. We're the only team this side of the belt that would know what it was looking at. I know we can talk about unmonitored rocks and that, but the outcome's—"

"—Unpredictable," said Rebekah, confirming her own thoughts.

The older engineer nodded. "Yeah. So, with the nanites, it definitely happens. And that load ..."

"Just the wealth of a small nation," Arin cut in. "Give or take."

"Exactly. With a reprogrammed navcom you could send the ship to an exact location in the black. Sophisticated piracy." Hendricks stopped her walking and gripped the back of the galley bench as she eyed Rebekah. "Or industrial espionage."

"Hoo-wee, that's some case of paranoia you got there," said Arin. "You still taking those tablets? You know the red ones with the little white stripes?"

"Har bloody har. You tucked ZZ3 in tight before you left?" Hendricks slapped her sub-engineer's shoulder, receiving a grin in return.

Savvo shoved himself away from the cupboards with his back, arms still crossed, wearing a worried frown. "To me it adds up to someone with a lot – and I mean a lot – of money. Big stakes, high players. And we just interfered with their plans."

"So, we're a target, perhaps? Retribution?" mused Rebekah, seeing where Savvo was leading and not liking it.

"We're a *nothing*," interjected Arin. "A spot on their arse. Look, if it's organised crime maybe, and I mean maybe, they'll kick our arses for getting in the way. But that'll make it obvious something shifty was happening, and Karal will go looking. Change their procedures even. If it's a big company, and we know they're a bunch of bastards, doing nothing and making sure we're not in the area next time is the most likely outcome."

"Or an accident," said Hendricks. "As they can happen on the belt, if you know what I mean."

"Okay," Rebekah grimaced. "Look, we stick to pairs. I think we all agree nothing is likely to happen but …"

"Shit happens," said all of them at once.

"Savvo, you got the feed cleaned up?" He nodded in reply. "Mind if I get the twins to give it another scrub?"

"Be my guest. See if they can get rid of Arin shitting himself after he scanned ZZ3. His expression will live with me to the day I die."

"Okay my marvellous crew, now some good news. Our billets ... we got District 2 Level 4. Grav heaven. I've sent the deets to your slates."

Rebekah leant her head against the door of the twins' quarters, calming her thoughts after the galley discussion. She drew in a few slow breaths, and began to run through her latest earworm, playing the lyrics in her mind and visualising the band as if on screen. Once set, she rapped gently on the door and stood back into the camera's view.

"Heki, Tremil. We need to talk," she said.

The door slid back, one of the twins facing her in the white and black diagonally striped skinsuit they both favoured. She had hoped by now they would have discarded their odd choice in clothing, but it seemed they were most comfortable when attired in similar materials they had worn when they found them in the lab.

"Heki?" she said towards the young woman. With her face set flat and unemotional, it was hard to tell them apart.

Her head tilted to the side, pale, almost white skin set with piercing green eyes. "Tremil," she replied, and smiled. It always appeared forced, but after four years in their company, she knew this was as natural as it currently got. There were moments, glimpses of who they could be. Hope.

"Tremil, we need to discuss protocol while we're docked."

Tremil stood aside, a stiff hand gesture showing her inside. Rebekah blinked, suddenly aware that the last time she had entered was when they had carried them both aboard – unconscious and bloody. She walked in, her earworm up to full blast.

The room came as a complete shock. Somewhere in her mind she had expected a sparse, unemotional space. Instead, the walls were covered in pictures of strange landscapes. Trees of all colours and kinds were a standard theme, beautifully drawn, not printed, the pencil marks, even to her unpractised eye, delicate. Loving. Heki sat on her bed, the one that should have been the captain's by right, a sketchpad and well-used pencils at her side. Her slender hands sat in her lap – clasped tight – and Rebekah was suddenly aware that she had invaded their personal space.

"I'm sorry ..." She made to leave, only for Tremil's hand to fall upon her arm. The shock of a touch from one of the twins knocked the earworm from her head, and the desperate need to be loved rolled over her in a wave. She staggered, and Heki rose to take her other arm before she fell. The depth of emotion eased back, becoming a blanket that swaddled instead of drowning Rebekah's mind.

"Stay, please," whispered Heki ... No. Not spoken. The words formed like pictures in her mind as they had back on Bustan 7. Rebekah rebuilt the earworm, and the pressing need reduced even more. Heki stepped away, the smile on her face almost taking Rebekah's breath away. "Sit."

Rebekah did as she was asked, reaching out a hand to check where the bed was before taking her place. Blinking, she caught sight of Heki's current drawing. It was much darker than those adorning the walls. She recognised it instantly, the stark, shadowed cell from which they had rescued her. Or was it Tremil? She couldn't remember – had they even known who was who back then? Both had been in isolation, though in starkly different circumstances.

"We are sorry, Captain. We can ... can tone our emotions down for a limited time when we have to, though it is a strain. We planned ..." Heki looked to Tremil, her eyes pleading.

"We planned for you to see our room. We felt ready to share more of us, but perhaps I should have asked you to wait a little longer," said Tremil, and she took a seat at the old table Savvo had acquired for them on their last but one visit to M2. Rebekah noted the objects organised in rows across the back. The closer she looked, the more she recognised them. They were anime characters, printed and carefully painted.

Arin, and most likely Hendricks.

Sometimes she forgot how much her crew meant to her.

"Thank you," Rebekah said. "For letting me see. Your pictures are beautiful. Stunning."

Both girls sat straighter, the wave of surprise threatening the earworm again before she turned up the internal volume in her mind a notch.

"We thank you," said Heki, and Rebekah could have sworn she wiped away a tear. She suddenly felt exposed, her own emotions rising unwanted in the background. Now was not the time.

"We are in dock," she said, dragging things back to business. "So, we will be off ship. I have sorted provisions, and," she eyed the toys, "connected the systems so you can download whatever you wish. Just …"

"Don't answer the door or the comms unless we hear the code word, nor step out for a tour," repeated the twins in unison. The emotional wave switched, and disappointment sat heavy upon Rebekah's mind. "We know."

"One day," she began, and the girls' expressions changed. They became sterner, stiff. "Sorry … how many times have I said that?"

"Ninety-seven," said Tremil. "And we know there'll be more. But we dreamt of the lab every night when we first arrived. Now, it is so much less. We know that *one day* we will be able to leave because of you all. We will follow procedure."

"Do you have the altered feed?" Rebekah asked as she stood to take her leave.

"Yes. We have done as you asked." Heki pointed to the private captain's console in the corner of the large quarters. It was bedecked with paper flowers. Heki's smile glowed again, so different to Tremil's. "And have removed anything incriminating, and added some radiation blackouts."

The girl blushed. Rebekah had never seen her skin have so much colour. "And Arin's ... episode."

"That'll please him," she grinned, enjoying the moment as the humanity of the girl shone through. She made for the door, turning back as it opened. "Thank you. Is there anything you need?"

"Chocolate," said Tremil. "Always chocolate."

Chapter 5

Savvo plonked the beer down in front of Rebekah, his eyes bleary and red-rimmed. She grabbed it, tipping the glass towards Hendricks and Arin – still amazed at how the liquid stayed within the open glass. "To District 2, Level 4," she said, only a slight slur to her words. "May the grav be with you."

"Captain," said Arin, his words annoyingly clear of any sign of drunkenness. "Are you, perhaps, inebriated?"

"I may well be. If I am, I think I have earned the right."

Arin clinked his glass with hers and downed the remains of his beer. "And I think I am in need of something a little stronger, and perhaps a card game or two. Coming?" Arin nodded towards Hendricks, who sighed in response and rose. She took her beer, raising both eyebrows to Rebekah and Savvo as she made to follow.

"Do you think he'll have the same success? No down-at-heel miners to take advantage of in this district," said Savvo, and he leant back against the plush seat, sighing.

"Possibly fewer beatings." She clinked his glass. "And a might less for me to worry about as a conse…consequ…result."

"Still not able to take your drink?" he laughed. "You had any more thoughts on what we discussed on the *Sunstar*. You know, the ... *issue*."

She frowned briefly. "Trying to enjoy the moment. We could be debt-free, Savvo. No more worries, and the ship ours again. That is something to celebrate. We'd be in serious shit if we lost her – with the twins and all. What would we do? Don't answer that 'cos then we're going to have to do that discussion stuff."

"We can't hide out here forever, Rebekah. Not as we are. Arin ... he chafes under the boredom. Hendricks ..."

"Knows no other life. And you?" she said, eyeing him above the rim of her glass. "You started this conversation."

He shook his head, fingering the glass before taking a pull on his drink. "Got to admit, four years is a long time to be hiding. Will they even still be looking?"

"The Almaar? Let me see ... Were our commanding officers the forgiving type? Mmm. Torture? On more than one occasion. Beatings, spurious orders, selfish and on a permanent ego-trip? Oh yes. And we stole their prize ... and deserted. I think they'll forget about us about the same time the Almaarian sun goes supernova." Rebekah knocked back half her beer, slamming the glass on the table. The noise caused a few customers to turn their way, muttering to themselves behind beautifully-manicured hands.

"As a group. With the twins in tow, I agree. But ..." Savvo's expression turned sour, a frown of surprise at his own words. "Sorry."

"What happens to them if we split up? Where do they go?"

"I was thinking, if we're debt-free ... if, then possibly in a year or so you could buy out my share of the *Sunstar*. I can't do this forever." Savvo stared into his glass, the words drifting off quietly.

"Is it just you?" she asked, her cheeks flushed with a rising anger. "Or the others? Do they want out too?" She stood far too quickly, her chair clattering to the floor. Flushed fingers flexed in and out as she stared at him, but Savvo refused to meet her eyes. Rebekah sensed the other customers were staring, and glanced over to catch the bartender rounding the end of the bar. She huffed, and turned away, heading out the door into the rock-walled corridor. She ignored Savvo's pleas and entered the crowds, heading home as the shuttle bays disgorged the workers from the Karal offices on M1.

Within five minutes the flush had died away, her anger having receded as reality hit home. It was bound to come, and she should have seen it beforehand. If the Calc was high, they could truly be free of the loan they had been saddled with. Buying out the *Mizza*'s contract had left them beholden to Karal. Being debt-free meant an opportunity away from the drudgery of daily life. They'd been crammed together for four years, and before that another three under the black ops arm of the Almaarian army.

The Breakers.

An irony that hadn't left her mind for a single day.

She reached the lift, her muscles tiring a little under the gravity. Giving in to the inevitable, she punched Level 4 and scanned her wrist ID. Within a few seconds the door slid open – and someone slammed into her back. She flailed forward, and arms took an iron grip around her waist, ramming her head into the lift wall. A wave of nausea rode the disorientation in her brain.

The arms let go, and Rebekah rolled onto her back, hand reaching inside her jacket. A heavy boot landed on her elbow. She screamed in frustration, glaring into the eyes of the suit-clad thug who had taken her down. A similarly dressed woman scowled beside him, her face flickering in Rebekah's mind as her activated chip recognised a holo-mask signature.

"Settle down," the woman growled, the words distorted in her brain. More electronic tricks. It gave Rebekah some hope in her alcohol haze. If she didn't know the face, well, perhaps she'd live. "Or Victor here will break that non-grav elbow and perhaps your shoulder with it. Yes?"

Rebekah nodded.

"Good. Now a message from my employer. You interfered today, understand? In our business. For that, there is a price. A warning." The woman mimed an explosion, glee in her holo-masked eyes. "Shame after you and your crew have become so debt-free, all of a sudden. My advice, take your money and go back to whatever hole you crawled out of, understand? You cost me a lot of money, and you live only because my employer says so." She leant down closer. "If it was up to me, I'd have your eyes as a trophy."

Rebekah headbutted the woman squarely on the nose, hoping her chip had got the image right. The crack was pleasing, the response less so as Victor slammed down on her elbow. Rebekah grinned back at him and flicked her other wrist. The embedded blade split her skin, extending out below her hand to ram into his ankle and slice the Achilles tendon. He toppled, Rebekah rolling away, only to receive a double punch to her kidney from behind. Sending a kick backwards, her boots hit something hard, and she wheeled about, bloodied blade ready to strike again.

The woman elbowed the lift controls, one hand palm out, backing away. "I will find you again, you bitch," she sneered, her other hand urging Victor out of the lift. "And I will have those eyes."

"Fuck you," Rebekah replied, and the lift door slid shut. She spat blood on the floor, then slammed her fist into the wall. Annoyed she had let herself be caught cold, but more so about the threat the woman had made.

The *Sunstar*, and the precious cargo that was on board.

"I'm coming," said the monotone voice. ZZ3 gently lifted one of its feet above the metal deck, its four red eyes locked onto the corner of the cockpit entrance. "I *will* find you."

The giggle echoed behind, the robot's head spinning about, its painted mouth now pointing towards the galley. "Are you two tag teaming me? That was a trick to distract me. I've played hide and seek with you frequently enough to know when I am being had."

The robot's head spun back, and he strode forward, deliberately clanging the deck as the heavy foot landed. It caused another giggle, this time ahead and inside the cockpit, the tone somehow different.

"Aha. It's Heki in there. I know that voice." He clanged another boot down, and the laughter spilled out uncontrolled. A third, and silence fell. The robot gripped the sides of the cockpit entrance with both hands and paused before thrusting its head through. "Found you!" The laughter exploded from the comms, accompanied by more directly behind.

"Argghhh," ZZ3 said, mimicking Arin's voice in a mock tirade. The bot's head spun about, its entire body readjusting, joints reversing as if it had turned itself inside out to peer the other way. He ran towards the galley, feet thudding when Heki appeared in the entrance, her tongue sticking out, and the door slid shut.

ZZ3 banged a gentle fist upon the door. "I'm done. You got me," the bot said in Hendricks' voice. "Bang to rights."

The door opened back, and Heki wrapped her arms about the lumbering robot. Its own hand rested on her shoulder, and as Tremil joined, on hers too. The three hugged, two girls and a huge robot, when the alarm resounded through the ship. Red lights shimmered, and the girls released ZZ3, disbelief on their faces.

"It's not us," they said together.

"Nor me," said ZZ3. Tremil's hands flickered with a complex pattern of finger movements. The bot dropped to its haunches, freezing into position. Heki stepped in, her own fingers running through a second algorithm in front of the bot's eyeline. ZZ3 shivered, then rose up in a whirr of motors and hydraulics. The metal hands spun, digits cracking as they flexed. Both girls stepped to the side and ZZ3 clanked through the corridor, heading towards the cargo hold with the twins following behind.

They remained silent as the alarms continued, but moved in unison. When ZZ3 reached the inner cargo bay airlock, Tremil stepped in behind while Heki took a position back down the passageway where the hold monitor screens were housed. Heki pointed to the screen, seeing the bay doors open a crack with three armoured figures entering, their lights blotting out the camera.

Tremil nodded. "ZZ3, engage protection protocol 'Kill the fuckers'. Action code HT." The bot's hands whirred, and as the hold filled with air, Heki opened both airlock doors simultaneously.

ZZ3 went to war.

Chapter 6

Rebekah knelt on the floor, leaning against the refuse robot that purred and beeped away at the side of the corridor. Feet clomped past in a blur, and the likelihood of a concussion dawned. Another wave of dizziness left her flat against the metal deck, an addled mind warning she was about to fall off. Her fingers flexed against the metal grate, and a blade glinted back, only curtailed by a thin line of drying blood along the edge. Automatically she reached inside her jacket and retrieved a plastic wrap. She tore it open with her teeth, managing to hit her mouth on the second attempt. Using the sterilised swab inside, she cleaned the blade's edge, and with a flick of her wrist it snapped back inside her skin. The drill, ingrained over the years, focused her mind, and with a thought, she engaged her chip. A warmth spread through her brain.

"Miss? Miss?" came a voice from someone standing above her. "Are you okay?"

Rebekah glanced up to lock eyes with a little boy, probably of no more than three standard years. His brown eyes and ochre skin shone in the corridor's harsh light, with his hand swallowed by someone she assumed was his dad who waited impatiently for the way ahead to clear. A tear formed at the corner of her eye, and despite the effort and disorientation, she smiled and nodded to the child.

"Yes, I just tripped. Banged my head."

The boy's face screwed up a little, something she took for concern, and he looked up to his father. With his other hand, he yanked at the man's suit trousers. "Father," he said, then repeated it louder. The man looked down, his eyes matching the boys in colour and to her surprise, in sympathy. Patting the boy on the head, he held out a hand.

Rebekah hesitated, then took it, making sure she hid the slit beneath her wrist. By the time she had regained her feet, the suited man held out an obviously pressed and newly laundered handkerchief. "You need that looking at," he said, pointing to the swelling on her temple. "Want us to come with you? There's a med unit one level down."

"No," she said, and despite the nausea, kept her balance. The warmth in her brain was spreading, and she began to remember the timescales of its effects. "I just need to find my crew." And then the next memory slid in. The miming of an explosion. "I must go. Thank you."

She managed to return the handkerchief, the man nonplussed as she shoved it into his hand and staggered away. With a little more focus, she kept on her feet, a distant voice behind asking her to be careful. Luckily, she could remember the one turn she'd taken, and the gentle neon sign of the bar appeared ahead. Rebekah pulled her shoulders back, needing to look calmer than she felt as she approached the security guard with a forced smile. He looked her up and down and was about to speak when a hand lightly touched her shoulder.

"Gana will let you through with me," said the suited man as Rebekah flinched. "Where's your crew? I need to be quick, Stig has only so much patience." He glanced behind, Rebekah following suit to receive a wave from the brown-eyed boy.

"I ... there," she said, pointing towards Savvo's hunched shoulders. She walked the last few steps and flopped onto the bench. Cursing herself, she looked back towards the good Samaritan who had half-turned to head off. "Thank you."

The man nodded in response; his smile warm and he headed out towards his son who had engaged the security guard in conversation.

"What the hell," said Savvo, his hands already on her temple. "You leave my side for five minutes and come back looking like you reenacted Bustan 7 on your own."

"I had some help," she whispered, wincing at Savvo's touch. "We need to get to the *Sunstar*. The twins ... just had a promise we were going to have our ride blown to pieces."

Savvo blinked, his alcohol shrouded mind trying to process Rebekah's words. "The *Sunstar*?" He was up on his feet before finishing the words, the table rocking as his knees struck it. The empty glasses tumbled and rolled to the floor. Rebekah couldn't make up her mind who was in a worse state to protect their ship and its cargo – a captain with a concussion and no weapons, or a second who'd caught her up in the alcohol stakes in the last ten minutes.

It wasn't looking good.

"Call in Arin and Hendricks," she ordered. "I'll check in with the twins, and hope we're in time."

She pulled out her slate, pleased to see it was as robust as the day she'd been issued with it. With two taps she flagged M2's comms system, requesting access. The asteroid's tunnelled rock wasn't the most conducive to communications, and they still had to reach across the hundred clicks or so to the M4 docking bay. The busy signal was greeted with a bout of swearing, and she tried again. On the fifth go, she secured a line, and hailed the *Sunstar*. "Gruesome twosome, this is Lily, come back." She waited, counting the seconds, and repeated. Relief washed over her when the comms clicked, and a monotone voice responded.

"Go ahead, Lily."

"You must lockdown all entryways. Double check all protocols. I have word of an attempt on the *Sunstar*. This is a Code 1, danger to life. Gruesome Twosome, confirm." Rebekah closed her eyes, willing the girls to be okay. Without any inflection in their voices, it was so hard to tell whether their response had been coerced. What would they do if a gun was pointed their way? A memory slid in, half her squad dead upon the floor, and a white lab coat splattered with blood and brains as the Bustan scientist eviscerated his own head to get Heki out. The bastard had deserved worse, but she had hoped the last few years had calmed their minds.

But trauma was so difficult to overcome. Especially in childhood ... as she well knew.

"Spot and Kitty confirm. All protocols are in place. Rebekah ... we may have done something very bad."

Rebekah leant her helmet against the cold hull, the inner plastic soothing her lump that thankfully had stopped throbbing with Savvo's ministrations on the shuttle. Behind, Arin waited impatiently, while Hendricks paced. Only Savvo remained calm, perhaps as a consequence of whatever tablets he'd imbued to clear his mind. Always a medic, even though he indulged too much for her taste.

With a sigh, she placed her gloved hand on the outer plate. The tingle of a scan and the thrum of recognition welcome as the airlock opened. Arin had paid a little extra for the lift platform, all of them having agreed the cargo doors needed to remain closed for now. The screams and pop of limbs still rang in her ears after watching the vid of ZZ3 at work.

The corridor was eerily silent as they emerged helmetless from the airlock. Not knowing what to expect, the hairs on her neck tingled. Adrenaline filled her veins, and Rebekah had to calm her body through the familiar routines of her past. Relying on the chip too soon was a pathway back to the numbness, the time when just one more death than necessary didn't really matter anymore.

With a signal to wait, she rounded the corner, turning left to peer into the galley. Both girls were sat there, faces frozen. Their struggles pervaded the air between them, and Rebekah's earworm kicked in. She turned the volume up in her mind. Somehow, she had to get the twins through the consequences of what lay in the cargo hold, and Rebekah didn't know if she was strong enough. Opening her arms wide, the girls exploded from their seats, arms wrapped around her, sobs shattering the silence. Their need threatened everyone's sanity, and with a dread, she kicked in the chip and the world went numb.

"They are asleep," said Hendricks, and squeezed into the bench, wrapping her hands around the flask of white, heavily sugared coffee. "How long was it last time?"

"Three days," Arin replied, washing his hands and collecting his own flask.

"That was the incident with the *Katrina*'s crew. A minor flare up and years ago," said Hendricks. "Who knows what would have happened if they'd managed to get further than the docking bay that time. Shit."

Savvo sighed, eyes flicking over to where Rebekah should be sat. The toll of the twins' empathic outburst had left her exhausted. He knew she had activated the suppressant wetware, black ops certified to keep you going when all around you fail. Out of habit, he tapped behind his ear, glancing up as both Arin and Hendricks nodded knowingly his way.

"I fucked up," said Savvo, sensing the mood switch. He ran his fingers over his scalp, knowing he had to keep going. To explain. "I told Rebekah I wanted out. Not now, but soon. If the score from the *Hatton* is as big as we think." Savvo met their eyes. "Don't tell me you haven't been thinking about it. We've been out here for bloody years. There's only so much isolation we can take." He took a sip of his tea, trying to avoid their gaze.

Hendricks' hand fell upon his. "I understand. I do. But …"

"The twins. Yeah, I know. What happens to them? If I abandon them to Rebekah, or if we all do, what then?" He took another sip, trying to force the redness from his cheeks and the treachery from his heart.

"We endure," replied Hendricks. "I won't … I can't … leave." Tears welled in Hendricks' eyes. "But I wasn't strong enough then, and I'm not enough on my own now. I owe Rebekah for what she did, and the twins for … bringing me back from the brink. Whatever you decide, Savvo, I'll still be here."

Savvo wiped away the first hint of a tear from the corner of his eye with his thumb, refusing to look at Hendricks, knowing if he did whatever resolve he had built up would crumble. "Where's your mind at Arin?"

"Me? For now, I have a cargo hold to flush, and a pair of twins to interrogate about how the hell they reprogrammed ZZ3. That protocol wiped my pacifist program clean out of its system."

"That's not an answer," said Savvo.

"It's as much as you're going to get." Arin knocked back his black coffee, his usual smirk replaced by a sour expression. "I'll think on it, okay? Is that enough?" He slammed the flask into the recycling pod.

"Arin."

"No, Savvo." Arin rounded on his second-in-command. "We *agreed*. You remember what that means? We all said that when we had doubts, we would talk them through." He jabbed a finger Savvo's way. "Not go off on our own and lay it all on the Captain. For fuck's sake, how much weight can you put on one person? She dragged us back from the pit and allowed us to be human again. Where would we be, Savvo? In a body bag, in the grinder as bad meat or still killing whatever the hell moved in front of us."

"I—" began Savvo, but Arin had turned his back and was halfway down the corridor.

Hendricks rose from her seat, hand reaching for his shoulder, but instead, left it to hover halfway between them.

"Captain," said Savvo, searching Hendricks' face for a shred of sympathy.

"No, Savvo. Not now, and if the truth be told, not then. Just a machine carrying out orders whether they were for good or ill. Arin's right. You should have brought this to us. He will calm down, and then we talk again. But," Hendricks leaned in closer, a mean glint to her eye that shocked Savvo back into the past, "hurt Rebekah any more, and I *will* have something to say, Marine."

Chapter 7

"This is Karal Mining Control, come back RCKN5QD. Rebekah, you there? Why are you not in our nice comfortable quarters right now?" Pike's voice echoed in the cockpit.

Savvo stirred, lifting his head from the galley table, blurry eyed. The crackle from the comms repeated itself. He reached inside his jacket and slid a stim from the box he kept hidden in an internal pocket. After dropping it on his tongue, the tingle of it melting stroked his mind before kicking it awake.

"Wrecking Squad, are you home?" continued the voice.

"Crew," whispered Savvo hoarsely. "Wrecking *Crew*." He walked gingerly into the cockpit, collecting the comms unit. "This is Savvo, Pike. Rough night. I'll wake Rebekah and call back."

"You'd better, she's going to want to hear this." The comms clicked off, and Savvo blew out a ragged sigh to find the smell of his own breath unappetising. "Shit."

"What was that?" said Rebekah from behind, and when Savvo spun about, she glared back having noted the swirl to his eyes. "This early in the morning? Maybe you *should* ditch, Savvo, if you need a stim to keep you going from the moment you wake up."

"About that ... about me."

A raised hand cut him short. "Not now. We have enough crap to deal with after the twins' actions. The rest comes after we know the Calc, then you can cut and run ... or stay."

He nodded, glancing to the floor. "That was Pike. Might be he has the figures? Said you'd want to hear him out and soon." Rebekah took the comms from his hand. "Want me to leave?"

"You're the second. You need to know what's going on if anything happens to me. Sit and shut the hell up." She shook her head with an exasperated smile, and Savvo slid into his chair. "Mining Control. This is RCKN5QD, Pike come back."

"Ah, at last. Why the hell are you sleeping on the ship? I got you the best quarters as a thank you." He sounded contrite, though not as much as she had expected.

"Had some issues on board we had to come back and deal with. Shit happens. We have the rest of the week to enjoy your generosity," she said, and winked at Savvo.

"Well, about that."

"Ah, come on Pike. Don't tell me you're backing out. The one time you've been nice." Rebekah felt her mood shift, but Pike hadn't sounded negative. Something was up.

"I know. I won't make a habit out of it. No, the quarters are there, but you might want to put a belay on that." Rebekah sensed Savvo stiffening, and she looked at him, querying his thoughts. He mouthed 'belay', and his reaction struck home. She had missed it. Not a common term, except in the Marines. Did Pike know?

"And why's that? Is the Calc so high we can move to District 1?" Rebekah kept her voice calm, despite the thud in her chest.

"I have the Calc figure, sending it over now. But I also have someone who wants to talk to you and your crew. They have an offer ... Look, I'm going to be honest. They asked for a rec for a job, said they had heard about your work with the *Hatton*. Offered to buy out a month of your contract with a nice cut for me." Rebekah placed her hands flat on the console, the fingers turning white as she used the pressure to help calm her thoughts. None of what Pike said sounded untoward. Crews were subcontracted all the time. But his honesty?

"Sounds like a catch in there somewhere," she said.

"Ahhh ... up to you. You can *skate* through this and enjoy the quarters. I'd lose my cut, but right now I'm grateful to still have a job after the *Hatton*. But I sent the offer over. Let me know, and if interested I'll set up the meet. Pike out." The comms went dead.

Rebekah made to stand when Savvo grabbed her hand. He had his screen up, the console aglow with its usual green when docked. There were two figures on the monitor and his grip firmed up as he read them aloud.

"There's enough Calc there to pay off..." he began.

"Another forty percent," Rebekah finished, and then she whistled. "And the same again for the job offer, with standard Calc to be added. Split four ways, the baseline is a year's creds. Enough to set you up, if I buy you out."

"Rebekah, you heard Pike. That's army slang he was throwing in there," said Savvo.

"Yeah, I did. SKATE ... *Stay out of trouble. Keep a low profile. Avoid Higher-Ups. Take your time and enjoy yourself.* Either Pike has made us, knows we're ex-army, and he's dropping hints that something stinks, or just hopes we know the parlance," Rebekah said, her eyes not leaving the numbers.

Savvo tapped the screen, deep in thought. "Or we only just noticed he slips into old habits."

"A dickhead. But an intelligent one. It's not a coincidence in my book."

"Sit rep," she said, eyeing the newly created sparkle of the cargo hold. Arin grinned manically, stripping off a pair of gloves and dropping them into the waiting recycle pod.

"I am yet to run a DNA scan, but I'd say the chems have degraded it enough for us to be in the clear. Just need to eject some excess baggage when we hit the astro field again." He let the pod lid flip back and paused a second. She recognised the hunch to his shoulders, the mood he was in. Arin couldn't hide anything from anyone. The old saying was 'your heart on your sleeve', though to her, it was 'baring your soul'.

"Say it," she said, eyes wandering over to ZZ3 whose layer of grime contrasted against the hold. Newly covered in the thin layer, she knew Arin had stripped and cleaned the bot first.

"Say what?"

"*It* ... whatever crap you're hanging out on the washing line. Come on."

"The cracks," he began, "and this offer. Shit, Rebekah, it's like everything at once. Too many thoughts going through my head. Savvo ..."

Rebekah grimaced and turned about as Arin sighed. "Is probably right. We've been out here too long. In a rut of routine where we hide from the truth. We don't even know they're looking for us – for them – anymore. But the job – I'd have jumped at it without Pike's words. And what about Hendricks?"

"What do you mean?"

"Small ship and all that. I assume where she goes, you go." She couldn't help but smile. This game of denial had been a running gag, one that warmed her heart, alongside the joy they took in each other's company.

Arin closed his eyes, lips mumbling.

"Can't hear you?" she said with laughter in her voice, tilting her head and cupping a hand to her ear.

"Don't make me say it … I don't think we're on the same page. She won't leave you, nor the twins, whatever happens." Arin blinked, eyes rising from the deck to meet hers. "And now I might have to actually think about it. The *Hatton*, it was kind of fun. An adrenaline rush. The only thing I miss from the Breakers. Being on the edge … you know."

Rebekah nodded, and patted ZZ3 on one of his metal limbs. "Whatever you decide, ZZ3 stays. You need to understand that. If I am to be alone, then I will need some muscle. Perhaps it's a good thing the twins stripped out the pacifist protocol."

"I put it back. Too dangerous to have a full warbot around."

"Come in, Rebekah," said Savvo over comms. "Pike on the line. He sounds … nervous."

"Go ahead, Pike. What's the problem, found a glitch in the Calc?"

"I sent that, all done and dusted, Bek." She glanced over to Savvo whose face was set hard. "My contact has sent a renewed offer. A large offer. One they'd like to talk through in person. They kind of … Look, Rebekah. Go and talk to them. Please."

"Ah. How much?"

"Double. And Calc, but only with a face-to-face conversation. They want to know who they're dealing with."

Rebekah suppressed the comms, the rustle from behind drawing her attention. Arin and Hendricks stood in the galley doorway and had clearly heard everything.

"Double," she emphasised.

"Pike's on edge," said Savvo. "And there were no dropped hints. Maybe his cut is enough to overcome his worries."

She turned her gaze onto the comms switch. Double, enough for Savvo to set himself up, Arin to find a new vocation and perhaps persuade Hendricks to join him. Enough so she could take the *Sunstar* somewhere quiet and live out her days with the twins until they were ready, or not, to face society. It spoke of hope, and maybe the glue to keep them together while they sorted new identities once again.

She blinked, then looked back to Hendricks and nodded. Her old Marine captain grimaced and did the same. Trust. Ever present since the fateful day Hendricks ordered Rebekah to take control of their squad. A moment that had bonded them as crew, or perhaps chained them, the links now working loose.

"Okay, Pike."

"Sending a location now, and the time. And Rebekah, thank you."

Flicking the switch, she slid off her comms unit and placed it precisely on the console. Firm hands pressed down her jumpsuit, and then she cracked a knuckle on each hand.

"Okay. You have thirty minutes. Hendricks, you're coming with. Savvo, you are to remain on board with the twins."

"I should come. They have ZZ3."

"No, they don't. Arin, I want you in the black with ZZ3. Tool the fuck up. You want your freedom? Then earn it."

CHAPTER 8

Rebekah sat in the deep chair, eyes fixed on the doorway where she and Hendricks had entered. A nervous tick tremored through her left thumb, and she wrapped her fingers around it.

Hendricks paced about the outer office as was her habit. Initially it had been just a step from side to side, but Rebekah recognised the nervous energy coursing through her ex-captain and soon she would take to pacing the entire room. It was the waiting. For years she had been cold, calculating. Dealing with the boredom between missions through constant training and analysis of the squad. When a new mission was assigned to the Breakers, she'd have the individualised reports on their slates before they were even awake.

And then the twins.

Just a nudge, a tentative touch. Followed by a wave of real, desperate empathic *need* that had broken Hendricks in a second. Restored the humanity she had locked away in one fell swoop, and Rebekah found herself in command of the feared Breakers, slap bang in the middle of a black ops mission. Breakers, because that's what they did. They had punched a hole through the Bustan defences, except the twins had torn a new one in each of them. Some bigger than others.

The sign above the door beeped, and it automatically opened. A woman stepped through, elegantly dressed but with an air of business about her. She held a slate by her side and lifted it to check something before producing a slim smile. "Captain Khan?" she said.

Rebekah stood, brushing down her jumpsuit and suddenly aware how out of place she felt. The simplicity of the outer office had lulled her thinking, and now it was on to business, and she was already on the back foot. She nodded, mentally kicking herself.

"And this is Engineer Bree Hendricks?" the woman asked, glancing down at her slate. Something that was easy enough to find out from Karal's files and the *Sunstar*'s roster. Even so, Rebekah noted the effort taken.

"I am," replied Hendricks.

"Good. I am Davina Connors, Mr Duboit's Personal Assistant here on M1. Follow me, will you?" The woman made to turn, then glanced over her shoulder. "You will be scanned, you understand? So, if you have brought any ... err ... inappropriate items then this might be the time to divulge that. It can be so embarrassing when all the flashing lights and alarms go off. And the security detail, well, they're *twitchy*."

"We're good," replied Rebekah, moving to follow. "We may be rough around the edges, but bringing a heavy wrench to a meeting is not our style."

"You'd be surprised how people think," Davina said.

Rebekah swept the room, noting where potential threats could appear from. She activated her chip, the wetware augmenting her brain's interpretation of what she thought she saw and the reality. By the time she had reached the centre of what was clearly Davina's office, she had picked out the signature of three sensory arrays and a hint along one wall of a hidden entrance.

Oh, and the robo guard disguised as a lamp on her desk. Expensive, deadly.

A double knuckle crack drew Hendricks' attention. An agreed warning. The ex-captain's chip had stopped working the day the twins blasted her with pure emotion.

"You can go right in. Mr Duboit is expecting you." Davina knocked on the door, and on opening it, stepped aside to let Rebekah through.

With a nod as a thank you, Rebekah entered. The room was lushly furnished, the cost of its transport likely more than its true worth, but still a sign of opulence even on M1 where Karal had its headquarters. To her lack of surprise, Mr Duboit remained seated as they entered, the brief smile on his middle-aged face as false as his appearance. A hologram.

Davina showed them towards a pair of chairs before his huge, wooden desk, and left.

"My apologies Captain Khan, for not being here in person. I am a very busy man, you understand." His smile hadn't returned, but at least he spoke first.

"I understand Mr Duboit," she replied. He had made no attempt to deformalise their names, which she found surprisingly comforting. She let the chip do its work. "This is my engineer, Bree Hendricks."

The holo's eyes flicked over to Hendricks, but there was no acknowledgement there. Rebekah decided the imagery represented the real Duboit there and then, not an altered simulation. Feigning the irrelevance in that gaze would have been a massive challenge. Duboit had asked for a face to face, and she had expected a sizing up exercise. She had changed her mind; it was so they could be scanned, and their biometrics cross-referenced. Be it the residue on a door handle, a flake of skin in the air or the sensor scans Davina had so carefully brought to their attention, they had been marked.

Good luck with that.

"So, to business," Duboit continued, his grey hair simulating movement as he tilted his head. "I must say, your crew were impressive in bringing in the *Hatton*. Did you know you were the fourth ship asked to intercept? No?"

Rebekah shook her head. She hadn't checked.

"Two others passed. The third couldn't maintain the course with the constant changes to the navcom. Impressive that you could."

"Perhaps a little luck," she said with a smile. "It was in the deceleration zone."

"But time was tight, and the costs in dear Mr Pike's mind, spiralling. One of the asteroids that sourced the PMG on board was mine. So, you have my thanks, and I ensured the Calc showed my appreciation." The smile that followed tightened her gut, apprehension sitting there and refusing to leave.

There were many players in the asteroid business. None of them poor, except perhaps, those who operated the machinery. The Duboit name wasn't one she knew, though a little private investment on the side wasn't uncommon either. But being unable to find anything about the man in such a short time had her on edge. Nothing. Yet he had an office on M1, and serious money.

Rebekah forced a smile. "Then you have our thanks. We just about cleared the loan against the *Sunstar*, which I'm sure you'll be aware of. We can finally start saving for our futures."

Duboit shifted position, clasping his hands on top of the desk. They hovered very slightly above, convincing Rebekah that she was dealing with a real person behind the holo. An AI sim would be too perfect.

"Well, about that. I have need of a crew and ship with your resourcefulness. And I might add, your skill set. You've seen my offer." He leant back; an eyebrow raised.

"I'm a details person, Mr Duboit. I have seen your offer, which could be viewed as generous. But that depends on what you want us to do. The risks. We have a chance to start making some proper creds with our debts cleared, we need to know why we would risk that." Rebekah refused to mirror his movements, and leaned forward, her hands resting on her knees. "You understand? We know this business, we're good at it. Safe."

Duboit seemed to consider her words. "You understand that I can't divulge details. Competition for information is rife in all walks of life. The cost of it getting out is too high."

"Give me the gist," she said, a quick look to ensure Hendricks was still focused. "Something I can work with. Otherwise, it's a straight no. My crew depend on me."

The contemplation on his face ended with a tight smile. "I feel I can trust you, Rebekah." There it was. First name. "So, I will divulge as much as I feel safe doing so. But …" His eyes flicked over to Hendricks.

"I can take a hint. Want me to leave, Captain?" Hendricks made to stand.

"I think so," she said. "Wait for me outside."

"Mr Duboit, a pleasure to meet you," Hendricks said, and turned to leave, closing the door behind.

Duboit's eyes hadn't left Rebekah. The rudeness played on her mind. She hated having her crew dismissed as unimportant. The Breakers, the Wrecking Squad – *crew*, she self-corrected – stood together. For now, at least. "So?"

"We lost a ship, out in the black. It's valuable, and should any of my competitors find out, then they'll be determined to recover it. Not only for what's on there, but for the embarrassment. You understand, Rebekah? The game of money relies on status, and I will not have it dragged through the newsfeeds on display as a petty victory." His manner hadn't changed, the voice remaining clipped. To her, he was holding the vitriol back, making her certain there was a large element of truth buried in there.

"Okay. I get it. Sending one of your own ships, or one of your normal sub-contractors, puts your competitors on high alert. Especially if you're doing something unusual like heading into the outer system. That I understand. But why us? Our ship doesn't have the acceleration capacity to catch anything moving fast out there. And we've no suspension chambers."

Duboit pursed his lips, then clasped his hands beneath his chin, one finger resting against his mouth. "I can only tell you so much. Let's say, it's not accelerating away. Rather, orbiting. And the recovery would be ... difficult."

Rebekah blinked, leaning back as her thoughts raced through the possibilities. Orbiting. That would mean the window of opportunity would be short from where the Minx asteroid field followed its own orbital path. And dangerous. Out in the black that could mean many things. But the *Hatton* had needed a skilled pilot, a space walk and auto-piloting auxiliary engines. And the sabotage still sat heavy on her. There was still some payback from Victor and the holo-masked woman in the offing to consider.

"That as much as you can let me have? How long? You know the specs on my ship. What timescales are we talking?"

"A month at most. Back here, docked and ready to spend your money. If you succeed."

"And the standard fifty percent if we don't," stated Rebekah. It wasn't a question; she was making sure he was aware of her terms. "I'll take this to my crew. You need to be aware, Mr Duboit, that with such sketchy info, there'll be dissent. I make no guarantees."

"I am sure you can see the benefits of all those creds for just a month's work. Be persuasive, Rebekah. Perhaps I can cut you in for a ... a little bonus."

"Hendricks," she said, turning away from the terminal to look towards the shuttle they had just exited. "What do you see over my shoulder?"

The engineer froze, face set firm, eyes scanning the terminal room. Rebekah felt the coldness seep into her ex-captain's demeanour. A bit of the past reborn. "Amid the chaff there's two, no three, onlookers. All three are marking the passengers, looking for a target."

"Threat assessment?" she said.

"The big one by the exit – in the suit. Threat point one. Cool as fuck. The two sat down, minor. Too much on edge." Hendricks tilted her head. "Not amateurs, just not cut out for their chosen target." There was no emotion there, no self-congratulation. Just cold fact.

"Mr Suit and Boot took me in the lift."

"When you were drunk and stupidly off-guard." Hendricks pulled at the collar of her jumpsuit. "No doubt."

"I slashed his Achilles. Quick healer. What do you think?" Rebekah knew what was coming. Run from a fight, you have to keep on running. Karal looked down on any violence in their low districts, even the upper ones nearer the core were policed. But the docks? You had to let off steam somewhere.

"Rebekah ..." Hendricks blinked, the coldness melting away. "I am not what I was."

"You take the two lowlifes. Leave the suit to me. You okay with that?" She squeezed Hendricks' arm. The ex-captain nodded. "But we can't be *seen*. You understand?"

"Yeah, yeah." She met Rebekah's eyes. "How many do I have to take?"

"Let them both hit you once. And don't kill them. Not even a little bit," Rebekah said, receiving a grin in return. She turned about and strode into the waiting area of the terminal. She noted the movement of the two sat down, their hands reaching inside their jackets. Either sending a comms signal, or reaching for a weapon. Possibly both. She ignored them, and took her turn at the console, scanning her wrist link and walking through when the security doors opened. They were up on their feet, but she walked on. Victor had slid through the doors into the corridor, likely heading for the locker room where crew suited up for the cold, airless docks beyond. Rebekah smiled to herself. She had some payback to deliver.

Once through the doors, she upped her pace, and soon reached the locker entrance. A quick wrist scan, and the door sprung open. It should be empty; she'd recognised no other crews on their shuttle. Instincts kicked in and she dived through the open space, the swish of something hard and heavy flying over her head. Coming up on her feet, the baton cut through the air again on a back stroke as Victor stepped forward. Threat poured from his reddening face, eyes narrow and angry. Apparently, he wanted some payback too. The chip activated, and Rebekah ducked low, hating the necessity as she couldn't monitor his shoulder movements for the tells that were key in battle. Instead, she eyed his hips, and the twist to his knee. Judging he would take the baton in two hands and elbow her in the back of her neck, she kicked his ankle.

The scream was a joy to her ears, the crunch of shattered bone and ripped cartilage a pleasure she had missed. Victor was about to collapse when her shoulder hit his chest, and she rammed him into a locker.

"You picked this place," she said, kneeing him in the balls. "Because they're not allowed cameras." As he doubled over, she rammed her elbow into his neck. His face slammed into the tiled floor. She crouched beside his head. "Good choice," she whispered in his ear. "Come for me and mine again, and I'll rip your fucking head off with the spine still attached. Am I clear?"

There was a muffled response.

"I said," she lifted his head by a few strands of hair just behind his ear. "Am I *fucking* clear?"

Blood poured from his shattered nose as a sound similar to a 'yes' slipped through swollen lips.

"Good, because that would be so, so messy." She let Victor's head hit the floor, stepping over him to peer into the corridor. Hendricks was taking a blow to her kidney from the remaining thug. The wince was feigned, at least to Rebekah's eyes, and the uppercut her ex-captain delivered, pulled. Even so, the thug clattered into the wall. With a glance to check the corridor camera was most certainly on, Hendricks then nodded her way.

"Any issues?"

"No. What did they want?" said Rebekah, unable to hide her grin.

The engineer peered down at the two unconscious figures. "Dunno. A beating, I guess. Don't remember pissing anyone off. But then, you have been recently drunk. There's always a problem after that."

They suited up, Victor curled up in the corner, pitiful moans emanating now and again that they ignored. On reaching the *Sunstar*, they checked for surveillance, and when sure the way was clear, entered the cargo doors. Once through the airlock, they were greeted by Arin, who hopped from foot to foot while Hendricks removed her suit and let him know about the attack.

"How many?" said Arin, trying to lift Hendricks' shirt and examine the bruise, only to be pushed away.

"Two. And they hit me because I let them. The Captain said we had to be careful."

"Too right I did," said Rebekah. "Stop fussing, and fetch Savvo. We have a decision to make. And Arin, we need to know what you and ZZ3 picked up."

"Yeah. You're not going to like it." Arin rubbed the back of his head. "They had the area jammed to high heaven and back. An exclusion zone. Only ever experienced anywhere that flooded once before – Bustan."

CHAPTER 9

"What do they mean, no?" Duboit spat. "No? To me?"

"Yes, Mr Duboit. I am sorry. The message was short and sweet. Without further information, Captain Khan does not believe they can afford to take the risks as they stand." Davina held her ground while Duboit seethed – wherever he was.

"Assessment," the holo snapped back at her.

"I do think she believed your version. The why and where. That this is about money and status. Her bio responses gave no indication she thought you lied. Either you choose to offer more detail, real or not, or you up the offer." Davina set her face still, neutral. "She is not as greedy as most we deal with and has genuine concern for her crew. There was obvious affection towards Bree Hendricks."

"Yes. And an odd choice."

"No. You dismissed her as inconsequential during the conversation. Hendricks was a test, which you failed." Again, neutral.

"Anything from the bio scans?" he continued, ignoring the comment. "Do they confirm who they are?"

"In some form. The idents are of Bustan origin."

"Bustan?"

"Common enough. Since the cessation, Almaar has needed more miners. Many of those disenfranchised by the Bustans have moved here for work, or to hide. The Senti have always transported whoever paid well. Criminal, or not." Davina swept her hand up, a holo screen appearing near the office wall. "We were thinking they were Almaarian, yes? An ex-Marine unit looking to hide from whatever horrors they suffered. Some of the officer-nobles had hunted down their old units after the cessation. Blaming them for the failures."

On the screen, the engineer, Hendricks, was up against two thugs. The fight lasted forty seconds, possibly a little more.

"What am I looking at?" said Duboit.

"A woman pulling her punches, deliberately letting herself be hit. By my judgement, she was never trained by a Bustan. That's Almaarian technique. Strikes me that they are playing a double bluff. Bustan ID is costly and much harder to verify. They *are* Almaarian Marines, but they must have chosen to hide as far away as they can from Almaar."

"Other than the Bustan system, yes." Duboit stroked his chin with his thumb, then stood up from his desk, resting his holo hands on the edge. "This is good. We can use this."

"You need to be careful, Mr Duboit. We know they entered the *Hatton*. They either survived the nanites, or got lucky. My guess is the former. Their interference cost you a chance to undermine Karal. To leave the company on the verge of collapse and an easy buy out." Davina shifted her position, moving to stand in front of the desk, expecting the order that was to come.

"Yes, yes. Even so, I need them. They want to remain hidden, and that's going to cost." Duboit sat back down, leaning back to smile at Davina. "Do I still pay them? Hmmm."

"My advice would be yes. Pissing off Marines can be costly in other ways. But it is your money."

"Yes. Yes, it is. But the Bustans will pay mightily for what's on that ship. And the Almaarian Nobility even more to keep it there."

Knock, knock.

Blurry eyed, Rebekah rolled over in the deliciously comfortable bed to try to focus on the wall clock. Her head beat with the sound of a thousand war drums. Or maybe it was the flood waters of the Spuran flash floods rolling down the winding valleys in furious anger.

Or perhaps just a hangover.

"Shit, how much did I drink?" Her hand stretched to the other side of the bed, to find the space cold and empty. "That, at least, is a bonus."

The door thudded again, and her addled mind suddenly connected the noise with one it may, or may not, have heard a few seconds earlier. Knocking? No one knocked.

But then, alarm bells can be silenced. She got to her feet and padded across the luxurious carpet to the door. A third set of thuds annoyed her. Did people not know she had a hangover? That they were risking losing an arm, only to find it stuffed halfway up their arse?

"Shhhh," she said, and with an effort pressed the vid feed to get a look at who waited impatiently outside. All she could see was the back of a head. Definitely a female body shape, and she baulked, realising that the chip wouldn't be able to discern any holo-mask through the vid feed. The figure turned, and Rebekah caught the swish of elegant hair and a face she had seen only a couple of days beforehand.

She pressed the speak button and blew out a long sigh as a hint. "I said no. Actually, *we* said no. Nothing more to say. I'm off back to sleep off a half bottle of Minx whisky." She let the button go, smiling as the lips moved on the feed but she had no need to listen. Until the banging started again.

"Oh, come on, have some sympathy here." She fumbled for the speak button, and missed, pressing the entry instead. As the door popped open, she quickly checked herself, relieved to find she had fallen asleep fully clothed. Not so fresh, but at least half-decent.

"I said no," she repeated as Davina nudged the door open.

"Here," said Davina, and shoved the takeout coffee her way. The aroma was tempting. "And it was two-thirds of a bottle with beer chasers. I think you may have forgotten the third bar. Or Savvo dropping you onto your carpet after you refused to walk another step."

Rebekah blinked. "You know what underwear I'm wearing?"

"No. You put those on when you were on your ship. Everything else, pretty much. Mr Duboit is the richest man you've never heard of. If he wants to know something, he will find out. Which is why I'm here." Davina handed over the coffee, scanning the chair crowned by Rebekah's boots. After making a show of removing them, she brushed the top and sat down.

How she sat had Rebekah on edge despite her current condition. Elegant, yes. But ready, and aware. Like a predator coiled to pounce. She kicked in her chip, took a sip of the coffee and let the pairing do its magic.

"I'll say that again, so the next part is easier. *If* Mr Duboit wants to know something, he will find out. That job lies with me. And I'm very good at it, and get paid an eye-watering amount to do so."

Rebekah sat on the bed, and ramped up the chip, turbo-charging it with the superb coffee. This wasn't going the way she wanted it. But she had suspected from the moment the crew had voted against the job that there would be a comeback. Only Savvo had dissented on hearing Arin's worrying information, and Hendricks' opinion, but had understood.

"I sense a threat in there. Spit it out, get the dirty done so I can decide whether I need a shit or a shower," said Rebekah, grimacing over her coffee's rim.

"I'd suggest both." Davina wrinkled her nose, leaving Rebekah unsure whether it was a joke or not. "Let me lay out what I know without any digging. You're not from Bustan as your ID declares – and by the way, those were a quality job. Whoever put the data trail together has my plaudits." Rebekah tried not to wince, hoping she succeeded. "And Hendricks' fight recorded at the terminal displayed too much Almaarian army technique. A giveaway. The fact she also took some punches that she could have avoided, well, is another hint you're an ex-army unit who doesn't want to be found. And the mess you left in the locker room? Apparently, someone opened a locker door on themselves according to the security records. Victor Goncho, by the way, has criminal connections on board M2 which take no digging to find. The fact you're not in a box this morning surprises me. Except, of course, I warned him off. For now."

"So, if I say no, I take it we're a target. Subtle."

"I suspect that wouldn't be the type of lever I need. If you and your unit went anywhere near Bustan, then you've seen far worse violence than Victor can even imagine. But it makes life awkward for you with Karal. You would be forced to move on to some of the less regulated companies. No. My offer is simple. You carry out Mr Duboit's request, and I don't start digging about who you really are. It wouldn't take me long, Rebekah, to find which unit and whatever noble officer-fuck you're hiding from." Davina set her hands in her lap; the smile tight.

"Hah. Bullshit. There's nothing stopping you from doing that, anyway. We're screwed if we do, and fucked if we don't. Not the way to start a business partnership." Rebekah swigged the last of the coffee, placing the cup on the bedside cabinet. "Is it?"

"You are aware, I assume, of the Incini Directive?" Davina said, her eyes catching the room's light. Or had they flashed?

"A little. Not my world, is it? Nobles playing politics, while the rest of us pick up the manure they leave behind."

Davina pursed her lips. "Perhaps not quite how I would word it, but agreed. I'm an Incini. When I negotiate a contract, it is binding. Whoever breaks such an obligation comes under the auspices of the Emperor, whose grandfather formulated the Incini Directive. Mr Duboit would have his assets *stripped*."

Rebekah stared at the woman. It hadn't occurred to her that Duboit was royalty, the holo a fake front. Maybe even a double bluff. She had assumed it to be real from how it presented, but was her thinking too naïve? A noble dabbling in a pot they didn't want anyone to know about. But then, the Incini would know who he, or she, or even *it*, was. However, the information was sacrosanct if she remembered right. Neutral. It didn't matter how dirty the contract, only that it was fulfilled.

"He could employ someone else to search," Rebekah said.

"Not Incini. That is how it works. And if we discovered he broke the contract, we would reveal that to the Emperor, or the foundation of our service would be nullified. Worthless. You have two hours. And I'm good, Rebekah. *Very* good."

CHAPTER 10

"No way," said Arin, eyeing the large case and the woman standing beside it on the vid screen. Her helmet visor clear, the eyes piercing him through the screen. "Not happening."

"We don't have a choice. It's part of the deal," said Savvo, his head in his hands as he leant on the galley top. "You heard the Captain. She's Incini. If she digs, we're fucked. All of us, Arin. Understand?" Savvo pushed himself up from the bench and leant in to peer closer at the small screen. "If she finds out who we are, and reveals that to the wrong people, there's nowhere in Almaar or Bustan we'd be safe. We will be stuck on this bloody ship forever, going bloody insane bouncing from one wild system to another at the whim of the mind-sucking Senti."

"Better than ... than this. The twins, Savvo. How the hell do we deal with that? For a month?" Arin eyed the woman a final time before turning away to face the co-pilot. "They come out, you know. When we sleep, they roam the ship. Stretch their legs, use the grav-gym, cook. Live. Breathe."

"We all know, Arin. But there is no alternative. Better that than being under some butcher's scalpel, or locked away in isolation while they mind-fuck them over and over. How the hell did this all go to hell so quickly after four years of hiding?" Savvo pressed his fist into the wall, before switching the screen off. With a shake of his head, he headed out the galley towards the cargo hold. "I'll recheck her cabin and the hold. You get your head together. First impressions and all that. Go let Rebekah know she's here."

Arin, hand on hips, watched Savvo until he reached the airlock doors. "Fuck," he said, then made his way to the twins' cabin. The largest room on the *Sunstar*, and what story would they be telling about that? That it was unused? Locked away for some secret reason that you can't tell the fucking spy on the ship? "A disaster. Why haven't I left yet? Why is Savvo still here?"

He stood opposite the twins' door, his hand held ready to knock when it slid open. Tremil faced him, her eyes wide and raw. However, her face was set rigid, stern. In control and only a nudge of her mood impinged on his mind. She didn't speak.

Arin fished in his pocket and drew out his latest creation. The toy felt pathetic in his hand. Irrelevant. But the switch in Tremil's countenance gripped at his heart. The joy on her face at something so simple doing what it usually did – reinforced the self-loathing at his own doubts about staying and protecting such precious souls. Tremil still didn't speak, but took the toy and eyed the collection on the old table behind where Rebekah stood watching him.

"She's here," he said, his voice hoarse, unable to make eye contact with his captain. "Rebekah, you sure about this?"

"No. And as we have two empaths listening in, they know I'm unsure *and* afraid of what might happen. But also, that the alternative is to be exposed. They understand and will play their part until it all goes to shit. First contact with the enemy and all that." Rebekah pushed herself away from the table she leant on, allowing the eager Tremil past so she could reorganise the collection.

Arin nodded and glanced over to Heki who had stood to peer at the new cartoon figure. His fingers alighted on the other toy in his pocket. One he'd refined and worked on for the past year. Each nuance of the design tweaked as the girls grew. He even had the striped skinsuits down pat. With a gentle stroke of the resin hair, he withdrew his hand. Now wasn't the time.

Rebekah led him outside, the door sliding closed as she gently gripped his arm. "This is difficult for all of us, I know. But if you show them any weakness or doubt, they'll feed off it. Despair. And you know what'll happen then. Insecurities we cannot help. But *certainty* that we will get through this is vital, or ..."

Arin nodded. "We're screwed. And everyone in the vicinity."

Rebekah gave him a reassuring squeeze. "On board a ship and out in the black. I can think of nicer places to lose my mind."

"I don't bite," said Davina, her arms at her sides. Rebekah thought she could detect tension there, as if she suppressed the urge to cross them defensively under the hostility in the room. "I am here to ensure the contract is fulfilled as per the terms agreed. That is all."

"And as agreed, everything other than the mission is private. That's right?" said Rebekah, keeping her face neutral. "Everything, under the oath of an Incini." Her crew pressed in eagerly, three sets of concerned eyes on Davina.

"Yes. You need to be clear that I have to judge what is relevant or not. My decisions, if contested, are overseen by the Directorate." The arms flinched just a little. Enough that Rebekah's mistrust grew another root.

"But this," said Hendricks, fingers pressed against the sugar and caffeine filled flask, "this Directorate, only intercedes noble to noble. We are mere crap on an expensive shoe to anyone of that status. We have no defence if you decide to renege on your word, and they won't give two hoots about us."

Davina raised an eyebrow.

"She means 'give a shit' about us," added Arin. "For clarity's sake."

The Incini shook her head. "This contract was not only sealed by me, but was also negotiated by myself. I assure you, it is … What term would suit you, engineer Hendricks? Ah, *rock solid*."

"But still interpretive," added Rebekah. "And this extends to *all* my crew?"

"As agreed."

"And all our equipment and working methods?" said Arin, with a wink towards Rebekah. "Don't want to be giving away trade secrets, do we?"

"As agreed."

"Just for the record, we don't trust you. It's nothing personal, but …" Savvo looked around the galley. "We have learned to rely on one another, you know. And, well, you are not part of the team. It goes for anyone we meet."

"And *just* for the record, Savvo, understand I know everyone here was in the Bustan war. I know you were Marines and have the skill set Mr Duboit requires for this mission. I know the names you have given, and that they are likely false, your IDs faked. As long as the terms of the contract are enacted, that is all I will ever know. Understand? It is that simple." The arms didn't flinch, the Incini's eyes steely as her gaze flicked between the crew.

"Okay. Any more words you need to piss on this fire with? No? Good. Batten down and buckle up. We take off in ten." Rebekah stood. "Why aren't you moving?"

And the galley emptied.

Rebekah ran through the preflight checks, eyes flickering over the list in a ritual that calmed her mind. Savvo waited impatiently as usual in the co-pilot's chair, knees bouncing as her need for routine gnawed at his impatience. Finally, she reached the final line and made the agreed adjustment to the flight plan and sent it off to the dockmaster.

"You think he'll buy it?" said Savvo.

"Money talks. Pike has had his cut, so there should be no issues." The lights went green, and the dock clamps snapped open. "If only the rest was so easy. Call us out."

Savvo pressed his hand to his ear, squeezing the dodgy speaker on the right of his comms unit closer. "This is the *Sunstar* lifting off. All checks in the green. Confirm bay is clear, dock tower."

"All clear, RCKN5QD. Good luck on the scavenger hunt, Wrecking Squad. Bring me back something shiny."

"No chance, Nicky. We find something nice out there, it'll be stuffed under my bed," replied Savvo. Rebekah recognised his grin; one she hadn't seen for some time. Relaxed, natural. Genuinely happy.

"And there it will stay, Savvo. There it will stay. Safe journey, tower out."

Savvo slid off his comms unit, tossing them onto the console where they maglocked, dodgy earpiece and all, making Rebekah wince. Doing her best to ignore his wistful look, she guided the ship clear of the clamps, and spun her about, gently adding a little thrust millimetre by millimetre as she shifted the paddle. Years of piloting dropships imbued a feel and touch, whether in or out of atmosphere, that she liked to sharpen every chance she got. As far as the tower were concerned, the computer was doing the guiding along its predefined sequence. Match that, as she always did, and they were none the wiser. "In the pipe," she whispered, and Savvo's grin disappeared into the ether.

"Aye," he said, quietly.

The huge scaffolding that jutted out from the bay slid by. The multitude of airlock ports for the main planetary supply ships empty, with the monthly jackpot of high-grade ore already headed for the factories closer to Almaar. She eased the ship about, a slow lazy turn that took them past the construction docks busy building the autodrives Karal used to transport the lower grade ore inwards.

"We are clear," she said over internal comms. "Accelerating in five, four ... did you remember your boots? No grav out here boys and girls ... three, two, one ... and we are a go."

Chapter 11

Rebekah recalibrated the scope, increasing the saturation and then counted the seconds until the blip returned. She pushed herself back into the pilot's chair, foreboding weighing on her shoulders. It could be a coincidence, but after the events of the last few days, it seemed unlikely.

They were being followed. Every fibre of her body, every element of her training, told her that.

"Savvo, Davina, up to the cockpit please," she said over comms, keeping her voice calm, emotions steady. For a second an earworm popped in, but she dismissed it. The self-defence strategy masked some of the emotions humans broadcasted when under stress. Right now, she was dealing with something she understood. Could strategise for. Unlike nobles and errant empaths.

With a prod, she adjusted the position of her comms unit, and cracked two knuckles with her thumbs.

"What's up?" said Savvo as he slid into the chair next to her. "You said please. Never a good sign."

His smile wasn't forced, more accepting. Perhaps now they were away from the promised land of M2 he could be a little more relaxed? Maybe.

She tapped the scope, and Savvo leant in as Davina appeared. Her hair was wet and tied back. For a moment Rebekah mused how she had coped with the strangeness of showering in space, but just put it down to Incini training. There didn't seem much they weren't capable of.

"We're being followed," Rebekah said, lifting her eyes to meet Davina's with a quirk of the eyebrow. "Mr Duboit making sure we're doing what we should?"

Davina eyed the screen. "No. That's my role. Mr Duboit doesn't waste money. Are you sure they're following us?"

"I agree with Rebekah's assessment. Too much of a coincidence. When is the course change due? When do we get to find out which bit of the bloody void we're visiting?" said Savvo. "That would tell us."

"Twelve hours."

"That's a long time to wait," replied Savvo. "What are you thinking, Rebekah?"

"I'm thinking we're still within decent comms range of M4, and Nicky would love to discuss your bed arrangements again." Her eyes slid over to Davina. "And letting slip we're off on a scavenger run hints at us having a tip-off to anyone interested. A sure thing. One that it's worth expending our time and newfound creds on. Possibly something we've sat on for a while and worth giving up getting drunk for."

Savvo nodded. "So hot, that we left the best billets in M2. Well, if I must chat with Nicky ..."

Rebekah stood, gesturing towards the exit. Davina stepped out, and they both headed towards the galley. The Incini was drawn by the smell of the coffee pot, while Rebekah made herself tea.

"That was a quick assessment," said Davina, taking a sip. "Astute."

Rebekah couldn't make her mind up whether the Incini was fishing, or just being polite. She opted for the first and tempered her words. "I could just as well be wrong. But the cover story could drag out some of the lowlifes. The scrappers have just about tapped out the remnants of the war, those who still ply the trade focus on the mined-out asteroids or defunct autobots and satellites. Slim pickings. Apart from the tower and the logged flight plan, who else would know?"

"The admin staff are nosy. Some are always looking for extra creds from whoever has a few spare for information, and they knew you had given up some prime rooms. *I* dropped the story in that pot to make sure it didn't develop into something bigger. Silence would have caused more of a stir." The Incini caught her disdainful look. "Secrets bleed out. Shape the story, before it shapes you. That's how I live my life."

Savvo walked in, his eyes a little distant, hand on his chin. "Nicky says it was the *Maverick* that took off an hour behind us. Registered to a scavenger crew led by Aidan Toms. Though the flight plan was more than a little vague and filed last minute."

"Toms? I don't know him, nor the *Maverick*."

"I do," said Davina. "I have employed their services from time to time. Scavenger is a loose term. Let's say he'd do just about anything for money. And a favourite of Victor's. I believe he has a share in the *Maverick*, though their dealings are hazy."

"You warned them off," said Savvo. "Am I right?"

"On M2. Not the same rules out here. Who would know if they stole your salvage? Especially if you don't come back. And they have no clue I'm on board. I registered myself as crew under a different name." Davina smiled then, almost revelling in her little bombshell.

Rebekah didn't give her the pleasure of any response. She had already checked through the altered manifest. If she'd had the creds for a bribe or two, she doubted the cameras would have shown her either. Or if they did, a much-changed version. Whatever they were out here for, Mr Duboit and his pet Incini didn't want anyone else to know. Covert ops. Why else would they want ex-Marines who had hidden away for so long? And whatever that secret was, what stopped them silencing her crew after the contract had been fulfilled? That was the true difference from a contract between those of noble birth, and one with peasants.

"We keep a twenty-four-hour watch on them, Savvo. Set up a monitoring alarm. Should they close, I want to know ASAP."

"Yes, Captain."

Arin ran his eye down the cargo list on his slate, tongue stuck firmly between the gap in his front two teeth. He sighed and scratched the back of his head.

"Fuck," he whispered to himself. "Start again."

He walked to the far end of the hold, checking each cargo code against his list. Wet and dry food stores, frozen goods. Spare batteries, clothing, additional suit parts to back up those they already had. The list went on. Each over and above what they would need for a standard run, he and Hendricks cooking up enough reasons to gather a year's spares for any on board issues courtesy of the mysterious Mr Duboit. Every contract had a little slack in there, but they had stretched this one a long way.

Across the other side, Hendricks ran through the machine parts for the ship itself. If the scavenger hunt paid off, and the crew went their separate ways, they would be leaving the *Sunstar* as the best equipped and spare heavy ship in Karal space.

Finally, Arin found the two anomalies on his list.

"Dricks. Over here," he said, the words echoing across the hold now it had been filled with air. The old engineer held up her hand while staring at her slate. She shook her head once, then began to wander over, talking to herself.

"You got a problem, too?" Arin asked.

"Mmmm, maybe. Some whippersnapper distracted me while I was thinking," she said, the grin genuine as the engineer peered at the heavy-duty boxes Arin stood by. "What's in them?"

"That's just it. They're not on the list per se."

"Per se? You been taking electrocution lessons?" Hendricks grinned and ignored Arin's half-scowl as she took the slate he handed over.

"Har bloody har. Elocution not electrocution. Those are heavy duty, Dricks. Almost …"

"Military grade. No almost about it," the ex-captain tapped at the metal lid. "Looked for any coding?"

Arin rolled his eyes. "Yeah, 'cos I didn't think of that before pulling you over. None. Either there never were any, or they were laser-etched clean."

Hendricks dropped to her knees, slipping a flashlight from her thigh pocket. The beam highlighted etch marks along the base, partially hidden by the vacuum-ready packaging the dockworkers had added. "Missed these. You still got a lot to learn."

"Wouldn't have if the teacher was any good. Army?"

"Navy, by the amount of numbers and letters removed. We'd better take a look." Hendricks ran her hand along the seams, lips twitching as she felt for any gaps.

"If it's not on the list, then it's been added by our number one fan, Davina. This wise?"

"Wise? No. Gave that up years ago. With age comes recklessness. Go get the breaker kit." Her hand pressed a pressure panel she had found, the lid flipping open to reveal a digipad. "We have need of your particular skill set."

Arin left, fingers scratching his neck as he headed off to the recovery bay where his kit, and ZZ3, were hidden amid random detritus with the added reassurance of a lack of atmosphere.

Hendricks checked her own slate again, and muttering to herself, returned to the stack of engine parts that had bothered her. She ran her finger down the list, and stared at the crates where she had first miscounted, shaking her head. "Damn if the manifest isn't right now. I need caffeine. And sugar ... lots of it."

The click of her magboots masked the scraping of metal upon metal above, and the gentle unscrewing of a vent, and its replacement.

"Do we keep it to ourselves?" said Arin. "I mean ... it's not that important."

Rebekah ran her hand over the helmet. Navy-issue and space-rated to go with the powered armour beside it in the crate. Not the full Space Marine kit – two sets of that would have filled a quarter of the hold – but standard issue search and rescue. Though modified for battle, with enough spare ammo to start a small war. It was two notches above what they had, and a lot younger. She couldn't see a scratch.

"And the other crate?"

"The same."

Rebekah glanced over to the second crate where Hendricks' face battled with the storm brewing in her head. "Can you keep this quiet, Dricks? You're looking mighty peeved."

"If the captain says so," she replied. Rebekah caught the look in her eye, the same as back at the shuttle terminal. Doubt. An uncertainty that a once sure mind had succumbed to after encountering the twins. It wasn't a lack of confidence in her abilities, more having your eyes opened to what and who you are. She wasn't a soldier anymore. And Rebekah had to question if any of them were capable of killing – until she recalled her encounter in the locker room.

No, she had been in control.

Just.

An alarm went off on her slate.

"Proximity?" said Arin, closing the lid.

"No. Time for the course change. Get it resealed, cover your tracks for now, just in case. And scan the rest." Rebekah turned away, only to sense Arin's stare upon her back. "If you're thinking I'm pushing too hard, just say so. But I'm thinking of you – all of you – and the demon we may have in our midst. Especially the consequences if we get it wrong."

"Come on, kid. Let's get to it," said Hendricks, slapping Arin on the arm. "Shield the fresh food, and I'll do a full cargo sweep, save some time. Then we'll unpack our steaks one by one."

"Yeah. Yeah. Good idea. Sorry, Captain. It's like we're walking on eggshells all the time with *her* on board." Arin's tight smile flittered, then fell away. Eventually, he walked off, heading, Rebekah assumed, for the shielding tarps.

The glance Hendricks threw her way was filled with warning, and then she followed the sub-engineer.

"Are you ready?" said Davina, waving the navigation command module in her hand. "I have Mr Duboit's redirection commands ready to go."

"So many secrets. It's almost as if he doesn't trust us," said Savvo. He recovered his comms unit from the console, and clanked aside, making sure Rebekah could see. "Go ahead."

The Incini slid the black box into the open slot on the console. The program flared on the screen, making micro-adjustments to the twin drives, then engaged a nudge from the steering thrusters. Just half a degree diagonally off the ecliptic plane, it would make tens of thousands of kilometres difference to their original path. Davina withdrew the box, pocketing it.

Rebekah and Savvo watched the *Maverick*'s blip avidly, expecting it to alter, though such changes would take time as they analysed the new trajectory. It took two minutes before their course corrected, and another five before it re-corrected. Their shadows had fallen a little further behind, but the difference was negligible over another week's burn.

"Paranoid? Is that what they're saying about me now?" Rebekah pushed herself away from the console.

Chapter 12

Five days later

The lights dimmed, signalling they had hit 22:00hrs ship time. Davina pushed the herbal tea around the table as her mind walked through the plans for arrival. Duboit had kept the details even from her, his mistrust running deep in his employees when dabbling in the shadier side of his business – and there was nothing as embroiled in shadow as the political game the target suggested he was playing. But that was the nobility for you, and the reason the Incini had been needed. To put it politely, they didn't give a fuck about anyone else. Status, power, wealth and the strategic manoeuvring within the Emperor's Court. You only had to look at the war, and their behaviour in the aftermath of its failure, to truly understand their motivations.

Me, myself and I.

Davina shivered. A coldness ran up her spine, and a sense of being watched weighed on her mind. The contrast was strange. There was more than one set of eyes upon her, and she accessed her sensory augmentations. Slowly, deliberately, she stood, scanning the galley. The data ran through her processing unit. Sensory only – as no one would trust a wet-wired human with secrets and lies – and she picked out scrabbling in the ceiling above her.

And inside the walls.

The ship's ducts, perhaps. She tried to recall the *Sunstar*'s schematics from the intricate visual memory labelling the Incini employed. It was distant, marked of lesser import as she had prepared for the journey, but as she crossed the galley to fetch a flask of water, it slid in. You would have to be slender, gaunt even, to be in the ceiling, and the ship's walls only had a few places where someone stick-thin could enter.

At the edge of her hearing, a voice whispered. Not words. And from a different direction.

She wondered if the isolation amid the lion's den of the *Sunstar*'s crew had begun to get to her. She swiftly dismissed the thought and ran a bio-check. No signs of true stress there.

The scrabbling above moved, its progress slow and in gentle spurts. Like a worm sliding through its hole in the earth. Ignoring it, she turned in the direction of the voice, taking a sip of water, watching ahead as she peered over the rim. The scraping was hard to define but hovered somewhere by the junction that led off to the quarters. Davina staggered, her mind suddenly filled with a weird sense of joy and fear, overlaid with curiosity and introspection. She blinked, and dropped the flask, reaching out to grasp the walls as her inner ears shuddered under the pressure. Her sensory augmentations screamed their pain and overwhelmed her thoughts. Row upon row of visions streamed through, each carefully labelled stack scattered to the wind. Anxiety crashed in and she hit the galley worktop, eyes falling upon a skittering lump of wheeled metal trundling towards the cockpit, and then her mind shut down.

"No," said Tremil along the corridor, her heart churning. Dread roiled in her heart, a single word forming in her mind. "Rebekah."

"Davina." The Incini's neck felt cold to Rebekah's touch. "Davina, the medscan is telling me you are waking up. You are in our medbay, Savvo has your vitals stabilised. Calm. Take your time, you have had a shock. A big one."

"She has too much bloody metal in there for me to mess about with," said Savvo, his fingers dancing over the medscan screen. "Eyes, ears, tongue. Nerve augmentation for touch. Fuck, it's like a spider's web in there."

"Damaged?" said Rebekah, her heart heavy as Savvo sucked in a breath. The consequences were stark. They might have to run if the twins had caused this.

"No. Rebooting, but slowly. The tw—"

Rebekah's fingers whipped out, alighting on his lips – a shake to her head.

"Davina?" she repeated. A finger twitched, and Savvo tapped at the screen some more. Rebekah detected a slight smile, and he gave a thumbs up. "Davina, can you hear me? Your systems are booting up."

The Incini's hand grabbed the sheets, fingers pulsing as if she had little control of the pressure she exerted. Rebekah took her hand, and the tremors slowed.

"Rebekah," slipped from Davina's lips, and both eyes fluttered, then opened, the pupils wide. "There's something in here," she said, the words raw. She squeezed harder. "On the ship with us."

"About that. We know. When you feel up to it, we can explain about them."

"No," said Davina. "Not the ... children? A bot. There was a bot headed for the cockpit."

Rebekah glanced to Savvo, who shrugged. There had been no sign of the girls extracting ZZ3 from the hold. It had been the first thing she'd asked Arin to check after discovering them both in a panic.

The ship shuddered, the drives stuttering. Rebekah held onto the edge of the medtable with one hand, the other on Davina's shoulder as a final tremor rocked the ship before the engines cut out.

"Shit," mouthed Rebekah, and pushed the Incini flat onto the table. Davina had mentioned the cockpit, and that's where she needed to head. "Stay there. Tell Savvo exactly what you saw."

Her boots pounded and clicked as she made her way towards the cockpit. The crackle of the internal comms echoed between the corridor walls nearest the junction. She stopped, thumbing the button on the wall. "Hendricks, come back. What's going on?"

"Complete power failure in the drives. Starting a diagnostic. Are we off course?"

"I don't know anything. Going to check the cockpit console. Davina mentioned a bot ... shit I'll get back to you. Keep me informed." She released the button, and a sudden, unwelcome thought encroached.

She hailed Arin. "Prep the suits. And prepare to move the twins if we have to. I want them in the main cargo hold if the scrubbers go down."

"Prepare for the worst. Aye, aye, El Capitaine."

Rebekah entered the cockpit, stopping herself from dropping into the seat as was her habit. She removed her slate from her left thigh pocket and checked the internal sensors. They were down, though she was far from surprised. She set the little slate into diagnostic mode and began running it over the console. She had no idea what size bot she was looking for, at least there was no sign of the telltale and hated nanite powder. The first sweep turned up empty, and Rebekah reached over the back lip of the console, scanning where it dipped into the nose of the spaceship. Nothing anomalous showed up.

"Shit, shit, shit," she said, slamming herself into the seat. A clunk drew her attention. Rebekah stood, warily sidestepping away. Nothing floated beneath her chair, so she knelt down, peering under the seat. Stretched across it were bands of metal, like a lattice work. She took a quick peek at Savvo's, noting it was absent. "Sneaky bastard," she whispered, and backed away.

Leaving the cockpit, she approached the wall comms. "Arin. Scrub that last order, bring your breaker kit, a suit and a steady hand."

"That doesn't sound good. Exciting, but not good. On it."

He was there in five minutes, suited up in the same kit he had worn to cross the void to the *Hatton*. Laying out a multitude of tools, wired boxes and a standard hammer, he pulled a strangely modded slate from a padded sleeve.

Rebekah cracked two knuckles, swallowing hard as a heavy gasp echoed along the corridor. It wasn't any she recognised, and she surmised Davina was up and heading for the galley. Even so, she watched Arin like a hawk. With no ZZ3 to pull him out of the shit, it was her job to keep an eye.

"Rebekah?" The Incini, her hair a mess, face sweaty, sat at the galley table, leaning over to peer down the short passageway. "You found it?"

Rebekah nodded, trying to keep up her intensity, annoyed that Savvo had let her out. She could hear the urgent click of his boots, and briefly wondered whether 'let' was the right word. "It's a camouflage bot. Lies in wait, then boom. Or in this case, drops a payload and then hides as if it had never been here."

"A payload? A bomb?"

"Unlikely," cut in Savvo. "More a data bomb if it's in the console."

A *whump* from the cockpit brought Savvo's words to an end, but Rebekah had been watching. Arin had boxed the little bastard up, wrestling its limbs like an angry octopus until he could shut the lid, and the bot had self-destructed. No evidence left to share with anyone. But then, five days out from the Minx asteroid field on an unchartered flight path, who would they tell?

Arin opened the box and ran his modded slate over it. Apparently satisfied, he clicked off his helmet, setting it aside on the cockpit deck and stood up. "Just ash and twisted metal." He cast the box aside and swept the slate over the console. It flashed red. "Someone's been a very naughty bot. We have a creeper latched onto the motherboard, and entering the other systems. Above my pay grade, Captain."

"You mean above your skill level," she corrected, and sagged onto the galley table.

"Who's the surveillance expert on your squad? Counterintelligence?" asked Davina. "Without the engines, we're screwed."

"Crew," Rebekah said quietly. "We're a crew."

"If it cuts out the scrubbers, we're doubly in the shit," said Arin, tapping his slate's screen with a tut.

Rebekah grimaced; her smile tight. Memories of Bustan 7, and the lab, spilling in. It had been the last time they had seen Angel, their counter intel operative. Her death, and the others, had felt so unnecessary at the time. Angel's eyes sorrowful before she had carved out her own brain. Rebekah had been too slow to react, they all had.

"You met them earlier. Know any bad songs with catchy choruses?" Rebekah got to her feet and headed down the corridor.

"What?"

"Savvo ... would you watch our guest. I'll see if I can persuade them to come out during the day."

"Does she mean the children?" said Davina, wiping the sweat away from her brow.

Arin dropped the containment box on the table. "You saw them?" he said. "No wonder you blacked out." He walked off, whistling to himself while Davina stared after him. His tune kept repeating the same line over and over.

"Savvo?"

He sighed, then sat down facing her. "You need to understand something here and now. For all your Incini ethics and private secrets, if you breathe a word of who you are about to meet to anyone, Rebekah *will* kill you. Understand? Even if all of us are sacrificed, she will not stop until she has your blood on her blade."

Another alarm blared, and the gentle thrum of the scrubbers died. The ship was silent except for the click of Arin's boots and the mournful sound of his whistling.

Chapter 13

Rebekah ushered the reluctant yet excited girls down the corridor. Her mind walled in, the earworm singing as the twins struggled to contain their emotions. She was quickly regretting her decision, but the crew had been right from the get-go. There was no way they could keep their secret away from Davina, and from the girls' own admission, their downfall had been obsessive curiosity. They had spent so much time researching what an Incini *was*, they had built up a mental pressure that was always going to blow at some point. Roaming the ship at night had been their usual release, and it just so happened that Davina was still up when they simply *had* to get out – as if she believed them.

"Is she okay?" said Tremil. "You know, h-her mind?"

"Yes, she's fine," Rebekah replied through gritted teeth.

"Will she be upset with us?" Heki said.

Rebekah didn't answer at first, having to contain her own emotions on that subject. They were, of course, focused on Davina in their excitement, and not the consequences faced by Rebekah and the rest of the crew for their choice.

She had never asked to be a parent.

How had that happened again? Oh yeah, being human.

They rounded the corner, and Rebekah asked the twins to wait – to calm and reel in rolling emotions that surged each time they lost focus. They were about to meet, and talk, to their first non-crew member since Bustan 7. This wasn't all about her, or saving the ship. First contact, well technically second, but the other hadn't gone so well.

"Savvo," she said and tapped her ear. He nodded, disappearing off to the cockpit to return with a set of headphones from the spare comms unit. She smiled at his attempts to get the Incini to wear them, resorting to reminding her where they had found her a few hours before and the bloody alarms that he'd switched off. Eventually he signalled Rebekah in.

"Careful, okay. I'll introduce you, then you get three questions each, one before the repair, two after. She will ask where you're from, so you have the cover story?" The girls nodded in unison. "Keep it simple."

"Yes, Rebekah."

With a shake of head and fleeting memories of her own behaviours at that age, she led the girls into the galley. They stood rigid, hands clutched together and eyes wide.

Davina blinked, clasping at the headphones.

Rebekah stepped forward, arms crossed, hands locked to her forearms. "Listen to the rhythm and the words. File that away and have them on repeat or they will so overwhelm you, that you won't be able to think. Let me know when you have it."

After thirty seconds or so, Davina nodded, and lifted away the headphones but left them dangling in her hand. The slight distance to her eyes gave Rebekah a little hope.

"This is Tremil," she said, and the girl gave a stiff nod, and a nervous smile. "And Heki." Whose eyes shone as she let out a nervous giggle.

The Incini's lips moved, but the words didn't emerge. It was the first time Rebekah had seen the woman with less than supreme confidence. Perhaps the risk was worth it.

Rebekah continued, "They are both part of my crew. You understand? Their presence aboard the *Sunstar* needs to remain our business. Not Mr Duboit's, or anyone else's. They are also our best shot at repairing whatever the cam-bot has done to the console."

"I …" Davina rubbed at her temples.

Rebekah glanced over to the girls who ignored her completely, their attention solely on the woman as if she was a new kitten they were dying to play with. And that was her major concern. Dying. She stood in front of them both, hands out and palms down, asking for calm. Their eyes glistened, but both girls nodded.

"I don't understand," Davina said, the words strained. "What is this? What are they doing?"

"They broadcast their emotions, as all humans do," said Savvo at her side. "Turned all the way up to eleven. And when together …" He stopped under his captain's glare, his eyes apologetic. He tapped his forehead, indicating it was a struggle to concentrate right now. Time to relieve the dam.

"They are orphans we found on Bustan 7 soon after landing. We were in the second wave, when things were still going our way. They were to be detained, separated and sent into the fucking camps." Rebekah recalled the real truth, letting the pain seep into her mind above the earworm. It always worked, and the tears came. "We just couldn't … we knew what could happen, but word was—"

"—The Scourge," said Davina, finishing the thought as Rebekah had hoped. "They were sending General Asham in to oversee the invasion. I know his reputation for civilian casualties."

"Our enemies named him the Butcher of Almaar. The Scourge is our moniker, taken from his ship. Even the girls knew his reputation," added Savvo.

Rebekah mentally crossed her fingers. Was it enough? How much humanity did an Incini have with all that tech in her brain?

How human am I?

"And so, you deserted – with two assets of great value to the war effort," she looked to Rebekah then. There appeared to be an element of sympathy in her eyes, a softness to the expression. But she was a trained negotiator of the highest calibre, and Rebekah could not afford to let herself trust this woman. "And hid."

Savvo nodded, while Rebekah took the cue to glance to the twins. "What else could we do? Now you know, they need to ask you their questions, otherwise I think they might burst. That okay?" Davina nodded. "Tremil?"

Tremil's stiff smile and squeeze of her fingers preceded a gabble of words that tumbled over each other in a torrent.

Davina held up her hand, a strained smile on her face, brow furrowed. "Slow down."

Tremil nodded, glancing over to Rebekah, who despite the emotional assault, gently smiled with what she hoped was reassurance.

"What's it like, at the-the college? The Incini College. I've researched and researched and ..."

"Tremil, is it? There's a long and short answer. We can do the long answer another time. In short, hard work. Tremendously difficult mental and physical training. Relentless."

The girl beamed. "Th-Thank you." The words monotone. A sure sign she was reining herself in.

Rebekah nodded to Heki, whose lips quivered. "The electronics, the parts they surgically added ... How did it ... change you?"

Rebekah's jaw dropped, the earworm collapsing in on itself. She was mired in their fierce self-loathing tainted by an urgent need for it to stop. Her legs buckled, and she lurched forward, grabbing the galley bench. Davina had wrapped in on herself, tears running down her cheeks as she shook. Heki stared, horror written on her face.

Rebekah gathered the girl in her arms.

"I love you whatever," she whispered in the girl's ear. Heki gave in and wrapped herself about Rebekah. "Breathe. Count. Calm."

She heard Savvo behind, helping Davina onto the bench.

"Come. We need your help." Rebekah pulled away from Heki, and reached out a hand to Tremil who looked on stiffly. "The console, we need it back online or we're stuck here with no working O2 scrubbers. In eight hours, it will start getting pretty urgent."

She led the girls away, calling for Arin over the comms to talk them through the creeper and what he knew of how it worked. Their emotions mellowed, and Rebekah sensed their minds focus on something bland – it was why they had immersed themselves in so much tech. There were no feelings to get in the way.

Arin clunked his way into the galley, eyeing the aftermath and sending Savvo a sympathetic nod. He swept into the cockpit with a flood of jokes and smiles, and Rebekah left him to it, pushing the bulkhead semi-closed behind her. She turned to face the galley, letting out a long sigh.

Welcome to my world. Handle with care.

Davina sat at the table, hands wrapped about a flask of tea. A faint whiff of peppermint pervaded the air, and likely for some time without the scrubbers. Rebekah nodded to Savvo, flicking her head towards the exit. His smile was grim as he slid off his chair and left.

Rebekah waited.

After a minute, the Incini glanced over her tea. Her eyes were red-rimmed, though the tears had dried.

"Hurts, doesn't it? Worse than a physical blow." She licked her lips. "I think Savvo will have warned you, but …"

Davina ran the edge of her knuckle under an eye, catching a last tear and wiping it away. "That was so raw," she said.

Rebekah was unsure if she was deflecting from the point she was trying to make, or had missed it.

"The warning… They are special to us, to me. You are the only one other than us who knows about the twins," she continued.

Davina blinked, giving the impression she was struggling to process Rebekah's train of thought. "I … the contract is clear," she said, and eased back into the bench, puffing up her chest as she straightened her shoulders. "Unless they interfere with its fulfilment, I have no need to report on them. In that case, your secret is safe."

"Oh, it'll be safe," said Rebekah. She slid off the bench and got to her feet. "Have no doubt about that. None. We are here because we were blackmailed, threatened. But that was in your environment, now you are in mine. You may think you have all the cards, but I am the type of person who makes sure you won't have the *hands* to hold them with."

CHAPTER 14

"Try that, Dricks," called Arin over the comms. "Come on, old lady. Get your arse in gear."

Heki giggled, leaving a slight smile in its wake. "You can't call her that," she said. "It's rude."

"She loves the banter," replied Arin, his personal earworm relaxing as the mood shifted. "And gives it back."

"I know," said Tremil, while her fingers flew over the console touch pad. "You should hear what she calls you when your back is turned. Just for us."

"PYP," said Heki, blushing.

"Eh? What's that for?" Arin tried to hide a smile, knowing what was coming, but playing along.

"Piss-your-pants," whispered Tremil, leaning in closer. "She said that's what you did when you scanned ZZ3 for the nanites. That you forgot it had a component of the same metal."

"What? Wait until I ... I need some new names. Fart knickers," he said, before remembering that was exactly what she called him.

Heki's giggle echoed about the cockpit. "You can't say that. And don't go telling her we told you." She leaned in closer, perhaps as near as she had to anyone but Rebekah. "Not a word."

The comms buzzed, Hendricks' voice cutting in. "There's some juice in the can, but no start up. Get your arses on the job. Come back."

"Okay, FK. On it," Arin replied.

"FK? Those girls had better not be letting out any secrets. You hear me in there?" The twins clammed up; their faces suddenly serious. "As *I* know what you call Arin. Remember that."

Both girls stiffened, eyeing Arin. He smiled and shook his head. "Relax. She's playing the game, that's all. She wouldn't tell me, but not all people are so trustworthy."

Tremil pressed a couple more buttons, while Heki's slate merged into a swirl of 3D images that passed too fast for Arin to recognise, before settling on the creeper. It had embedded into the motherboard, metal limbs dug deep in a block of electronics.

"You mean Davina, the Incini," said Tremil. "Don't you?"

"I do." He handed over the link driver, and a collection of wiring clips that Heki pointed at. "She has a set of rules, but people with power like to bend or even ignore when rules are broken if …"

"It suits them," said Heki, her hands working inside the console, while her eyes watched the slate's screen. "You fear we understand the principals of social interaction, but have no practical experience."

Arin nodded. This was how they spoke whenever such questions arose. Switching from teenagers to a textbook. Of all the things he worried about, it was their isolation that galled him the most. How would they ever learn? Or be released?

"Got it," said Heki.

Arin glanced over at the complex and precarious bypass of wires and clips.

"The *old lady* can try again," Tremil said, smiling.

Arin whistled. "Flying close to the wind. Hey, Dricks, come back."

"I'm here getting my old lady pants in a bunch. We ready?" crackled the engineer's voice.

"Aye, FK, we are."

"I will find out what that means, and when I do ..." The ship rumbled to the sound of the autodrives. "I will forgive you all. Woo-hoo, we are up and firing on all cylinders."

"Cylinders?" said Heki.

Arin shrugged his shoulders and mouthed 'old lady'.

Rebekah inspected the creeper, the bot's appearance much like a woodlouse. Seven sets of limbs that crawled through the electronics, hunting for its target and then digging in, bypassing systems. Once the primary mission was complete, they dropped in a virus, usually with a secondary goal. In this case, the oxygen scrubbers.

"Give it back to the twins. I'd bet they can repurpose it. And Arin, thanks." She tilted her head towards the cockpit. "For in there. For what you did with the twins."

"You heard that, huh?" He collected the errant bot. "We all love them, Rebekah. We just don't have your strength."

"Captain," came Savvo's voice from the cockpit. "You need to come look at this."

She clunked her way into the cockpit, taking her seat as Savvo pointed at the console screen. "The bastards are still following us." He tapped at the pad, numbers flying as he ran a calculation. "We should have hit a hard burn to slow down two hours ago. They must have been upping their acceleration when we went dark, and now the *Maverick*'s on their steady slow down."

"Get to the point, Savvo."

"Point one, we're going to bypass the target unless we use an extended hard burn. Even then, they'll likely be there before us. Point two, they bloody knew when the creeper would act. They timed their speed changes for maximum gain." He glanced over, and Rebekah made no effort to hide her anger.

"And point three, if they set foot on whatever we are here for, they'll have the salvage rights, and we're screwed."

"We still don't have the scrubbers. If the girls can't strip out the virus, by rights, I'd be recommending we turn around, head for SK7 on the spin." Savvo pushed himself back in the co-pilot's chair, waiting for the tirade.

"An aborted mission? And the girls are involved in how it came about. Read the fucking small print, Savvo. It would get bloody messy." She spun the chair, heading out the door. "For all of us."

"You're going to have to trust me," Rebekah said. "No choice. I'll be putting the twins out too." She held out the tablets in one hand, in the other a hypodermic. "Either I do it, or you do. The needle is the fastest, and we're already short of time."

Davina rolled up her sleeve and took the needle. "And you?"

"We trained for years under heavy G. We pair up, watch each other's backs. It'll be shit, but like old time shit." Rebekah grinned. "Always nice to know what's coming."

The Incini expertly injected herself, rubbing the spot before rolling down the sleeve. With that, she sat down upon her berth. Rebekah pulled at the straps, buckling them to check they worked.

"Can you reach?" Rebekah pointed to the waiting catheter. "The drugs suppress the colon, but not the bladder. Have fun."

With that she left, taking a breath before knocking and entering the twins' room. Her internal song was up at maximum, and she had the spare headphones if things got really messy. When you were raised in a fucking lab – poked prodded, drugged day in and day out – what she was asking them to do was horrific. Only the alternative could be worse.

She exited after five minutes, her soul sore, tears on her cheeks. The girls had been sat waiting, already prepared as if they were test subjects going through their daily routine. It was Tremil who had spoken, a tremor to her lips.

"The alternative is to run," she had said. "And you have sacrificed so much for us already."

Fuck.

She checked that Hendricks and Arin were safely in position in the engineering room, then clicked her way through to the cockpit and took her place.

Savvo tapped the comms. "We are entering hard burn in sixty seconds. There'll be a ten second count down. Arin, you got those spare pants with you? Dricks, the hammer in case you need to shut him bloody up? I have a set of headphones if you need them."

"Har bloody har. May your stomach have a party in your mouth," Arin responded.

"Hey, didn't you black out the last time, Savvo?" said Hendricks. "I'm sure you missed that slow down to Erinta."

Rebekah grinned, the memory flooding back. "That was *after* the party in his mouth. Major Rin never forgave him. Shit, I never forgave him. Hendricks, can I swap places?"

"You want Arin for company? Sure."

Savvo cut in on the comms, "Too bloody late. Hold your water, we are engaging hard burn in ten, nine, eight …"

"Been a while since we talked like this," said Rebekah. "Maybe it's time."

"One … engaged. Shhhiiiiittttt."

Chapter 15

"Coming up," said Savvo, and he sent the images onto the galley screen.

Three asteroids spun about each other, each caught by the slightest of gravity and clearly related to each other. An asteroid family much like Minx, except they were smaller, closer and according to the sensor pings, filled with smaller debris they couldn't make out at that distance.

"We're at ten thousand clicks, so this is just about in real time but artificially enhanced based on the last hour's light stream," Savvo said. He pointed to a small glimmer of reflected light. "That's the *Maverick* coming to a stop. They have three hours on us if we hard stop. Five if we take it easy and wake the others up now."

"But we're beaten," said Rebekah, her shoulders hunched as she looked away from the screen.

"Only if they get on board. Look at the angle of spin on those rocks, the speed. That isn't natural. Someone has spun them up and set them orbiting each other," said Savvo and Arin nodded beside him.

"I agree on that. Even ZZ3 would struggle to navigate through that shit despite its reflexes." Arin stood and pointed to the centre of the orbit. "This rock seems to be the key, Savvo? You think?"

"We should run some simulations on it. Perhaps get the twins involved. But it certainly looks that way. That's some serious effort to protect whatever's inside. I wouldn't give up hope just yet. I don't know this Aidan Toms, but he must be on a huge bloody bonus if he tries it."

Rebekah stood and walked closer to the screen. She stared at the swirl of rock. "So why us? Why Marines?"

"That's the wrong question," said Hendricks. "Why a tested recovery squad with Marine experience? Two parts to that conundrum. The first is staring you in the face. The second is waiting for us on the other side of those rocks."

Rebekah watched the two space-suited figures, their flight packs jetting as they micro-adjusted to the flow of rocks that flashed across their path. They were a click south of their last attempt, now strewn with the extra debris of their recovery bot. She made an informed guess that the suits were being remotely controlled from the main ship. If it was her, they would be packed with recording equipment, learning as they went. Her smile tightened as the first suit stopped, having, she assumed, entered some clear space.

Davina squeezed in next to her on the bench. "Your assessment?" she enquired, tilting her head towards the screen.

"I'd give them about six out of ten for effort. Four for the fluidity of movement."

Davina smiled. "Yes. And their chances?"

"Nothing bigger than a bot is getting through. Tremil and Heki have run the simulations over and over. It's suits only. These have as good a chance as any. But should they reach whatever is in there first, we're screwed." She glanced over to the Incini. "So, a clue as to what is in there would help determine our priorities."

"I don't know. I have further instructions to read and share with the crew on your first visual contact with whatever is inside." Davina's fingers thrummed on the tabletop. "Not ideal, but contractually set."

"Most likely to prevent what has already happened. Losing out to another salvage group. Are there stipulations for that?" Rebekah leaned in closer and raised an eyebrow. There was the slightest tell in the movement of Davina's left eye. "There is, isn't there?"

"I can't confirm, nor ethically deny."

A light flared on the screen, the pack of the stationary suit exploding then quickly fading away. A trail of debris strung out behind it, though thankfully none of it appeared human. Rebekah watched the second disappear behind one of the asteroids. It didn't reappear.

"Well, you may not have to action those non-existent instructions. Unless the *Maverick* is packing a serious number of suits on board. We'll be at a stop in an hour, and you know what I'm going to do? I'm going to scan this bastard asteroid family from every angle I can. I get one peep at what's inside, from whatever distance, and you are contractually obliged to kiss my arse."

Arin felt the comfort of ZZ3's limbs wrapped about his midriff, his suit adapting to the curve of the bot's torso as they exited the cargo hold.

"You ever been this far out into the black, ZZ3?"

"No, our glorious leader, I haven't. Though, according to my scanners, it is very much like every other bit of space." The warbot's thrusters ignited on their left side, sending them into a curve that skirted the edge of the rock curtain whirling about the asteroid family. "Except emptier."

"Heh, I think you're right there. Deploying probe one. Deployed." The tiny satellite-cum-drone spurted forward, closing in on the orbiting debris. "Take us ten degrees to this axis."

"Actioned."

Arin gave it a little longer, then set the second probe free and its remotes kicked in. They repeated the process seven more times, before heading back on their own outer orbit towards the *Sunstar*.

"Glorious leader, my sensors detect an anomaly."

"Explain, ZZ3." The bot spun about, and a smaller screen appeared in Arin's HUD in the top right corner. He eye-clicked, dragging the image down for a closer look. "What am I looking at?"

"Ship debris," said the bot. "Without a cross-referenced analysis, I could not designate its origin with any certainty. Watch the spin of the third asteroid."

Splitting the screen, Arin matched his view to ZZ3s additional screen. The red marker flagged up, enabling him to visualise its position. They zoomed in as close as they could. It was definitely from a ship. "Hazard a guess. Another salvage ship? Are we the last desperate choice of a greedy royal bastard?"

"Unlikely. Analysis shows armoured plating. It is likely of Almaarian Navy origin."

Rebekah huffed, hands on her chin. Davina sat beside her as the probes drew a complete, spherical image of the asteroid family and its siblings. With each pass and angle adjustment, they added another layer of information.

"This standard recovery equipment?" asked the Incini, fascinated as the complexity increased.

"It is when you have bored twins with nothing to do all day and brains the size of a planet," said Rebekah, looking back over her shoulder to ensure Savvo was on the monitor. The *Maverick* had been manoeuvring, searching she believed, for another possible way in. At what point would they risk everything, or withdraw, leaving at a big loss to their coffers? Or would they wait on them and try and grab what they could? She was certain they'd snuck the cam-bot aboard, and at the moment held out hope they had planned to help them on the way back. But then the scrubbers ...

"It's just tech adapted and used in a different way. They think differently. But," she glared at the Incini, "it was our choice to use it, understand? Not theirs. See them as our tech supplier, and we simply use those tools to do the best job we can." The image was complete, the probes now on their second sweep. Rebekah wasn't so sure it was needed as something familiar caught her attention.

She tapped her pilot comms unit. "ZZ3, sending you coordinates now. Focus on the flag, at the designated axis point and angle." She clicked on her slate and sent the data direct.

"Adapting for our glorious leader," replied ZZ3.

"Glorious leader?" Davina repeated, shaking her head.

"Like I said, space is boring. Days of nothing to do. It's alright for a few months," Rebekah said.

"But after four years, I bet the cracks begin to show," Davina said, and she locked eyes with Rebekah.

She couldn't read what lay behind those Incini eyes, and was forced to look away. The change in image saved her before Davina started to inquire further, but there was no way she missed the affirmation in Rebekah's eyes. The image resolution continued to increase, the ship's computer enhancing the layers of images the probes produced. A flicker across the screen indicated ZZ3 and Arin's arrival.

She wanted to revel in the victory, except the image brought her up short. "You see it, Arin. You got eyes on?"

"You mean do I have eyes on the fucking Almaarian cruiser? I can't unsee it."

"We've cleared the virus from the scrubber system," said Heki.

"And the probes?"

"They tried and failed." Heki handed over her slate, running her finger down the list of hacking attempts on the probes. "I mean, the code cracking is about four years out of date. A child could have kept the *Maverick* out." Heki caught Rebekah's smirk, and the girl's surge of anger and frustration caused her to wince. "I am *not* a child."

"I agree. Can you send that to my slate?" Rebekah said, and rubbed her temple. "Quietly."

"Sorry." Heki clomped off down the corridor.

"She could have sent that from her room," said Savvo. "They are testing their boundaries. We have unleashed the beasts of war." He tapped Rebekah's shoulder, smiling at her concerned look. "It's what teenagers do, and for the best. Though the timing could have been better."

"About right, I think." She pointed to the enhanced image. "Assessment?"

"It's holed here and there. Could be attack damage, but I am more inclined to say some of the minor asteroids have kicked out of their orbit from time to time. No markings. They have scrubbed her clean. So, no way to tell who she is until we get into the main navcom." Savvo looked to his slate. "There are at least thirty ships of her class destroyed or missing from the war. Could be any one of those."

"Or any that were declassified since. Fruitless. The only way to know is to get aboard. But before then," she eyed Davina, "I take it you've accessed the stipulations?"

"I think you have pushed the boundaries of the contract," she replied. "But considering where we are, and the competition, I have. You may want to see this on your own."

"You employed *Marines*, Incini. We don't act alone. Duboit knew there was a Navy cruiser, and we are most definitely not here to collect on its salvage. It's most likely a war grave, or at the very least, an accident that'll come under that statute. Unless you tell me otherwise, we are not going near it."

"Under Almaarian law, the ship was declassified and engaged as a private transport. It was on route to the Senti transport hub when it disappeared." Davina threw up the ship's limited data onto the screen. "It was returning high-ranking Bustan prisoners. And … this."

The screen filled with a containment unit. A rectangular box, about two metres long by one metre in height and width. They were often used to carry sensitive equipment.

"So that's our primary target? What's in there?"

"An AI."

"From Bustan 8? We lost thousands on that bloody planet." Savvo kicked the bench.

"I don't know which, just that its dangerous and needs to be kept in the containment box." Davina tapped the screen, and the information stream dropped off to be replaced by something far more familiar. The suits currently residing in the cargo hold. "We suspect the ship had more than just human guards. Standard designation would point to autobots. You're going to need more than your old recovery suits."

"They were going home, why would the Bustans need guards?"

"Not everyone trusts what they were told. Besides, according to the logs, this was a secret exchange to seal the cessation. Secret even to the ship and its crew. Nobody wanted word to get out." Davina left the details of the suit and the weaponry up as she turned to face Rebekah.

"All that fuckery points to it being the Battle AI from Bustan 8. You know what you are asking us to do? To monetise our dead?"

"I concur with Mr Duboit's assessment that this is a fully legal contract under the auspices of Almaarian law. You are contractually obliged to engage in this mission. If you renege, then you know I will have to dig." She glanced towards the corridor and the cabins beyond. "And likely not very deep."

"You're unbelievable," said Savvo. "I was just beginning to like you."

Rebekah glared at the Incini. "I wasn't."

Chapter 16

Rebekah donned the helmet, and with the gentlest of twists, the electronic motors whirred, and the hiss of its seal echoed through her comms. She eye-clicked the cursor blinking at the bottom right of her heads-up display, and selected the communications tab. With a few more clicks, she removed the echo.

"You losing your touch, Arin? I thought you tested these navy skins?" She lifted her hand, pulsing her fingers to test the gauntlet's movements. She had to admit, they were top of the line, perhaps a notch up from the black ops kit the Breakers had used when they were atmosphere surfing.

"I have to leave one fault so you can beat down on me some more. Checking suit links in one, two, three, … now." Arin eye-clicked the auto connect. Rebekah felt her suit sag, then stiffen. "Relax your limbs, people." Rebekah's knees pumped, then her powered arms. Savvo's mirrored hers.

"We're good?" she asked.

"A-okay. Recovery program engaged. You get killed, I get to play with your body."

"There's better ways to explain recover and return protocols, dickhead." Rebekah slapped Savvo on the armoured shoulder, giving him the thumbs up. To her shock, the suit's HUD overlaid her second-in-command's laughing face onto his helmet visor, as if she could see inside. She half-looked away, the image clearing as it reached the edge of her vision, and filled in Arin's when she glanced his way.

Eye-tracking too. Impressive.

Savvo's comms clicked on. "Just like old times, except Arin is just a touch more insane." He flexed his wrist from side to side, and twin barrels flicked out. "These work the same, Mr Glorious Leader?"

"Six shots each on the right, over and under grenades on the left. External hip packs I've emptied and replaced with our old kit. Fucked if I want to be relying on weapons I've not stripped and prepped."

Rebekah grinned, catching herself, trying to overcome the sense of warmth coming over her. Was it right to feel comfortable as they tooled up once again? Yet the atmosphere was electric, each of them slotting back into the old ways – their old roles – and the morbid banter that had kept them tight and alive as the shrapnel flew.

Should I have missed this as much as I do?

She checked her weaponry, and the auxiliary pack augmented with basic salvager's welding and chem-entry paraphernalia. Low duty, ZZ3 carried the heavy, industrial kit.

"We are in the green, Dricks. Good to go, come back," she said.

"The *Maverick* hasn't moved, but I'll keep an eye. Good hunting …"

Rebekah tensed, feeling her fingers pulse. *Good hunting* was an old Breaker refrain, one of their ex-captain's favourites.

"…Wrecking Crew. Bring back something shiny for Savvo to put under his bed."

She sighed; relieved Hendricks had used their new title. Right now, Davina had enough hold on them. One whiff of them being the Breakers, and she suspected the whole mission would fall apart.

Savvo pointed his middle finger towards the hold camera, his smile wide and savage.

"ZZ3, activate escort protocol, activation code Wrecking Crew," said Arin.

"Active," replied the bot, extending its jointed limbs, and lifting the cumbersome looking rig secured to its back. Rebekah watched as the additional arms and their various attachments sucked back into the solid box wired into its main torso. It nearly doubled the width of the bot, and had been a bone of contention with Arin. But having to come back through the hell of a maelstrom surrounding their target was a far worse option. Take everything you need. One trip in, one trip out. That was the plan.

They all collected their auto-jets, large backpack style jetpacks designed to save their suits from expending any fuel. Rebekah slotted into hers and confirmed the connection with her suit's systems.

"We all synced?" queried Rebekah, and her HUD beeped. The jetpack's thrusters gently throbbed.

"We are on trajectory," said Hendricks. "Main doors opening in three, two, one. Engage."

All four lifted off the hold floor and exited in unison from the *Sunstar*. The synced auto-navigation set their suits on a curved path away from the ship's orbit and on towards the middle-sized asteroid. Rebekah, as she felt on the rare occasions she joined her crew on recovery missions, was in awe of the sheer depth of space. The black called to her, the mere pinpricks of light in the distance singing to her heart. She had always refrained from identifying Bustan's star and the visceral, painful memories it carried. Doing so would add a cloud over her love for the freedom space inspired.

"Check in," she said. Each of her crew called back, confirming what her HUD told her. They were in the green, and in the pipe, heading into the unknown together.

And it felt good.

The sheer silence swallowed her, and as the jetpack carried her onwards, began to realise that it was true silence. No earworm required, nor the defensive walls as her crew bickered. Not even the bustle of the Karal docks and quarters to intrude.

Utter silence.

Mesmerising. And too dangerous – for the mission, and for her sanity. A glimpse of what could be ... if she just gave the twins up.

Her breath caught, sickened at herself for that unbidden thought.

They are human and they need to be loved.

"Target in sight," said ZZ3 over the comms, the robotic voice thankfully cutting through her thoughts. "Permission to sync packs with my navcom."

She checked her HUD for the crew's status, and satisfied, replied, "Granted, ZZ3. Action code, Wrecking Crew."

ZZ3 was ahead of the three of them as they approached the spinning asteroid. Its surface pockmarked, rough. In places small canyons gouged the surface, and from others sharp, flint-like cliffs rose in hooked, menacing curves. The twins had analysed the asteroid field's orbital patterns, discerning multiple routes amid the probes' constant feed. Except not one would see them all through safely. Instead, they would be scattered across the field in pieces or cut off and alone. Rebekah also had half her mind on the *Maverick*, which hovered with intent. If they had set the cam-bot on their ship, then what would stop such a devious crew from intercepting them on exit from the asteroid field with their prize? Especially if they came through alone.

It had been Davina who had cut through it all with simple logic. She noted that the outer asteroids now bludgeoned their way through the maelstrom with very few impacts. And she simply asked why. Within minutes, they and the ship's computer had worked out a plan in tandem. Ride the smaller asteroid's spin until they were on the inside of the rocky maelstrom, and then back out. Its trajectory already set, with the likelihood of minor rocks deviating from their swirling orbits within safety limits. Well, the 'safe limits' set in a contract that promised Calc.

With the *Sunstar*'s orbit altered, they were now closing in on completing the first stage.

After that, anything could happen.

ZZ3 fired dual pinions twenty metres above the target surface. They winged their way downwards, driving into the surface in a section clear of any ultra hard rock. The first stage hit with an impact explosion, the second drove them deeper and the holding pins fired, extending to grip the asteroid.

"Testing," said ZZ3, and Rebekah imagined the whirr of its motors pulling at the pinions. One gave, ripping the surface and she swore as it clattered back into the bot. Their time window was small, and any increase in momentum would require additional fuel expenditure to arrest. That, or they flew into the swirling rocks and were smashed to pieces. The second line went briefly slack, then tightened, and ZZ3 reeled itself towards the surface. The thick synth-rope began to angle away as the asteroid spun, and Rebekah's jetpack suddenly surged. She flicked her eyes to the HUD, calming her heart, noting the other packs had also engaged in sync and were heading directly for ZZ3. Within ten seconds, ZZ3 was feet down on the surface, with a member of the Wrecking Crew wrapped in three of its limbs.

"Group hug," said Arin. "Just want you to know that each one of you is special to me."

"Fuck off, Arin," said Savvo.

"Can it, both of you. Focus," Rebekah ordered, and scanned the black above her. Rocks peppered the sky, reflecting the weak light of the distant sun as they careered on. The criss-cross patterns set a dread deep in her chest, and the silence she had revelled in earlier was broken by the beat of her heart and hoarseness of her breath. It would take just a micro adjustment for them to collide, to be deflected off their path. One pebble, travelling at colossal speed, could not only penetrate her suit, but would rush on through with hardly a stutter. Flesh and blood were such insignificant barriers to the madness of space.

"Recalibrating release," said ZZ3. "Time window begins in fifteen seconds."

"Check in," she said, the words spilling out in a hurry.

"Green," came back the dual response.

"Adjusting release," said ZZ3, and the bot's head swivelled, red eyes flashing. An image flowered on Rebekah's HUD. A rock disintegrating, the individual sections flying apart. Her boots rumbled, with her chest vibrating as ZZ3 burst off from the surface. Still held tight by its arms, she thrashed her head, searching for a glimpse of the danger when something struck the bot's metal hull. It gouged a scar across one shoulder, the deep scratch glowing hot before rapidly cooling. A second glanced off its forehead, smaller and scoring an electronic eye.

"Shit." Rebekah's stomach lurched as they entered a spin. "Status call."

"Green," replied Savvo, a strange wetness to his words.

"Yeeha," said Arin. "I'm in the green."

Rebekah mentally checked herself, focusing on one point on her HUD as they spun away from the smaller asteroid. Nausea roiled, sinuses screaming as her ears protested.

"Clear," said ZZ3, its voice the usual calm monotone. "Spinning down."

The flare of the bot's thrusters lit up the black, repeating gentle patterns. Her head began to clear as the momentum stayed and the pressure thankfully dropped. As the last rush in her ears calmed, she found herself looking upon their target – the central asteroid. Its spin was slow, almost majestic compared to what they had just been through. On the surface, the Navy cruiser sat waiting for them. The dread that had entered her chest dropped like a stone into her stomach. She couldn't explain it, but the sight of the stricken ship set her on edge, weighed her down. The last time she had felt like this, Hendricks had ordered her to lead after Tremil's empathic assault. The sheer pain in her captain's voice had entered her mind and never left. She had feared what she would encounter – and found her squad mates' minds and bodies decimated – and the end of the Breakers.

"We good, ZZ3?"

"Yes," said the bot. "Though I have been forced to use more thruster fuel than expected within the mission parameters."

Anxiety squirmed inside. "Explain," she said.

"I may, as our glorious leader puts it, be running on fumes for the return journey."

Chapter 17

The twins sat wedged together on the galley bench; their eyes glued to the large screen while sharing the butter-flavoured popcorn Hendricks had made from a large domed bowl. Each crunch set Davina's teeth on edge, and she had resorted to the headphones, while the warm, buttery smell had major disagreements with her nostrils. Luckily, she hadn't needed to worry about the girls picking up on her discomfort, they were engrossed in Rebekah and her team's efforts. Their nerves, Davina considered, perhaps contributing to her nausea despite the loud music ringing in her ears.

Hendricks sat with her, the engineer's lined brow rising and falling with worry as the crew alighted on the asteroid. After the first pinion gave, the wave of concern from the twins had played across the engineer's face, the pain obvious but the stubborn woman refused to give in. A mere rub of her temples the only admission to the effects of the girls' fraught emotions. When the spin of the asteroid brought back their target area into view, the team's absence was a relief.

Hendricks drew out her slate from a thigh pocket, and tapped at the screen. There, in simple green text, sat a message from ZZ3 confirming they had got through. "Interference," she mouthed. "Over the comms."

Davina nodded, feigning a smile she did not feel. At first the contract had seemed clear cut, but the staged reveal of the target had set her nerves on edge. Whatever she had admitted to Rebekah had not fully reflected her own views. Duboit had pushed the boundaries of acceptable protocol as laid down by the Emperor and the Incini. Pushed, but not broken, though it left her in an awkward position. If the AI was the target, and it was the Battle AI as Rebekah feared, then the laws became decidedly murky – and the point where *intent* encroached. What the hell did he want it for? To return it to the Bustans? Unlikely, unless it was for a price. Or to develop it for the Almaarians? But the nobles had banned such technology as dishonourable, though in truth, they feared it usurping their status. For personal use? That scared her the most.

With the bowl empty, and the screen filled with the same lonely image, the girls got up and made their exit. Once they were in the corridor, Davina removed the headphones, though her ears still rang for a few seconds afterwards.

"How do you get used to it?" she asked as she attached the headphones' magnet to the table.

Hendricks looked at her intently, and she could sense the engineer was measuring how far she could be trusted. How much she could say. The brow furrowed a little more, the lines on her cheeks joining in.

"Practise. My own personal box where I put my thoughts. They are learning all the time, and we hope that once they get a little older, and their biology changes, their control will develop even more." The engineer pressed a hand into the small of her back, sighing as she did so.

"But why do it? It must be horrendous at times." Davina pushed a little, her curiosity urging her on.

Hendricks gave her a tight smile. "Is this where you lead me down the alley, then bash me over the head with a tangential question? The simple answer is that there was no one else to do it. The complicated answer requires a heart, a family. Love. Nothing that makes sense written down, or reported to a commanding officer. Or your boss."

Davina considered probing a little more, but it dawned on her she was just distracting herself from her own concerns, and by doing so was adding to Hendricks' worries.

A red flash filled the room.

"Shit," said the engineer, who quickly stood and headed for the cockpit.

"What was that?" Davina asked, standing up and ready to follow. "Are they in trouble?"

"No. We are. Proximity alert. That bastard Toms has ... no. Not the ship. Shit, he's sent boarders." Hendricks looked over to Davina with her lips twisted into a scowl. "Two, maybe three suits out there. They're trying to get aboard. They're after the salvage. To steal it."

Reality hit home, the thought of the cam-bot and the scrubber virus at the forefront of Davina's mind. They weren't playing games. No laws and stipulations out here. In fact, the *Sunstar*'s crew being dead would make their lives a hell of a lot easier.

"What do you want me to do?" she asked.

Hendricks ignored her, clicking through the screen menu, eyes roaming over the options. She selected, and an image popped up that looked to Davina like a short-barrelled gun. A little hope flowered until Hendricks started thumping the top of the console. "The point debris cannons are down. Not just down, offline." She clicked deeper into the menu. "Look at that."

Davina peered closer. The *Threat to Life* message blinked back at her. "Can't you switch it off?"

"The options greyed out. I bet you a bang to a buck the fuckers snuck in a second target for that virus. This was planned." Hendricks looked up at her. "You any good with a gun?"

She nodded. "On the range, I'm a damn fine shot."

The light flashed red again, a clang echoing across the ship, followed swiftly by another two. Hendricks bent over the console, tapping away at the screen. "Shit. They're not boarding." She flicked the screen around where it displayed a scavenger's industrial laser clamped to the hull. A large, gloved hand appeared over the screen, and then it went dead.

"Of course they are, they're just cutting their way in."

Hendricks shook her head. "No. Easiest way in is through the airlock failsafe systems. But those are hard to rewire if your intentions are not good. They're going to empty the ship of its atmosphere. Forcing us into the rescue suits, and when their air gives out, we're fucked." Her eyes glazed over, the lips quivering. "It's what I'd do. Shit, it's what *I've* done. Take down the enemy, while minimising your own casualties."

Hendricks leant on the console top with both hands, her lips twitching for a few seconds. Davina remained quiet, letting the ex-Marine think. She was, after all, her best hope of survival.

"I need to go out there. Buy some time, stop them if I can. And you … you need to watch over Tremil and Heki. Understand? If it goes shit-face up, keep them safe. Promise me."

"I can't … I."

"They hate the spacesuits, you understand? The claustrophobia sends them wild, takes them back to when we first found them. Those bastards breach this hull, get inside, they'll be the first to go. They will dump the air from whatever hidey-hole they take up and then you can sit there with your guilt until the fuckers come for you." Hendricks pushed past her, heading for the corridor, shouting over her shoulder. "And put your bloody headphones on."

"What about the rest of the crew?" she said, trailing behind while fiddling with the headphones.

"Message sent," replied Hendricks. They had reached the twins' door, her hand hovering over it. "Strange they didn't jam that, unless of course they're doing it some way I can't detect."

The door slid open before she could knock, Tremil stood there in her *Sunstar* jumpsuit with Heki standing behind in hers. Their faces were flat, lifeless. "We got some of it through," said Tremil, her voice monotone. "The message. Text only and bounced off their ship. But the frequencies are now flooded." She tilted her head, the movement stiff. Davina felt the tinge of her presence against the barrier of the music. It scared her more than the waves of need they had overwhelmed her with before. It was a void, empty. A soulless abyss that she daren't investigate in case she found the answers.

"You know what's happening?" said Hendricks. Her hand reached for Tremil, and the girl flinched away, eyes like death falling on the engineer.

"Yes," said Heki from behind. "But not what to do."

A clang not dissimilar to those from before resounded through the ship. A wave of fear rode through the abyss and assailed her music, and Davina staggered, grabbing hold of Hendricks.

"Sorry," said Tremil, a flicker of pain rode the mask of her face. "It is too much." She glanced back to Heki, and to Davina's surprise, reached out a hand. The girls stood there, hand in hand, looking so young. They knew nothing else but each other and – for the last few years – the protection of the crew, and it was about to come tumbling down. Faced with the technology of the creeper, they had shown little concern. Their thoughts clear, the resolution swift. But people?

"What are we going to do? By the time they get the message – if they get it – we'll likely be dead," said Heki. There was a tremble to her shoulders and Davina could see the mask wouldn't last long.

"I'm going to delay them." Hendricks eyed Davina, watching her as she spoke. "Heki, Tremil, go and hide. Find somewhere quiet. Take an O2 bottle and the survival clothing from your locker. It's going to get damn cold. And stay quiet until you hear Davina, understand. Listen for her voice, only come when she calls. No one else." Hendricks nodded to the girls, sending them a wink, then stomped off down the corridor.

Both girls looked to Davina but struggled to maintain their stern faces. Their nerves pressed in through the abyss, niggling at Davina's own drive for preservation. She upped the music, clinging on to the repetitive rhythm of words.

"O2 bottle?" said Tremil, her eyes flat. "I don't understand."

Davina felt an urge to reach out and touch the girl, but battened it down. "They're likely going to turn off the air. Force us to surrender," she lied. The music helped. That and the abyss the girls had forged between them. "You know where to find them?" Both girls nodded. "Then get gone. This part is up to you." Hating herself, she turned away. Thoughts of a spacesuit and finding her own place to hide paramount in her mind.

Chapter 18

The cruiser appeared to be more damaged than Rebekah had expected. The images built up by the probes gave the impression the hull was intact but holed. Now, as ZZ3 guided them closer, she could see the ship had suffered under some form of barrage. Likely rock debris from when the asteroid family had been set spinning, up until it consolidated into a more consistent orbit. As they closed, most appeared minor except for one breach near the base, likely where the ship had been set down on the highly uneven, rocky surface.

"How's it staying there?" said Savvo over comms. "By rights, it should spin off."

"The simulations agree," replied Arin. "So, it must be embedded somehow. Jammed in, perhaps."

Rebekah had an urge to check her HUD, rerun the downloaded sims. But the ship's presence in her visor was ominous, a creeping sense that the whole mission was a shitshow compounded by the malevolence it exuded. Unpleasant, brooding, and right now she feared talking about it would spook her crew. Deal with the facts. Plan, prepare, and act on what happens.

"Drop us down near this breach, ZZ3." She eye-clicked the exact spot on her HUD. The bot responded and recalibrated its flight. She desperately wanted to sweep the whole ship, but thruster fuel was tight, and getting back relied on the bot's sensors and flight sync systems.

It wasn't long before the side of the pitted spaceship loomed above. Its armour plate scarred with multiple strikes, a myriad tiny holes that penetrated the outer hull. Whether the ship's inner protection was intact was another issue. Cruisers were tough, built for battle in the outer regions of a solar system. This one looked as though it had fought valiantly, and then died upon the asteroid. A grave indeed, especially if there were multiple internal breaches.

They slowed on approach, dropping beneath the grey metal hulk towards the browns and blacks of the asteroid's rocky surface. With a minor adjustment, they closed to where the ship's keel met the asteroid. A twisted set of docking clamps rose from a smoothed strip of rock, and were bound tight to the ship. The hull was scraped and scarred, as if it had battled the clamps to get away. On closer inspection, what she had taken for a major breach, was where the main engines had ruptured at the rear.

"What the fuck," said Arin. "Am I seeing what I think I'm seeing?"

"Leave supposition until we have boots on ground," snapped Rebekah.

"Yes, Captain," he replied. "ZZ3, escort protocol pinion ..."

"Alpha," replied Rebekah. "Twenty metre spread." She eye-clicked the location near the clamps.

"Alpha positions. Action code Wrecking Crew."

"Confirmed," replied the bot, and they flew lower in a spiral until satisfied with the chosen position, and the bot drew the multi-barrelled pinion gun from its back. Inside two minutes, ZZ3 secured anchor points in a twenty-metre square next to the twisted clamp. They waited until the debris had drifted harmlessly from the surface as the asteroid spun, and ZZ3 took them in.

The bot's sync escort system brought them all together, wrapped in a limb each, as the bot secured itself to a pinion. With affirmation from Rebekah, they de-synced and their jetpacks powered down.

"Savvo, Arin. Dynamic synth-ropes along the outer perimeter. Static within. Move Marines," Rebekah ordered.

They both disengaged from ZZ3, drawing out the coiled and linked synth-ropes from their hip packs. Thin and super strong, it was a recovery squad's prime tool when working in space. A simple clip could save you from a long, lonely death.

After they had tested and then attached themselves to a driven pinion, she left them to it and examined the docking clamps. Eye-clicking the HUD, she drew the images in closer, assessing the damage. She dismissed their first thought of a crash; it had never explained the orbiting asteroid family. There was no way the cruiser could have entered and remained in one piece. To her mind, the asteroid shield had been created around the ship, and at an extreme cost, though the skills to achieve such a feat were evident right across the belt. She could name three companies without thinking who could have made it happen. But out here, in the depths beyond the inner system, the logistics were phenomenal.

And logistics, and costs, spoke to her of the Almaarian Navy, even the Emperor and the Court.

But that didn't explain why. If they wanted to prevent any eyes seeing what was on board, why not just blow it up?

Unless this was all about the Bustan AI, and it was the Court they were hiding it from. The nobles and their fear of being usurped.

What the hell had they got themselves involved in?

"ZZ3, what's the likelihood you could find more of your thruster fuel aboard the cruiser?" she said.

"Under normal circumstances, one hundred percent. If any humans survived and attempted escape, the odds drop significantly," replied the bot. Its red eyes whirred about to look towards the ship. "Autobot guards were mentioned but standard cruisers carried three warbots during the Bustan War. All AD units, attack and destroy." The eyes whirred back, the bot dimming the glow to peer straight at Rebekah. "They are, of course, completely compatible with my systems and fuel requirements."

"Then that is priority one," she said, her HUD pinging with an image of the completed safety perimeter. She clicked on the comms as Savvo and Arin returned. "We set this area as a base of operations, and we only enter the ship when we have accessible areas mapped. I'll get the shelter up. Savvo, I want the comms relay running and the zero-g drones prepped. Arin, you and ZZ3 find us the nearest entry point and attach a dual access line. This is what we do, what we know. The Wrecking Crew." She glanced up to the looming wreck.

So, when do we become the Breakers again?

ZZ3 lifted gently from the surface, and with Arin clamped to the bot's chest, spun to face the stricken Almaarian cruiser. Analysis flowed into Arin's HUD. Details of the armour thickness, assessment of the visible damage, extrapolation of possible conditions of the inner skin. ZZ3 scrutinised the information as they rose, narrowing down their options until settling on three within line of sight.

Arin eye-clicked through the list, assigning an order that would use the least fuel. They flew to the first, but Arin couldn't help checking and rechecking the fuel monitor. Even by his basic mental calculations, he knew the bot had little chance of getting back to the asteroid entry point. Leaving ZZ3 to find its own way, he set his suit computer onto the task of planning the crew's synced route out of the asteroid field. He needed to know their leeway for his own peace of mind.

"On approach to entry point one, glorious leader," said ZZ3. "Enhancing image."

The image grew in his HUD, and Arin eye-clicked the shadowed metal inside the razor-edged hole. "That inner skin is intact," he said. "We'd need to cut through. Where would we come out?"

"That is classified information," recounted the bot.

"Override protocol, action code Breakers. I repeat, what's on the other side?"

"Minor fusion generator for the lower rear deck," replied ZZ3. "The inner hull is about seventy-five centimetres thick."

Arin whistled. "So that'd be a *no*, then." Arin mentally kicked himself. How long had they been out of practice? "Assess the other two entry points using the cruiser schematics, evaluate parameters based on ease of access using current equipment."

There was a pause, then the bot spoke. "Access point three would bring us out in the lower deck galley. Inner hull skin would be twenty-five centimetres thick. Standard cutting time thirty minutes for safe entry."

"Take us there."

ZZ3 complied, and after a minute, they hovered ten metres from the breach. The edges of the hole were peppered with embedded rock fragments, but the inner was hard to make out. They moved closer, ZZ3 engaging its headlight. The beam struck a wall of red – all swirls of scarlet and crimson that covered half the inner skin in a hardened shell.

"Someone has sealed a breach. Survived the crash. Maybe there's people still in there," whispered Arin.

"Unlikely," replied the bot. "Is further assessment required?"

"Check the temperatures, drill a pinprick hole and test the atmosphere. We don't cut until we know it's clear."

ZZ3 hovered in closer and clamped two limbs to the ship's surface. A third limb's tip pressed against the red material, and data ticked off in

Arin's HUD. Without analysing the composition, he wouldn't have a clear picture of the heat exchange properties, but right now the temperature matched that of the outer hull. ZZ3 twisted the limb back in as a chamber at its hip broke open to reveal a variety of attachments. After engaging the selected augmentation, the limb extended, its tip glowing with a very thin white lance. The bot paused as if selecting a likely spot, then pushed the lance into the material. Crimson flowed from the hole like lava, freezing solid as it pillowed over itself. ZZ3 extracted the lance, and already prepared, Arin slid in his suit's probe. It self-cleaned on the other side, and the temperature readings flooded in, counting down as the hole cooled.

"We have warmth, and atmosphere. Shit ZZ3, there could be survivors."

"Possible," replied the bot. Arin's HUD flickered with additional data. "Bio readouts would indicate minimal airborne bacterial activity. Recent human presence would seem unlikely... there is an anomaly, glorious leader."

Arin tensed. "Explain."

"Organics in the atmosphere that are not in my database."

"Eh? Extrapolate," Arin said, his heartbeat rising. He glanced at the red swelling bulging from the inner skin, finding the colours suddenly unsettling.

"Not of the Almaarian system, nor Bustan. I cannot explain further."

"Is it present in the material used to fill the breach?" he asked, unsure he wanted to hear the answer. He drew the probe back, scraping the inner wall of the red substance.

"There are multiple organics present," the bot replied, and Arin steeled himself. "Both human and the unclassified organic. Also, synthetic beef, soya extract and various chemicals used in 3D printing."

The dread shifted and encased his heart in a cold grip. "Captain, we have a problem."

Tethered to the safety lines and huddled together beside ZZ3, all three stood and watched the 3D map form on their HUDs. The zero-g drones were steady but slow, and the inner structure took time to come to light as they roamed the areas of the ship devoid of atmosphere and warmth. They came across numerous bulkheads and were forced to turn around and head back, their electromagnetic fields bouncing them off the walls to career back down the wide corridors of the large ship. Within an hour, they had a map that covered a third of the cruiser – the rest inaccessible as far as they knew. Some sections had taken severe damage, she assumed from rock strikes penetrating deep into the ship. But they needed eyes on. The drones had provided a rough map, anything more detailed would require hours. Time they didn't have when they were relying on their suits' scrubbers, spare batteries and limited filters. Rebekah wished for one of the orbital probes to sweep the entire ship's hull before going in, but wishes meant little when you had an asteroid family swirling around you.

"We can abort," she said, sensing Arin's glare fall upon her. "Return to the *Sunstar*, call it a bust. No one can say we didn't make the attempt."

"And we risk dying on the way without ZZ3," Savvo said, so that Arin didn't have to. He also left out 'and leave ZZ3 behind'.

"We go in, find ZZ3's fuel, then make a decision," insisted Arin, the comms doing little to hide his frustration.

"With what ZZ3's basic analysis is telling us, we're going into an unknown situation. No evac, no backup. We have had zero comms response." Rebekah eye-clicked an uncharted section of the map – now overlaid with the expected schematic – close to the ship's main bay. "The warbots are stationed here when not in use. Their armoury and fuel stored next to it."

"Aye," said Savvo. "The cargo bays are double reinforced with the inherent need for the door to repel shelling. Cutting in will take longer than if we enter this breach." He eye-clicked a sector ZZ3 had scanned and tethered on their way back. "We already have this entry prepped. Longer walk, but worth it."

"Agreed," Rebekah said, and turned to face them both. She leant in, and all three helmets pressed together, eyes to the rocky ground. "From this point on, we are Marines again. The Breakers once more, understand? Whatever happens, you follow orders, you kick fucking arse, and we protect each other's backs."

"Yes, Captain," they both replied. "Nobody breaks the Breakers."

"Nobody," she reiterated.

"Heh," said Savvo. "Pike would have a bloody field day. If only he knew why you hated being called The Wrecking Squad so much."

"Crew … we were a crew." She eyed them both again. "And now we are a squad once more."

Chapter 19

Hendricks' left magboot adhered to the airlock floor, and she swung the right onto the third rung of the exterior ladder-cum-handhold. Cursing the rescue suit, she reached up and clipped her lifeline onto the safety rail, and then gripped the rungs with both hands. Releasing the boot still inside the airlock, she eye-clicked the HUD. The airlock didn't budge, and she swore, reaching over to press a panel in a coded pattern. A flap flipped open, and she depressed the button. To her relief, the airlock slid closed.

"Bastards have hacked more systems than we knew," she muttered, and made her way up the rungs until the curve of the hull allowed her boots to lock onto the metal surface. She still knelt, testing the knee motors of the spacesuit. Satisfied, she rose and slipped the Marine-issue carbine from the back sheath. Clicking off the safety, Hendricks tried to focus on the flat part of the ship, and not the curving hull that would lead her eyes out into the black. Even the thought of doing so sent her weak at the knees, and testing the motor again, she stiffened the joints.

"We were never meant for combat in space. Why would you? One snick of the suit, and you're pushing up frozen daisies."

She reached down and unclipped the tether, adding it to the safety bar that ran along the topside ladder. With a heaviness to her lungs despite the lack of gravity, she lifted her leg and dialled down the electromagnet on her boot, then tested it. The grip broke away easily, and she shook her head. "Why the fuck did I ever join the Marines?"

Hendricks matched the new setting on her other boot, and bending low, started to walk along the ship. The gentle grip and click was silent on the hull, but the softness of her movements was not mirrored by her hardening mood. She checked her HUD; the timer approaching a fourth minute. If the *Maverick* crew were using an industrial cutter, that was as long as it would take to breach the plate and inner hull.

Her hands ran over the carbine, working by memory as she adjusted the safety and ran through the three triggers. Satisfied, she finally reached the curve of the engine mounts, and ducked lower to peer over the hull side, trying desperately to focus on the metal and the enemy, and not the void that menaced around her.

A gentle pull away from the ship lifted her suit and tugged at her boots, the grip wavering. Ignoring it, she took two hesitant steps towards where she expected the cutter and its crew to be working. A helmet came into view, bobbing in front of the thick barrelled cutter and the top of its extended limbs that adhered to the ship. If she risked the shot, the second salvager would be alerted, reducing her chances, and she de-clamped her right boot, ready to take another step.

It was then she noticed the tether. Another lifeline attached to the opposite bar from hers. Her heart stopped, time slowing down as her eyes followed the line out into the black. Trying to ignore the void, she caught sight of a pair of boots. Smoothly, she lifted the carbine, trying to keep the movement natural. Whoever was out there, didn't have her experience or skill with a weapon. They were a salvager; a scavenger who decided murder was the low-risk path to a big score.

Hendricks pressed down towards her weapon, then jerked upwards, wishing for her old Breaker suit – recalling how the HUD would sync with the weapon's digital sight and arrow in on the target. Good times, until they weren't, and were forced to confront what you had become. To be swaddled in a child's fear and loathing, wrapped in their pain as you stared down the barrel of your own gun.

She remembered blinking, suddenly aware of the taste of metal in her own mouth. How it had got there remained a blur, aware only that she hated what she had become, and it was time to end the pain. To wipe away the devastation she had wrought in one simple act. Her finger had hovered over the trigger, begun to press, the first click making her wince. Gun shots rang. Blood spattered her neck. And a young girl's hand touched her cheek, eased her finger away from the trigger. Their eyes had met, the overwhelming need to live within them demanding her help.

A tear formed as she pulled the trigger, the bark of the carbine lost in the silence of space. The bullets sped from the rifle, spraying the tethered figure. Her boots broke from the hull, and Hendricks found herself lifting away when a wave of bullets smashed into her suit, cracking the spinal plates. Blood spilled as she spun from the ship, pain wracking her nerves, emptying her mind. As the tether yanked her to a stop, she drank in the ink black of space before she finally closed her eyes.

With both legs halfway into the spacesuit, Davina pulled on and activated the magboots. She freed herself of the tether and yanked the rest up and over her hips. The slate by her side flashed, and she swiped the instructions over to the next page, her fear-filled mind having forgotten the procedure in the panic. One slip, one seal inaccurately bonded, and she would be wasting precious oxygen. She slid her arms in next, and the rear of the suit moulded to her back. Picking up the gauntlets, she quickly added these, checking their seals before donning her helmet. With a final twist and click, the basic survival suit ran through a system check, pinging back a yellow warning. She tapped through the simple HUD menu, and identified a crack in the shoulder membrane, probably from age and lack of use. The crew clearly had never put much store by the backup suits and had not bothered servicing them. With a prayer, she instructed the HUD to seal the rent and after a few seconds felt the warmth of a liquid seep from the inner lining. A minute of dread soon passed, and she ran the check again, rewarded with a green response.

Davina picked up her slate and eased it into the flap pocket on her thigh. She eyed the navy battle suit that lay in the cargo box Duboit had added to the manifest, jealous of its armour and weaponry. But she had as much chance of operating that, as flying the *Sunstar* itself. And it would also make her an obvious threat, and therefore a target. The only way, she surmised, of getting out of this mess alive was to play to her strengths. She just had to live long enough to get the chance.

The suit's HUD was button controlled from her left wrist, basic forwards and back menu choices with a select button. She clicked into comms, hoping with the lack of choices, that it was linked to Hendricks.

"Hendricks," she said, a waver in her voice. "How's it going? Have you found them?"

Nothing but silence responded, as empty as the surrounding void. She tried again, with the same result.

"Shit." Her heart pounded. Options were low, and if Hendricks was dead or captured, they had just dropped another notch.

A clang echoed through the corridor, louder than before, followed by a series of smaller noises that seemed to be coming closer. At first, she thought the salvagers had entered, and were clomping down the metal corridor in search of the crew. But that didn't match the tactics Hendricks had suggested. She stood, flexing the suit's joints and satisfied, walked over to the hold door controls and the screen above it. Flicking through she stopped on a view of the galley and the metal disc that clattered against the wall, before spinning away down the corridor. Yes, they were in. The *Sunstar* breached, and between her and death was the survival suit's oxygen supply.

"I need more," she said, kicking herself for skipping the safety briefing the crew hadn't bothered holding. Or asking the twins.

The twins.

Shit. That was it. Her best chance of surviving lay in those girls.

She sat back down, staring at her own image in the suit's HUD, and hating what she saw.

With a sigh, she clicked the comms, and chose the wide broadcast option. "This is Davina Connors, calling from the *Sunstar*. I repeat, this is Davina Connors. I am the Incini to the contractor of the *Sunstar*. I say again, I am an Incini with an offer for Aidan Toms, captain of the *Maverick*."

"Just get on with dying, will you," came the hoarse voice over the comms. "You're jammed, no one but us is going to hear you."

The voice grated on Davina's nerves. She hated dealing with lowlifes. "Assuming you are crew on the *Maverick*, I have something of huge value aboard the ship. I repeat, an auctionable asset. A weapon. Your captain *will* want to know about it."

The hold lights dimmed, then flashed. The monitor screen in the wall filled with an emergency message. She didn't need to read it.

"Then die, and we'll collect it afterwards, Incini. I can wait as long as it takes, but I need a shit, and I'd much prefer to do that out of a suit. Hurry will you."

Davina swore. The powerful rarely dropped into threat mode at the beginning of a negotiation. Doing so was crass, and unhelpful to both parties. She checked her gauge; the temperature was falling, and the suit's heating system had activated. Her hand dropped to the hip pack on the suit, flipping it open in hope of a spare battery she knew should be there.

Damn.

One hope now. "This weapon ... these weapons are alive. Human telepaths, you understand. They die, their value drops to zero. Nothing. They live, and there isn't a noble out there that wouldn't place a bid. A guaranteed score, unlike waiting for this crew with no certainty they'll find whatever lies inside that asteroid family."

"You lie," said the crewman.

"You can't risk that. And besides, I am Incini. This is a contractual offer. My life, and theirs. Without me shutting them down, they'll be worthless. Why the hell do you think I'm on board? For a fucking no hope mission in the black, or the chance to earn the contractor some real money by acquiring two valuable assets?" The gauge on her suit indicated the atmospheric temperature was dropping rapidly. She'd be fine until the battery gave out, but doubted the twins had more than thirty minutes, possibly less. "Time's ticking, they die in here, then your captain's going to be mightily pissed off."

The comm went dead. Silent. Davina's heart thundered in her ears, and a *need* pressed on her mind. Filled with fear and dread. She attempted an earworm, trying to push away what she assumed to be the girls' worries – clearing her mind.

The comms crackled. "This is Captain Toms." The voice sounded distant, faded. "I understand there is a deal to be made."

"There is. But you don't have long. The temperature is dropping rapidly, and I am relying on oxygen in my suit. The *assets* do not have suits. If something doesn't change soon, a lot of creds are going to slip through your fingers."

"And how do you suggest we proceed?"

Davina enjoyed a brief smile. "How long will it take for you to get here with spare suits?"

Chapter 20

Rebekah's boots clamped to the metal deck's cold surface, and she unhooked her tether, adding it to the two others on the external pinion, while she removed the jetpack. She manually checked the gauge. ZZ3's efforts at getting them to the asteroid meant her tank remained two-thirds full, with the gas jets they used safer, but to the bot's detriment, burning a different fuel than its thrusters. She switched on the pack's maglock, and the casing softly rang as it attached to the deck by the breach. Something about the hole felt off, odd. But she couldn't put her finger on it.

"Savvo. Watchtower," she said. Her second-in-command nodded, and detached a spherical device from ZZ3's back that, on first glance, looked like an octopus. He unfurled the six legs to reveal a dual-barrelled mini-machine gun, and tapped away at the small screen. A blink in Rebekah's HUD was greeted by her eye-click confirmation she was 'friendly', and knew both Arin and Savvo would be doing the same. With that, Savvo guided the device towards the corridor ceiling where its legs attached. One blink of a green light, and the barrels whirred, picking them each out in turn, before settling and aiming along the passageway.

Rebekah indicated down the corridor. "Dark camera feeds on. Savvo, take point. ZZ3 watch our rear. Standard spread."

Savvo led off, his carbine cradled in both hands. Rebekah clicked into his feed, noting the image enhancement provided only six metres vision ahead of the squad. Not a lot in potentially hostile territory, and as they slowly travelled the corridor to the first junction, the heavy vibration of their boots grated on her nerves – each step announcing their presence to anything sensitive ahead. The dark was oppressive, her thoughts wandering to the uneasy feeling she already had about the ship. She toyed with switching over to the armoured suits' lights, but knew reliance on them caused shadows and light spots that created additional dangers.

"Halt," she ordered, and the squad paused. "Arin, send one of the zero-g drones down both sides, then set it twelve metres ahead. Semi-remote. I'll have your back."

"As always," replied Arin, and he collected a small drone from his pouch. "I only have three," he reminded. The oval device lifted from his glove, spun once, then rose to eye level before flying past Rebekah and down the left passageway. Their mapping indicated it was blocked by debris from a strike about ten metres down. Arin confirmed this and spun the drone back to check on the opposite side.

"Clear up to twenty metres. Nothing, not even dust," Arin said over the comms.

Rebekah desperately wanted to know if it was clear all the way down, but time was of the essence, and ZZ3 had their rear. "Affirmative. Bring it back and station it ahead."

Arin eye-clicked when the drone was ready, and Savvo led them on. Rebekah resisted the urge to have the drone's feed up in her own HUD. She couldn't control everything, despite the constant desire to know. The atmosphere in the ship was bad enough, without adding an edge of paranoia to it.

"There's a second junction ahead," said Arin.

Rebekah ran through the map. Left led to a sealed bulkhead, beyond that the engineering access for the starboard manoeuvring thrusters. To the right more of the same. She hated walking by and not knowing what might be on their six.

Arin seemed to read her mind. "I can set a second drone to auto sweep any junction passages. I don't have to pilot; I can set the threat detection up high. We'll get some false positives, but hey, that's the story of Savvo's life."

"He's so funny at times, just not today," came back Savvo. "This place is kind of creepy. Finding nothing seems weirder than if it were piled with bodies."

"Do it, Arin. And yeah, I'm not liking how this sets up. Analysis, ZZ3. Assessment of what we're seeing," Rebekah resisted the temptation to glance back to the bot. She knew it would have reversed its limbs, walking backwards so it could watch their rear. It never looked right, too far from the normal order of things.

"Swift depressurisation would seem the most likely statistically," said ZZ3. "Everything was pushed out of the breach. Although—" Just what Rebekah didn't need, a pause. Arin had a lot to answer for. "—it was deliberate."

That did it. She did turn about then, pushing down the unease at the sight of the twisted bot. "Explain."

"The inner hull bent outwards, away from the ship. It would indicate there was an explosive placed on the inside," finished the bot.

"Shit." Rebekah's mind wandered back to the breach and its sense of oddness. "Maybe someone who couldn't reach an escape pod," she offered. No one else spoke. Speculation wouldn't help, nor did the beep from the second drone. She clicked on its feed, and it appeared in the corner of her HUD – a red square placed over something wrapped about a bulkhead wheel. Arin had taken control, and focused the drone's camera closer. The image was unclear, and she ordered her HUD to enhance it. She blinked.

"Is that..." began Arin, his voice tentative, weak. "Is that an arm? A hand?"

Rebekah stared at the image, and amid the odd swirls of frozen flesh, the part Arin had eye-clicked could well have been a human hand. What protruded from the fingers, however, could only be described as barbed tentacles.

"ZZ3, protocol guard, activation code Wrecking Crew. Watch this end of the corridor." She sent the bot the image, adding it to the list of threats in its database. "Savvo, lead on."

Ten metres down the passageway, Savvo warily approached the bulkhead door. The last stretch of the metal walls scored with multiple deep scratches in long criss-crossing patterns. Savvo pointed out several barbs remained embedded in the metal, too deep to be retrieved. As they walked closer, the camera forged a monstrous apparition against the bulkhead. Multiple, elongated tentacles were frozen to the door, sprouting from a central torso that set Rebekah's stomach lurching. Amid the swirls of icy flesh were shreds of clothing – a uniform.

The implication sent her thoughts spinning until Savvo grunted.

"Lights?" he asked.

She agreed, ordering Arin to do the same. To flush the corridor behind them of the dark malevolence that lurked there.

Rebekah briefly closed her eyes, and on opening them, allowed the helmet to adjust the lumens let through until she was comfortable. She instantly regretted it. Among the maelstrom of twisted limbs, two icy eyes stared back, sat above a wide, tongueless mouth filled with black teeth.

"Fuck," she said.

Savvo retched, turning away. They had shared many a moment of horror together. The squad mates they had sent home in body bags after collecting their pieces from among the carnage. Target buildings they had scoured filled with the dead and dying desperately calling for their help. The hundreds they had killed in the moments of battle, or those presumed a threat blown apart from a thousand metres away.

The families, the children.

You can't break a Breaker.

Fuck me, this was close.

"What?" said Arin. "What the hell?"

Rebekah assumed he'd checked his feed. "Eyes on our fucking six," she ordered, then forced herself to turn back. Somehow her hand reached out, the shake more prominent than she would have liked. A single finger landed on the hand they had first seen on the drone camera. It was solid, frozen, and brittle. Despite her gentleness, the palm shattered, icy dust shimmering in the airless corridor. The hole it left showed no sign of bones, just a powder of scarlet and mauve that floated within the hollow.

She swallowed and slid her carbine into her back-lock. Extracting a sealed box from a pouch, she coaxed some of the dust inside before replacing the lid. She wiped off any remains from her gauntlet on the metal wall, only for it to catch on something. One of the barbs, protruding from the metal. Rebekah took a set of pliers from her small tool belt, and grasped the end, expecting it to shatter. Instead, the tooth came out whole. As she held it up to the light, it appeared canine.

"Fuck me," she whispered, and showed Savvo who merely shook his head, his skin white in the harsh light.

"Is that …?"

"Human? I don't know. I don't even think I want to know." She dropped it into the same box, ensuring she didn't lose what she already had. The option to use her suit's probe had crossed her mind, and she would if she really had to. But ZZ3 waited for them and their grisly prize, and it seemed a far better solution.

She passed Arin and asked him if he wanted to take a closer look. To understand what they faced. To her surprise, his reaction was muted, yet he followed her words as if they were an order, and walked over. His wince was accompanied by a glance to Rebekah, who simply nodded in response.

"What in hell's name happened here?" he said.

No one answered, no one knew. Did they want to know?

Rebekah squeezed Savvo on the arm, signalling for him to lead them back. With Arin in the centre, she took the rear, a constant fear tapping on her shoulder, reminding Rebekah what was at her back. This wasn't a fucking war zone, it was the devil's graveyard, and they'd been forced to play.

When they got back to ZZ3, the bot reported what she already knew. No contact. She handed over the box, brushing her glove on the corridor wall afterwards. Its huge hand swallowed the container, and tipped the contents into a panel on its arm next to where its limb augmentations were stored.

"Lead us on, Savvo." She caught his look and nodded back. "Keep the fucking lights on."

"Thanks, Captain," he replied, and hefted his carbine. "Too many monsters on this fucking ship."

"There's only been one," piped Arin, his drone winging its way ahead.

"Like he said," Rebekah cut in. "Too many monsters. Now stow it, and focus."

Taking the chance, she pinged ZZ3, eye-clicking a message that the analysis results were to be FCEO – For Captain's Eyes Only – giving her activation code. Right now, she was spooked enough, and didn't need the others snowballing the whole thing. The last time that had happened, she'd had a rapid field promotion to captain and four years hiding in an asteroid field.

She checked the map again. Another thirty metres. Two junctions and then pay dirt – the bulkhead they needed to open before making their way to the ship's warbot storage. With the lights on, shadows played at the edge of her sight, the sweeping movements of Savvo and Arin's beams delaying the HUD's adjustments. It gnawed at her nerves, but after that thing they had left behind, lights it was going to be.

The supplementary drone swept down the side passages of the next junction, flying twenty metres in both directions and returning nothing. Both these central sections of the ship were classed as production areas. Mini-factories that supplied the endless needs of the ship's crew. The drone had flown past a multitude of standard doors. Each was closed, and that was good enough for Rebekah right now. They had enough on their plate without risking opening more boxes of horror.

"Captain," said Arin. "Check the feed ahead. Target bulkhead in sight. Fuck."

She eye-clicked the feed, blinking before gazing at the drone's eye view. "Oh God."

"Ain't no gods here," said Savvo. "Just demons."

Chapter 21

Two salvagers filled the small airlock, their suits pressed against the inner walls as the cutting machine worked. Hendricks had used the digipad on the outside, and when Davina had attempted to let them in, the system had refused to open. Everything was in the red, and she feared the virus may have spread or Hendricks had shut it down for some reason. Either way, her plan had reached a crossroads. Slicing open the airlock as the salvagers were, the *Sunstar* would be next to useless, and she needed to be aboard the *Maverick*.

The airlock doors folded away, the newly cut metal edges glowing hot until the coldness of space hit. She backed off, checking her tether, and allowing enough space for the two suited salvagers to clomp inside and attach their plasma cutter to the deck. The doors cooled quickly, and checking her own gauge, fear for the girls' safety and her survival ticket rose. They needed to act fast. The ship's systems had prevented too rapid a fall in temperature, but her gauge quickly let her know that was at an end now the airlock was exposed to space.

"You got the spare suits?" she asked, her tone brusque. "They'll be dead if we don't get them inside."

The first salvager seemed to pause, his visor clearing to show steely eyes set beneath a shaven and scarred head.

"Now." Davina didn't have time for this bullshit. "Otherwise, Toms isn't going to get his prizes. No money for dead telepaths."

"Yeah. I don't trust you, and now I know you're an Incini, I definitely don't fucking trust you. So, this goes how I say it goes. Understand?" He stepped closer, his suit glove filled with a pistol. "Understand?"

Davina stood her ground. "Yes. But it remains the same problem, does it not? A dead asset is worth shit."

"Yeah. Where are they?"

Davina noted the second salvager was dragging an extra tether line, coiling the synth-rope as he walked. "In the galley."

"Lead on." He flicked the weapon towards the front of the ship.

Davina turned, magboots clomping as she headed that way. Both girls were slumped on the galley benches, wrapped head to toe in survival suits, their noses and mouths covered by masks, with tubes attached to simple oxygen tanks. Davina couldn't tell with all the wrapping whether they still breathed.

"What have you done with them?" he asked. "They dropping into hypothermia?"

Davina glanced back, with three suits now filling the rear corridor. One occupied by the second salvager, the others he hauled untidily their way. They were old spacesuits, but perhaps that was an advantage. Wide and bulky.

"They will if we don't act soon. I persuaded them to take the retardant we used when decelerating, with a little extra to help them sleep." Davina glanced towards the salvager. "I didn't know what else to do."

"It should buy some time. It might even be enough. Clever. Sasha, bring the spares." The man swore and dragged the two dirty spacesuits through the opening into the galley. He prepared one, removing the helmet and unclipping the upper half. "Now you get one of them inside, yes? And you are right, you need to be quick."

While the surly salvager directed, Davina eased Heki into the lower half of the suit, aided by the removal of her magboots. Her survival clothing was bulky and thick, but combined with the girl's thin build, the suit still had room to spare. Sasha had stripped down the other, and she repeated her actions with Tremil while he sealed Heki into the upper half and locked the helmet in place. Eventually, both girls were in the protective suits, and to Davina's relief, the chest panels were flashing green.

"Wrapped up nice and warm, body temperature a little low but survivable." The salvager nodded to himself, his eyes flickering, Davina presumed, over a stream of information displayed on the inside of his helmet. "Thank you for our presents." He raised his gun, the barrel pointing straight at her, an evil leer on his face. "Now, if I were a kind man, I would shoot you. But I'm not. I am a bastardo. Enjoy your slow death." He backed away, Sasha dragging the two weightless girls behind.

Dread took hold. A starkness far greater than the fear of an Incini negotiator meeting their match. Losing your life was vastly different to losing a percentage.

"You need me," she said, trying to keep the pleading out of her voice. "I know how to control them. When they wake up."

"Wake up? Who says we will allow that?" Sasha had reached the airlock, and was connecting the tether he'd bundled up to one of the suits, probably Heki.

"If they stay drugged, how will you know I wasn't lying?"

"True. You can think on that while you suffocate on your own carbon monoxide. Or perhaps, you'll take a coward's way out, and remove your helmet. I will enjoy dreaming of all the ways you could die, Incini." Sasha finished attaching Tremil, and both girls were pulled out into the black. Davina caught a last glimpse, their suits still flashing green, before they slipped out of view. Sasha then collected the hand cutter and clambered out of the airlock.

She knew there were only a few moments of hope left, and all she had were words. Davina eyed the bastardo, his grin stretched from ear to ear. In all her life, she had battled the nobility and their advisors in trials of mental combat, and won. And here she was, at a loss to a lowlife.

Sasha flew to the side of the airlock, guiding in a second jetpack.

"Adieu," said the bastardo, and slid into the pack. He spun about and followed Sasha out into the airless void. Davina checked her own tether, then walked over to the open airlock. In the distance she could see the two girls, a third member of the *Maverick* crew towing them towards the ship.

Perhaps she could unclip and join them. Take one last trip into space, enjoy the peace.

"I lost," she said, and thought of the twins. "Maybe."

The comms crackled, and she winced, waiting for the last goading words of the salvager. A final riposte perhaps.

"Hurting bad ..." The words were barely a whisper under the hiss of whatever jamming the Toms and his crew had used. "Don't want to die out here ..."

Davina clomped back inside, checking her oxygen levels, and realising that whatever help she could offer would be short-lived. Either way, she passed through the galley and the discarded oxygen bottles, grabbing both and shoving them into the wall grips as she reached the cockpit monitor. She tried to recall the menu sequence Hendricks had gone through, and with a brief misstep, eventually found the external cameras. A few clicks, and she had a view of two spacesuits. One was shredded; the occupant clearly dead with the last vestige of condensation slipping from the suit. The other bore *Sunstar*'s insignia on its chest, and had clearly been hit by some form of weapon. As it gently spun, she could make out Hendricks' face, the eyes shut but her skin appeared warm and normal except for a streak of blood from the nose.

She wrist-clicked her comms. "Hendricks? Can you hear me?" No reply came. "Hendricks, this is Davina."

"Davina? I don't know a Davina," the engineer said, the words distant.

"Damn," mouthed the Incini, thinking. She needed a spur, something for Hendricks to want to live for. "Dricks," she said, attempting to keep the voice as monotone and robotic as she could. "Dricks, this is Tremil. I need your help." She suddenly felt ridiculous. Perhaps the stress and the thought of oxygen starvation had got to her. Another dead end.

"Tremil? I know a Tremil ... and a Heki. Good girls ... mostly."

"Dricks, I need help. Please."

"Help?" The spacesuit shifted in the camera view. It spun about, though under little control. "Tremil? Are you okay?" As Hendricks' face rotated back into view, Davina saw the eyes were open. The engineer's hands moved down to the lifeline, and she began to pull herself slowly in.

"No," said Davina, keeping her voice flat.

"Ow ... shit I hurt ... I'm coming."

The engineer reached the *Sunstar*'s hull, boots adhering to its surface. Pained grimaces showed on Hendricks' face as she moved slowly towards the rear of the ship. There was a hitch every time she lifted her left leg, the distance she could stretch limited. But it was hope, and that was in short supply.

The movement stopped, and heavy, ragged breathing echoed in the comms. "I hurt, Tremil ... I've been shot. The suit must have sealed but fuck, it's agony." The engineer bent over, fiddling with her boots. Standing straight, she attempted to lift her right leg, and a howl of pain forced Davina to cut off the comms. The woman wavered back and forth, the boots still as her body shuddered. Eventually she bent down again, and after a second adjustment, she tried again. This time the boot lifted with a hitch, and Hendricks barely lifted the left before placing it down again. However, she had moved forward, and centimetre by centimetre, Davina watched the engineer make her way around the hull and towards the airlock. Halfway, she staggered, and Davina realised Hendricks had forgotten to switch over the tether that trailed behind. In horror, she watched as Hendricks withdrew a cutting tool from her belt pouch. With a snick, the synth-rope parted, leaving only magboots to prevent her from spinning off into the void – and they were set very low.

Hendricks continued on her way, and Davina opened the comms to discover the engineer was babbling away to Tremil.

"I dream of it ... you know that? When Angel opened your cell door. There you were, in your striped skinsuit amid your own ... own shit, your head locked in that ... that foul helmet. I remember her eyes when she knocked off the lock, her face ... god, her face. Then I knew how worthless I was, we all were. Murderers dressed in a uniform, blinding our eyes to the senseless death, closing our ears to the screams of the innocent."

"Dricks, you are near the airlock. Can you hear me? They cut open the airlock."

"Huh?" Hendricks paused, swaying. One boot lifted from the hull, but she didn't place it down right, the heel catching a rung. The second boot shifted, and the moment seemed to stretch out before Davina. She couldn't help but visualise what was about to happen – and she pounded out of the cockpit. In her mind, Hendricks was floating away, spiralling into space to die alone. For some reason, she couldn't let that happen. The engineer represented a light in the dark, a sliver of hope she needed to cling on to.

On reaching the junction, she turned and ran as fast as her boots would allow. In her mind's eye, her tether wouldn't be long enough, or it would snap, and together she and Hendricks would tumble out into the black. A leg appeared, hanging below the airlock aperture. Without allowing herself to think, Davina toe-clicked both her magboots and leapt out the carved-open doorway.

Chapter 22

"Fuck," said Savvo, one gloved hand stalled in the air, halfway towards the frozen body.

It was as if the woman had melted in boiling lava, her upper torso perfect, with arms outstretched, reaching in desperation for the bulkhead door. Her face glistening; cheeks smooth. One touch, however, and Rebekah knew it would crumble. The lower half merged into a mound upon the deck. Ripples and bubbles poked from a split uniform like a boiling mass of flesh frozen in time.

Half a monster.

All terrifying.

Rebekah blew out a long breath, calming her thoughts. Their lights were a sanctuary, a shield against the dark. But all she could think of was what lay beyond. Waiting.

"Leave it," she said. "We need to be through that door, Savvo."

Backing away, ashen faced, he glanced over at her, then nodded and approached the door. The mechanism was the usual electronic recognition system, and without power would have deadlocked. One tap on the screen revealed it was functional, and the green glow lit his visor. The response, however, was slow. It took much longer than Rebekah expected for it to deny Savvo access.

"Did the door say 'no'? Damn, perhaps it's a hint that we should go back – where there are no monsters to chew our faces off," said Arin, though he didn't move.

"No *in*, no fuel. And we leave ZZ3 here. You want to be the one to tell it, glorious leader?" Rebekah kept her eyes on Savvo as he worked at the pad and screen.

"Har, I think that's the captain's job. I'm just a lowly lackey."

A puff of dust wafted by her boots. She turned to find Arin with a rueful look on his face, peering over his shoulder, only for it to dawn on him what he'd just stepped in. The brief moment of fear that crossed his face was swiftly replaced with a shrug, but she'd seen it. Felt it. Was fucking living it.

A gentle grind of metal upon metal brought her attention back to the door. Savvo had his hands on the bulkhead wheel, tugging it clockwise with some effort until it jarred to a stop.

"I've switched the deadlock to manual, but something's stopping it from disengaging." He slammed both hands on top of the wheel. "Perhaps ZZ3?"

Arin ordered the bot forward, grimacing as its heavy limbs brushed through what remained of the dead woman. The corridor filled with her dust, billowing like burnt ashes in their lights. Rebekah tried to push intrusive thoughts out of her mind. How would she have responded to such a horror if they were still on active duty? The Breakers punching a hole through enemy lines? Soulless, emotions deadened by their relentless reality – a shroud the twins had lifted from their minds.

Those that had lived through first contact, anyway.

ZZ3 gripped the wheel and yanked it sideways. The lock shuddered, creaked, then gave. The bot spun it open freely then pushed the door inwards. A rush of air and warmth registered on Rebekah's suit, condensation sweeping into the corridor.

"Hurry, ZZ3," she said, and the bot complied. It kicked aside the pile of debris in its way and took a position five metres further along the dark corridor. Savvo followed, carbine pointing ahead, eyes sweeping the area behind the door. Rebekah went through next, and finally Arin. Rebekah shoved the door to and spun it to close the seal.

When she turned about, she retched, dry heaving. All of them, ZZ3 included, were covered in blotches of grey and red, immersed in the remains of the woman-cum-monster from the other side of the door.

"Shit," she said, wishing Hendricks was there, needing the ex-captain's calm reassurance. "Savvo, take station ahead. I want a sit rep. Arin, spin the drone back up. ZZ3, atmospheric analysis. Action code Wrecking Crew." All of them reacted as if breaking from the glue of reality. Almost pausing, thinking, then taking on board their orders and acting swiftly. She needed that to stop, both for her benefit and theirs. It would get them killed.

She checked the debris that had been piled against the door. Two thick bars, likely cannibalised from a door frame, appeared to have recently been twisted in half, probably as a result of opening the bulkhead. The rest a mixture of piled filing cabinets and desk tables, now crushed by ZZ3's bulk as it crashed through.

"First analysis suggests a breathable atmosphere. There are no known pathogens in the composition, but I detect the unknown organic's presence …" That pause again. Why the hell had Arin programmed a dramatic fucking pause? "Which we are also covered in."

"Say that again," she whispered, then said it louder. "Explain."

"The corpse is only partly human. The rest composed of the unknown organic. I do not have the programming for any further analysis."

"Is it a danger, ZZ3?" she asked. "From what information you have." But she knew the answer. They were covered in it.

"In consideration of the data and witnessed facts, I would suggest humans avoid direct contact, and the area to be quarantined under Almaarian medical guidance." The eyes flashed red, and the bot seemed to turn to face her. Or was it the stress? "But as we are trespassing on a Navy grave, that may not be viable."

The woman's uniform. Navy-issue. This wasn't a private, company-owned ship. Just one pretending to be. Too many secrets, not enough facts.

"Noted, ZZ3," she said. "Savvo, sit rep." Her eyes flicked up to her HUD, her second's feed showing a familiar corridor set up.

"No movement. Seems clear." His camera glanced towards the ceiling where a string of red lights glowed. "Emergency power is on. Could explain the warmth and the atmosphere."

"Okay. Arin?"

"One junction, both sides barricaded before a second bulkhead door." Rebekah checked her HUD, the image coming back very basic, but enough to show both off-passages were accommodation areas as predicted by the schematic. The way ahead led to the lift and stairwell, and their target.

"Can the drone get through the barricades?"

Arin coughed. "Want me to risk it?"

She knew they only had three, but accommodation meant people. Crew, or the Bustan prisoners, if they really existed, and it wasn't just another lie. They needed to know what had happened on board. Scrub that. *She* needed to know, and if there were any survivors. "Yep. But wait until we reach the junction."

Savvo remained on point, and with ZZ3 at the rear, they carried on. The gentle clang of their boots now echoed along the corridor, their careful movements only reducing the noise. On an active ship, they would have been barely audible. But on an empty husk, each step played on Rebekah's mind. After what they'd witnessed on the other side of the door, she wanted them to go unnoticed for as long as possible. Of course, ZZ3 was hardly inconspicuous, but even the bot could adjust.

On reaching the junction, she ordered them to dial down their boots, and switched ZZ3 into stealth mode. The bot's movements would become slightly delayed as it analysed each movement, but she considered it worth the risk.

The barricades were thorough. Metal objects and furniture carefully interlaced rather than a hurried, defensive barrier. On closer inspection, she found a section on both sides where the metal exploded outwards, as if something seriously strong had yanked it out from their side. Like a tentacle.

It was through one of these that Arin sent the drone, the gyroscopes and motor adjusting as it weaved its way through. The first few doors were closed, their frames roughly welded shut, and an X scorched across the outside. Arin glanced her way, his lips thin, white. She ignored him, watching the feed as Savvo and ZZ3 protected their backs.

The drone moved on to find the next doorway was partially open. As Arin guided it through, the machine bumped into the door, wheeling about as the gyroscopes tried to adjust. Blurred images flashed until it settled. The room was a standard berth – a cabin with a space for an absent desk, the bed also missing with just a mattress on the floor. On top was something smooth, like a sack, with the weak emergency lighting unable to pick out exactly what it was composed of.

"Lights," said Arin, and he flicked on the drone's meagre light. The sack consisted of something he recognised – the scarlet and crimson material that had blocked the inner skin of the hull. Except this version undulated. "What the f..."

Where the light fell, the sack shifted, shuffling away in ripples that sickened Rebekah's stomach, acid bubbling away. It left a smear of red upon the bed, while strings of sticky crimson stretched to breaking point and snapped as the drone adjusted its beam.

"Monsters," whispered Arin.

But all Rebekah could think of was Savvo's demons.

"Cut the light, bring the drone out," she ordered. "Carefully."

Arin complied, and the picture swung away from the foul, bulbous sac. But a little too late for Rebekah, as the outline of a human face appeared, pressed against the membrane, stretching it thin.

Had she imagined it? Overlaid a sickening expectation over what was really there? Then her thoughts flicked back to the half-woman behind the bulkhead door, and those tentacles wreathed in human teeth.

The drone slammed into the wall, causing Arin to flinch. The image in Rebekah's HUD shook and died, and she took an involuntary step back. There had been no sign of what had smashed into the machine, but the screech emanating from the corridor was clue enough. They had awoken something. And it knew they were there.

The scrape of claw upon metal echoed along the corridor, followed by the wrench of a door opening, and a slap of something wet upon the walls. A second moist noise slithered along the passageway. Rebekah turned her lights on full, the beam stretching into the darkness. A horror awaited her there, and her finger pulled the trigger.

Bullets barked, flying through the passageway to drill into the human head that roared in anger and pain above the writhing torso. It hung in the corridor, tentacles gripped onto the walls. Human legs dangled below, the pants blue and of Almaarian Navy origin, but what hung on top dripped blood and mucus.

Arin fired through a second gap, the burst controlled, and the skull shattered. A mass of flesh and tentacle splattered the corridor with a wet slap. The upper tentacles – they may once have been arms – snaked out and hooked into the deck, dragging what remained towards them. She engaged the second trigger, and it clicked back, before taking aim and fully pressing. The grenade flew, smashing into the mound. The explosion's flash was muted by her helmet, the sound rolling over her amid relief as the corridor walls were smothered in whatever had come for them.

"Fuuuuck," said Arin.

Somehow seeing it in the flesh, and that it could die, steeled Rebekah. It was no longer an unknown in her world of certainty.

"They die," she said. "And that's all that matters." She slapped Arin on the arm. "You hear that, Savvo. They're not demons. They can be killed. We just have to work out the most effective way."

"Grenades work," came back the reply. "But we didn't plan on a war zone, or a horror show. I'm packing six."

"Same," said Arin. "Let's just hope there's less than seventeen left. Hey ZZ3, what's the standard crew size of a cruiser?"

"Two hundred and twenty-one personnel …" replied the bot. "Plus the captain, and any Marines they may be carrying."

"That's cheered me up. You missed out the warbots," said Arin. "What if they're functional?"

"To be honest, Arin, I think you're pissing up the wrong tree. If they were functional, they would be the first thing you would deploy. If this is an infection," Rebekah gazed down the corridor at the mess she had caused, "then bots and drones are ideal. But we need that fuel, so let's go find out. Savvo."

"Yeah, I know, take point. Seems the safest place in this deathtrap."

Rebekah stared back down the corridor they had already covered, and towards the junction. The pieces were slotting together. An infection, the crew turning on each other, and likely the survivors had tried to get rid of it by blowing the monstrosities out of the hull. They died – be it from the cold, the lack of air, or being spaced. But not all of them. Or the infection lingered somehow and had taken more of the crew.

She checked her bullet count and reloaded the top grenade launcher.

"Move out, stay alert."

Chapter 23

"Red, red," Davina repeated, her mind fogging. She yanked at the tether, pulling herself in a little more.

Too slow.

Hendricks' bulkier suit bumped into her back as she tried desperately not to gasp for breath.

Red.

Steady, take it slow, calm your breath.

There had been no time, and without thinking she had leapt for the engineer. A moment of joy followed as she caught Hendricks in one hand, and as they sailed into the black, a jerk of her tether encouraged a whispered prayer that it wouldn't give way.

And here she was, anchored to the ship. Except the engineer's foot had caught her helmet, and the oxygen pack at the rear. The pipe had snagged and broken away. The spurt sending them both into a slow whirl. She had counted the seconds, expecting death to come when Hendricks' hands tapped at her helmet, and fumbled with her pack.

The seconds had turned into a minute, with no word from Hendricks between.

Red but not dead.

She pulled again, timing each attempt with a gentle, long breath. Calming her heartbeat.

And again, and again.

The whirl settled as the tether shortened, and with the ship moving in orbit, the effect was more like being dragged through space. She caught sight of the asteroid family over the hull, the sheer weight of swirling rock almost overwhelming. Caught in the orbital patterns, her mind focused on one ...

No ... no. Concentrate.

She pulled them closer, and with a second yank, they floated at the periphery of the airlock. Red flashed, a deeper scarlet than usual. Her eyes flicked up to the gauge.

Two percent.

Calm.

Shaking gloves wrapped about the tether, and Davina slowly eased them both inside, turning as she did. Hendricks carried on past, the momentum sending the engineer head over heels towards the inside of the ship. Davina's panicked hands fumbled with the second clip, swearing as the rope began to tighten. With relief, the karabiner snapped open, and Hendricks bounced down the corridor.

Davina pulled herself the last metre, and on through the damaged airlock to the corridor. Chest tight, she clamped down on the deck.

"Where?" she gasped, her addled mind trying to recall what she needed, where it would be.

The incessant noise blared and blared, the red lights flashing.

Focus.

Her vision narrowed, but her boots moved, and she began a slow walk down the corridor. She didn't know why, but she turned to the right, chest tight, pain taking hold. A weight she couldn't shift. More panic, but stride followed stride.

She rammed into the galley bench, her thigh and knee catching its edge. Pain rode her leg, numbed by the scream in her chest. Another step forward, followed by a stagger, then a second and third, saw her crash to her knees, knelt as if in prayer as both boots disengaged from the deck to stare at the glowing cockpit screen.

"Why am I here?" She collapsed, her helmet hitting the deck before she began to float upwards. And there, on the wall, Tremil and Heki's oxygen tanks.

She blinked, everything was red.

And then it went black.

"Easy." The voice was pained, gruff. She recognised it, had heard it before. Perhaps recently.

"Slow breaths. Ease in and out. Hypoxia can cause damage to your lungs. Swelling. It may hurt, but don't gulp."

Hendricks.

Davina's gloved hands pressed against the deck. The *Sunstar.*

She coughed, her throat itchy, whereas her lungs felt wet and angry. She forced herself to take each breath slowly, and after six, opened her eyes. Blurred at first, her vision cleared. The engineer's concerned, pained face grimaced back from inside her helmet.

"Guess," Hendricks winced, adjusting her leg where she knelt on the floor. "Guess this makes you crew. Thank you for the rescue. What happened? The girls won't answer."

Davina blinked, trying to drag back the memories. She pushed herself up to lean against the co-pilot's chair.

What to say?

"They took them. Left me to die."

"Took? Why would they?" Hendricks stood up; a slow, laborious movement clearly mixed with pain. The confusion on her face didn't mask the worry.

"I ... I told them they were valuable, an asset worth keeping alive." She held up her hands as Hendricks' eyes widened. "It was the only way. They would have died ... we would have died."

"To save your own skin? What did you tell them? That they needed you too?" Hendricks' voice rose. Not shouting – commanding. A captain.

Davina blushed, though with her blue-tinged skin she had no clue whether it showed.

"You did, didn't you? Of course you did ..." Hendricks turned away, the comms hissing slightly. "It makes sense. A familiar face. How did you get them into suits without ... you know ..."

A sharp pain invaded Davina's left lung, causing her to gag as the nausea rose.

"Ah. Leave that for later." Hendricks said. She staggered. Her knees buckling and eyes unfocused.

Davina found herself on her feet, arms wrapped about the engineer to prevent any more injury. Both lungs screamed at her, and she slowed herself, taking gentle, ragged breaths before disengaging the engineer's boots.

With her tether still attached, Davina awkwardly dragged Hendricks through the galley and on into the corridor. Eventually, she reached the first junction and turned right towards the small medbay. Relieved to see the door sealed, Davina pressed the release, and eased Hendricks inside. She undid her tether, attaching the clip to the handhold outside of the door before pulling herself in and shutting the door.

The room was small, barely enough for both of them. Her first aid was sketchy at best, but this was a Karal contracted ship, and to be certified, they had to maintain a certain level of medical systems. That included a medbot and at least grade IV software. She didn't know how it would work when the injured party couldn't remove their suit. But perhaps a diagnostic would help.

With Hendricks strapped to the medtable, she tapped at the medbot's console. It lit up, a menu ran down the screen – a welcome idiot's guide – and relieved, she got to work. Step by step, she connected the old suit Hendricks wore with the medbot, all the while expecting incompatibility issues. Below the *Sunstar*'s logo on its chest was a scuffed patch. It didn't take much for her to work out the suit's origins. Marine-issue, probably five years old, possibly longer.

With relief, the medical assessment pinged through. The suit must have been far better maintained than it appeared.

Two gunshot wounds had penetrated the armour. One had hit the engineer's left hip, and the bone was shattered. The suit had compensated. No, overcompensated – you keep your Marines in the fight – the long-term prognosis wasn't good. Another had passed through her left thigh, causing muscle damage. Both wounds had been sealed by the HUD computer applying the same hardening foam as it had used to repair the suit. In fact, the closer she looked at the images from the medbot, the more convinced she was it just plugged any hole it could find. Hendricks was glued in, and would require careful extraction. That and enough pain meds to knock out an army. Davina set the medbot to sync with the suit, and after a few twists and turns with the menu, applied the meds directly through a linefeed. Within five minutes, Hendricks was floating on the inside, as well as the out.

Davina disengaged the medbot and found the setting for her own basic suit. Once synced, it gave very little information. A simple warning about hypoxia, and the potential side effects based on the recorded data. With no way to run a full scan in the cold and airless ship, she set the medbot to deliver a cocktail of the advised drugs, removing any that would cause sleep. Having administered that through her own feed line, and with the pain in her lungs a reminder of the risk she was running, Davina left the hold.

Re-tethered, she headed for the cargo hold, ticking off a mental list of how she could increase her chances of survival. Number one on that list was keeping Hendricks alive. She could teach her how to use the navy-issue armoured suit. The built-in scrubber would give her extended breathing time, though it would also require sourcing charged batteries and filters.

Davina rechecked her O2 gauge. It hovered below the midline, in the yellow. All her plans would take time, and so she returned to the cockpit and collected the second bottle. It had barely a third left, but better than nothing. By the time she had returned to the galley, her comms was crackling.

"What the hell did you give me?" came Hendricks' voice.

"Enough drugs to knock you out for a while. How the hell are you awake?" replied Davina, diverting back towards the medbay.

"Heh, if only you knew just how many drugs they pumped into the Br ... into the Marines. I must be immune. Where are you?"

"Here." The door slid open, and she re-entered to find Hendricks sitting up, one strap over her lap. "Your hip is screwed, you know that?"

"We're on an airless shit heap in the black. My hip is last on the fucking list." Hendricks eyed the O2 bottle. "That ain't going to keep you alive, either."

Davina laid out her plan.

"Not much better. Maybe we get a few hours each, perhaps the crew return in that time, maybe not. But I don't feel the engines. Is that because of the shit you put in me? Because if they're out of commission, then we're truly fucked. We can't recharge the batteries, nor clean the filters we have. It'll be a race between the cold and hypoxia – and your lungs are already on the fritz."

"The bearer of good news. Remind me why I saved you?" Davina said, looking at the two-thirds empty tank. The tickle in her raw throat made itself known, and she coughed. "I could use a little hope right now."

"Heh. I'm an engineer, baby. If anyone can work this shit out, it's me. But I'm going to need more pain relief. Our medbot is touchy about over-subscribing. You know which room is Savvo's?"

"Yeah, I do. Why?"

The lights cut out. Flickered once, then died. Within a few seconds, the room glowed a sullen red. The medbot sagged, the console switching off.

"Fuck. We were on the standby battery. Now we've hit emergency back-up. Get going. Savvo has a side table, pull out the drawer and tap out the base. There's enough stims in there to keep me going." Hendricks eased herself from the table, gently touching her feet to the deck and deciding against attaching herself, floated over to the door. "Meet you in engineering."

Chapter 24

Savvo heaved at the wheel, shifting it a few centimetres before it refused to budge. He stepped back from the bulkhead, eyeing the pad which showed the door was deadlocked but ready to be opened. "Guessing they barred this one too." He looked over to Rebekah. "A staged withdrawal?"

"After what we just saw? It'd be my first guess. ZZ3, open the door." Rebekah stepped aside, while Savvo backed off from the door. The hulking robot placed two limbs on the wheel and motorised joints whirred in protest as it heaved. A second tug, and something snapped the other side, scraping against the door. ZZ3 spun it the rest of the way.

"ZZ3 enter, secure the entrance to the stairway. Action code Wrecking Crew," said Rebekah, and the bot heaved the door inwards. Metal chairs and tables clattered as the bot ducked and shoved its way through, striding past the detritus. Savvo stepped inside, his light beam illuminating the hallway. It was clear of bodies, but the deck was scarred, dried blood amid the torn metal. He swept behind the door, then carried on through, taking a position to watch over the dual lift doors. Rebekah followed, then Arin, the second drone buzzing behind. Once he was through, Rebekah shut the bulkhead, spinning the wheel.

"We're cutting off the retreat," said Arin, his eyes distant as he instructed the drone to hover near the stairwell.

"I know. But threat assessment ..."

"You mean green tentacled humans with teeth for hooks aren't your first choice to have at your back? You disappoint me." Arin chuckled as he spoke.

"They die, just like your jokes. But I'd rather know what to expect if we return this way. Send the drone down," Rebekah checked her HUD map, "one level. Should mirror where we are now. Same layout."

Arin affirmed, and the drone sped past ZZ3 and down the stairwell. The emergency lights were on, and the drone detected no threats. "Clear."

"What about the lifts?" said Savvo. "Shouldn't we check them?"

"The ship's on emergency power. They won't operate, so whatever is in there can stay in fucking there," replied Rebekah. "ZZ3, descend to the next level. Guard, action code Wrecking Crew." The bot rapidly descended, all its limbs acting as legs as it practically ran. The thud of its arrival made her flinch. Combining codes had always been an issue since Arin's adjustments, so stealthy descent near-on impossible. They paused, listening.

"Savvo, Arin." She signalled down the stairs, and after they reached the small landing that sat halfway, followed, with a last glance to the lift doors. Once at the next level, they were faced with the dilemma of yet another layer below and a potential source of danger.

The drone buzzed as Arin ordered it down. Dark, foreboding, and again mirroring their current level. Except the bulkhead was open, with a worrying stain upon the lower seal and the door itself.

"Fuck," said Rebekah, the size of her crew – her squad – gnawing at her. The Breakers always operated light, tight-knit and at speed. They blitzed a target, smashing through while other soldiers followed behind to mop-up or cover their backs. "Set up a watchtower guarding that lower level, Savvo."

"Aye," he said, sounding distracted as he glanced at the drone's feed. "Will do. It's the last."

While he worked, Arin read the door pad menu. Once Savvo was done, Arin tried the wheel, surprised to find it give after an initial squeal. "Captain?"

She ran through the options and decided on the human one. Unbarred meant one of two things. They used the door regularly, or they hadn't had time to block it. Either way, human decision-making would be key if there were survivors.

"Open it, Arin." She eyed ZZ3. In times past, she would have sent the bot in first. Preserved her squad, or Hendricks would have at least. "Savvo on our rear." There was no bite back. Good.

The door spun open, and Arin threw himself to the side. No bullets flew, no screams or the wet slap of tentacles. The sub-engineer-cum-Marine spun back warily, eyes looking down the sight of his carbine. "Enemy sighted," he said. "Multiple targets, permission to fire."

Permission to fire, so no agreed and immediate threat. Rebekah eye-clicked his feed, the HUD aligning with the carbine's sighting software. The corridor was dark except for the fleeting beams of Arin's light. It caught six, maybe seven bulbous sacs along the first section. Three clung to the ceiling, four against the wall, spreading out into the corridor. Scarlet, mauve and crimson swirled on their membranes.

Kill the lights was her first thought, if only to get time to think. But they were Breakers, and couldn't leave an enemy at their back. "Permission granted. Target the lowest." Arin opened fire, and she knelt on the other side of him, her carbine spitting bullets in turn. The first sac split, yellow and green mucus spilling into the air. Something slithered out, white skin amid the foul mess. Her bullets shattered the elongated head.

"Grenade!" Rebekah prepped the trigger and fired. They both pulled themselves to the deck, helmet down and away from the explosion. Debris spewed from the entrance, and returning to their positions, fired another burst into the maelstrom. Amid the mucus and blood, all the sacs emptied their contents. There were no howls of anger nor screams of pain, just the thud of bullets. "Hold fire."

A mist milled about the corridor, entwining with the shredded sacs that dribbled slime into the weightless passage. Globules of red and green drifted their way. The rest was still.

"ZZ3, threat assessment, action code Wrecking Crew." Rebekah stepped aside as the bot strode into the swampy remains.

The bot's eyes flashed momentarily, and raised two hideously stretched heads. "Cold. No sign of life. Zero threat."

"Cold? Explain," said Arin.

"These were not alive at point of contact." The bot dropped one of the deformed heads, its limb milling about in the detritus to retrieve another. "This hybrid had developed more than the rest." The bot swung the skull towards them. The eye sockets were covered in scaled, white skin above a stretched nose. The mouth was a long, vertical slit from which a thick tongue lolled. "But also failed."

Rebekah stared at the head, the skin flapping loosely. She had images of it sloughing off, exposing the skull. But that would require gravity. It was dead, and if it hadn't been before, it certainly would have succumbed to their onslaught. But amid all the gore and mucus, they had once been human. A living breathing person, with wishes and memories.

"That's enough, ZZ3. Is the same organic present?" She hesitated to say it. "The same alien organic."

The bot paused. "It is, though I would shy from labelling it 'alien'. My programming states the Senti are *alien*, but I do not have their biology in my database. I, therefore, do not recognise their biology in these ... hybrids."

"Okay." Rebekah checked the FCEO flag in her HUD, confirming a match with ZZ3's previous analysis of the powdered body and tooth. She dismissed it and eyed the mess they needed to walk past, a lot of which clung to the bot already. "Fuck, we need to go through."

"Hey, I'm on the rear now. Good choice, captain." said Savvo, looking back to peer along the corridor. "Make sure you sweep up after yourself."

Arin threw a middle-fingered response over his shoulder.

Rebekah sighed. "ZZ3, clear a way through. Guard five metres past, action code Wrecking Crew. Arin, send the drone in after. I'll have your back."

"Got an umbrella?" he said, watching as ZZ3 swept body parts and gelatinous sacs to the side of the corridor before moving on. The unwholesome mess began to seep back, and he sent the drone ahead, swiftly following.

Rebekah reloaded and raised her carbine, keeping her eyes on Arin's back. The occasional squelch made her stomach flip, but she made it through to find the next space bare of bulbous sacs. The corridor veered to the left, and she knew it opened out onto the secondary cargo bay. All they could see, however, was an ominous black void. No emergency lighting was going to fill that space, though there should be lanes traced in LEDs once they got closer. Along the left, the schematic indicated two large doorways. One led to the warbots, the other to their armoury. Target in sight.

"Drone," she said. Arin sent the little machine further ahead, taking over full control as its gyroscopes and sensors detected zero input to align with. The camera picked out the blue and green LEDs Rebekah had hoped for and tracked them to the centre. Broken crates littered the bay, their contents snagged to the deck, or swinging softly as the low rotation of the asteroid took effect. Most displayed multiple scorch marks or wood pitted with scratches.

"It's a wreck," said Arin. "Someone's hit this bay like a hurricane."

"Or some things," added Savvo. "With tentacles and teeth. Two hundred and twenty-one crew, remember."

"Plus Marines," said Arin. "Fuck." The drone paused, hovering above a section of ATVs and their armoured counterparts. They were burned out. Crushed and hammered, their batteries or fuel cells having exploded and fire likely to have spread rapidly from the centre. Amid the destruction lay buried the shell of a warbot, its four limbs twisted and bent around a holed torso. Greasy chains swung above, attached to the bay ceiling.

"Closer," said Rebekah.

"Chains," said Savvo. "Chains with screwed up gravity ... shit. They shouldn't hang straight."

The drone squealed as it was struck by something the camera didn't catch, spinning about only to be lashed a second and third time. The feed stopped, but the noise carried on across the otherwise silent bay. A screech of metal upon metal, followed by a tiny flare of light that signalled its demise.

A second screech, this one organic, though Rebekah doubted any shred of humanity lay within it, scraped at her nerves.

"The warbot room, now," she ordered. "ZZ3, escort protocol, defend. Action code Wrecking Crew." Taking the lead, Rebekah ran along the wall, her beams highlighting the metal sides and their bloody scars. The space was littered with the contents of shattered crates that spun away as she ran through. Rebekah shouted a warning – a cracked helmet, a split suit, and they wouldn't need to worry about the fucking hybrids or whatever they were.

Her HUD pinged, the map flagging where the warbot door should be. She pulled up, her lights highlighting the razor-edged gap ripped through the holding bay wall. Arin clomped behind.

"Cover my rear," Rebekah ordered, and with carbine high and synced to her HUD, entered the completely dark room. Shadows flickered wherever her light hit, the chaos of bent and misshapen machines causing her heart to thud. She stilled it, activating her chip, letting the warmth seep in.

This was what she was.

A Breaker. In, assess ... Kill.

She slowed her breath, sweeping the room, ignoring the clamour behind. They knew their job, and she hers. This was the target, and she sensed something waited in the dark for them. For her.

The HUD flashed, and she eye-clicked Arin's query about sending in ZZ3. She replied in the negative, then swept her beam to the right. It caught white flesh, and the slightest of movements. Softly, she brought the carbine around, and with finger on trigger, switched her beams to full.

The figure screamed. Eye sockets wide, sallow skin stretched across them veiling whatever hell lay inside. Its neck squirmed against a metal collar, red and raw. The light shifted with her head to pool upon the hybrid's body strapped to a table – no, a curved metal hull– with its elongated arms spread wide, and far too long legs plunged into a metal casing. The slitted mouth opened wide, exposing a thick tongue flapping from side to side. A screech assailed her comms, but not of flesh – of metal. The hybrid flexed, knees bending while motors whirred, and the hellish blend of human and warbot rose to its magnetic feet.

Rebekah fired, the flashes sparking across her light beams, drilling into the torso and head. Blood flowed, but the warbot lashed out, its forelimb sweeping towards her vulnerable helmet. She ducked, awaiting her death.

Metal met metal; Rebekah suddenly aware she was still alive. ZZ3 blocked the warbot's forelimb and smashed down onto the hybrid's skull, splintering the bone. It made no difference, the machine lashing out at ZZ3 which the bot only just managed to block. Rebekah threw herself to the side, dodging the flailing limbs of the two huge machines. With her boots unclicked she flew into the wall, nervously eyeing the sharp edges of the hole as she spun away.

"Grenade," shouted Savvo.

Trusting his judgement that she was far enough away, Rebekah grabbed the broken crate by her feet and pulled herself behind. The explosion filled her comms, the HUD quietening the noise to within safe limits as the impact reverberated through the decks. Few grenades could do much damage to a warbot. Their armoured hulls were protection against most low-level explosives and even some artillery shells. However, grenades also filled the air with smoke and light – a useful distraction and a chance to run away. And run she did.

The magboots clamped down, and she powered for the ragged exit. Dropping to her haunches alongside its outer edge, she peered back along her carbine's sight towards the ensuing fight.

"Sit rep," she said, and Arin's gun barked once behind.

"There's something out there," said Savvo. "And it's playing games."

Rebekah watched ZZ3 reel from a heavy punch. "And in there," she said. "Nobody breaks a Breaker. Except, perhaps, for a fucking weirded out warbot."

Chapter 25

Hendricks sighed, the stim Davina fed her through the feed line easing into her system. The engineer's eyelids flickered once, then she set about the piles of electrical boards and fibres her arms were immersed in.

"If I can bypass that fucking virus, and the safety systems, I think I can restart the links to the beta fusion engine. The primary has shut down completely. A missile up its arse wouldn't wake that one up." Hendricks dragged out another section of the linkage. "Hold that," she said, and dropped a pile of interwoven wires and fibres into Davina's hands. "And do not move." The engineer had slate in hand with a probe attached that she repeatedly pressed into sections of the console. Each beep or ping was received with a tut or a shake to the head.

"And if not?"

"The solar panels are no use out here. Sun wouldn't heat a gnat's arse, never mind charge a battery."

Hendricks hadn't looked at her as she spoke, Davina taking that as bad news. "Last chance," she whispered.

"Eh? Possibly. Thinking." The engineer stretched her right leg, wincing as she moved it back under the chair Davina had acquired from the galley. "Talk to me, keep me focused."

"What about?"

"The twins. How did you get them into suits? I remember warning you." Hendricks flicked the slate's screen, changing something that brought a sliver of a smile to her face that abruptly disappeared.

"Would you believe me if I said I asked?" Davina coughed, her lungs protesting. "You don't trust me, none of you do. I can't say I blame you in the circumstances."

Hendricks leant back, her eyes sliding over to meet with hers. "Trust comes when someone has your back. So far, you've had mine. And you are telling me the girls are alive. Considering the state of the airlock, your story rings true. But ..." The engineer returned to her job, tongue poking out of the corner of her mouth.

Davinia's lips twisted. "I lied to them. Does that help? I told them you were going to kick the engines in at full power. Break away from the people on the roof so you could fix the ship. That they had to take the retardant so they would be okay. If I'd told them that you were dead, what do you think would have happened?"

The engineer frowned. "You have absolutely no fucking idea. Everything you think you know about empaths," she bit her lip, "fuck ... When I first met them, they had me putting my own gun in my mouth. The hate, the self-loathing. They poured it in there and shook my mind like a cocktail. Angel took off the first restraining helmet, Tremil's, and she just stood back. Those eyes."

"What happened?"

"She cut them out. Drew her knife and carved her own face." Hendricks stopped working, leaning her forehead onto the tops of her gloves. She sucked in a breath. "Rebekah. The dropship had been shot down. She came in looking for the squad and found us all on the edge of madness. Everyone seeing not only their own failures, but all the hate and loathing that had been forced upon the girls. Can you imagine that? You walk in and your squad, those who have had your back for the past three years, are all in various stages of killing themselves."

Davina adjusted her position, trying to catch Hendricks' eyes. Drawn into the story and needing to know how it ended. But it hadn't ended, had it? They were still living it. The helmet mentioned likely a psionic restraint. A Class A illegal piece of unregistered scientific equipment.

"They weren't a family you found, were they? The girls, they were a Bustan experiment. Their genetics programme."

"Like I said, everything you think you know, you don't. They were our target. Simple as. And if you want to know why, and what happened next, you'll have to ask our captain – if she's alive out there. I'm telling you as a warning. They know when you lie." Hendricks painfully rose from the chair, dropping the remnants of the console into the open doors. She held out her hand, and Davina gave her the pile she had been holding on to. The engineer shoved it inside with the rest then turned away.

"Is that it? You've done it?"

"Can't be done. The reactor has gone too far for recovery." Hendricks glanced her way, the look apologetic. "I don't go telling people my life story when I think they'll live to retell it. It's a rule I have. Sorry."

"*Sunstar*, come back."

Davina's mind whirled, grappling in the dark, fighting off the grinning bastardo as he fumbled with her helmet.

"*Hey, you were going to die slowly, Incini bitch. But I changed my mind.*"

The fingers drummed at her helmet, slapping at the sides. Suddenly she knew they had gripped hold, and she beat at the arms, desperate to stop the salvager.

"You is going to suck vacuum. At first the breath will be torn from your lungs, then they will fill with liquid. That's the point when you know you is about to die."

The click sent her heart racing.

"*Sunstar*, come back. This is Tremil – Davina, Dricks, you there?" The voice was monotone, steady. "Come back. Please be alive."

Davina woke with a start. Eyes flicking towards the scrubber filter gauge on the navy suit Hendricks had talked her into. She coughed, suddenly remembering the dream. The salvager. She lifted her head from the galley table. With her mind slightly fogged, she panicked as her chest constricted, and checked the filter on the suit again.

Calm. Breathe.

Another hour before the next change. Hopefully the battery would last a little longer. Rebekah and her crew had taken the spares.

"Please don't be dead, we don't know what to do," echoed in her comms.

What the hell? She reached for her wrist, but realised the controls weren't there. She scanned the eye menu, finding the comms and attempted an eye-click. She missed, but backtracked, getting it right the second time.

"Tremil, come back. Tremil, this is Davina." Her feet met the deck, the magboots clicking, and she pounded towards medbay. "What's happening? How come you can talk to us?"

"Something bad's happened, Davina." The monotone broke, the voice cracked. "Really bad."

"But you're alive. Heki? Is Heki okay?" She opened the door, finding Hendricks laid upon the medtable. Her eyes were closed, probably swimming in pain meds as their time slipped away.

"She's not well. We … we did something."

"Fuck it."

"Davina?"

"Not you. Listen, I'm waking up Hendricks, okay. She'll know what to do. How to help." Davina dropped the stim through the feed line and eyed a second. The engineer stirred, and her eyes popped open.

"What the f—"

"They're alive. Tremil, Heki. Both of them. On the comms."

The engineer sat fully up, clearly ignoring the pain as the stim kicked in. "Tremil?"

"Oh, Dricks … Dricks. We need your help. We need to know how to fly the ship. The *Maverick*."

"What about the crew? Toms?" said Hendricks, but it was clear she already knew the answer, her eyes locking with Davina's.

"They're dead. All of them. I … we couldn't control it." Tremil's voice broke completely. "I thought we were better. Healed. But we're not, we're monsters, Dricks. Monsters."

"Those salvagers attempted to kill all of us, you hear? You hear me? Me, you, Davina. They decided we should suffer the most horrible way to die, knowing it's coming and who did it and that they're laughing at you as you take your last breath. Out here in the black, alone. I'm sorry you had to go through that, but don't mourn them. Don't grieve." Hendricks looked to Davina, her face imploring.

"Tremil, listen," Davina said, thinking on her feet. "We need you. Understand. We don't have long left. The air is short, our batteries low. I understand your pain, but you have a chance to rescue us. To make it right." She hated how that sounded, and the accompanying wince from Hendricks. Nothing would make what they alluded to right, but nor would her death.

There was silence, Davina realising there was no crackling either. The jamming had stopped.

"Heki is here. What can we do?"

Hendricks patted Davina's shoulder, and spoke. "Remember the ship simulator? The one I added to your slate?"

"Of course," said Heki cutting in. "High score every time."

"Yeah, well forget that shit. Arin coded it, and he couldn't fly a bus on the moon." There was the briefest of giggles in response. "So, we don't want any of those PYP moments, do we? So, we follow my lead. You at the cockpit console?"

"Yes, Dricks," came back the reply, the voice once again monotone and firm.

"Good. Now these fuckers, excuse my language, set a course over here when they grabbed you. So, check through the menu and then—"

"Got it. Keyed in. Autopilot?" said Heki.

Hendricks grinned. "Yeah, clever girl. Punch them both and holler when you're near. Does it have an ETA?"

A brief silence followed. "An hour. There's a modifier to adapt it. We can shave twenty minutes."

"Yeah, higher burn, more thruster fuel use. But select that. Happy flying, trainee pilot."

Davina grabbed the engineer as she keeled backwards, her eyelids fluttering before they settled. "Next stim might do for me," she said. "I can hear my hip grinding, and my back is murder." The flow of words stopped, Davina panicking until she caught a twitch in Hendricks' nose and lips. She had passed out.

Patting the woman's arm, Davina left, heading for the cockpit. The ship's systems were on emergency power, and the girls had patched through onto her suit comms. But they were close. Could she find a way to get a message through to the crew? What had Hendricks said? Text only. A data send. And data was her thing.

She clomped into the cockpit and settled into the pilot's chair. Her hands flickered over the console, hoping to bring it to life. Nothing happened. No sign at all. She leant back, unclicking one boot and resting it on the console. As she peered at the ceiling, the HUD assumed she was requesting the menu and flickered into life.

Am I thinking too small? This is a navy suit, not the old rescue kit.

After a few attempts, the HUD flared, and a swirling picture of the asteroid family appeared. She eye-clicked some more, but it didn't register any comms links in its vicinity. She frowned, then analysed the menu again.

And a thought dropped in.

"*Maverick*, this is *Sunstar*, comeback."

"Receiving," said Tremil. "Are you okay?"

"At the moment, all is fine. Though I warn you, Hendricks is injured pretty bad." She had a second thought. "Is there a medbot aboard?"

"I think so … Heki has gone to check," replied Tremil.

"Good. Tremil, am I right that you are the surveillance and comms specialists on this crew?"

"Oh yes."

Chapter 26

ZZ3 was on its back, the deranged warbot of whatever hellhole ship this was, on top, feet maglocked to the deck and ready to strike. The other three limbs had ZZ3 pinned, arms useless and stuck under its torso.

Rebekah fired, the grenade ramming into ZZ3's assailant just below the threatening arm. The joint ruptured, and though the limb swung, it flapped harmlessly against the bot's torso. ZZ3 bucked, trying to throw the warbot and its bloody passenger off. The maglock was obviously too strong, but it managed to free two arms that grasped the warbot's forelimbs and squeezed.

"Shit." Rebekah flipped open her pouches to gather the last two grenades. Reloading, she glanced behind, with both Savvo and Arin focused on something out in the murk of the bay. The occasional flash of a bullet winged into the dark, but no answering cry of pain followed. She latched both grenades down, locking them home, and made a decision.

"ZZ3, pacifist program ZZ, negative protocol, I say again, negative protocol. Action code … Breakers." The red lights on the bot's face flickered, then flashed, a pattern whirling until it settled into a steady, rhythmic pulse.

Rebekah released another grenade that struck the warbot's chest. The remains of the hybrid splattered over ZZ3, but more importantly, it rocked backwards. ZZ3 took the opportunity, its jointed hips flailing upwards, and the bot de-clamped, falling to the side. Rebekah expected a flurry of limbs, for ZZ3 to try and roll on top of the bot.

But it was in AD mode, attack and destroy – with enhancements. Two new limbs appeared from ZZ3's back, their ends flaring into life. Plasma torches, the additional heavy cutting tools the bot carried. Without a pause, both torches drove into the warbot, burnt hybrid flesh and seared metal filling the air. The warbot flailed, but ZZ3 pushed the plasma deeper and deeper into its chest. The pulse of its eyes rose until they flared manically. The two cutting limbs ripped sideways, opening the warbot's torso like a can of beans. ZZ3 drove its spare limbs into the innards, ripping a thick, black box free and flinging it aside.

Rebekah heard the occasional burst of rifles from behind, her mind running through the options. This was not a war zone, there could be survivors, and the warbots were notoriously poor at deciding between fear and aggression. ZZ3 pulled itself up and locked to the deck, gaze settling on her, the pulse of its eyes slowly returning to the steady beat of assess and survey. Fuck, she had forgotten how bestial they could be. Cold killers.

One that had just saved her life.

"Threat assessment, survey this room ZZ3, then stand guard, action code Breakers." She turned her back to the warbot, leaving it to carry out the set order.

"Sit rep, come back," she said, running low in her armoured suit to kneel beside Savvo.

"Arin has flanked back towards where we came in." Savvo flicked the feed over, flagging it for her attention.

Rebekah eye-clicked and analysed the image. Arin was up high, the faint shine of the corridor's emergency LEDs reflecting off the cargo box he was clamped on. He began to skim through the spectrum, each change to his lights altering the feed as the HUD adapted. Hitting infrared, smudges appeared, dotted throughout the bay. Nothing strong enough for an ID, and each stationary and barely different from the surrounding temperatures. The switch to ultraviolet produced nothing of note, useful in space but …

"Arin, prepare to flood the bay with your UV lights. Savvo, alter your visor for ultraviolet," she ordered.

Rebekah checked over her menu, and eye-clicked the adaptation. On their own helmets – those they used for salvage and rescue missions – the auto switch over was a normal part of the software. Not so for the Breakers' kit, and so it proved for the navy-issue.

"Ready, Arin." A clomp and whir from behind had Rebekah looking over her shoulder. ZZ3 stood at the torn open wall, the plasma torches stowed, and forelimbs extended – on guard. She nodded and looked back. "Now."

The ultraviolet flooded the centre of the bay, spreading out in a triangle towards the back. Frustrated by her position and what she could see, Rebekah clicked on Arin's feed. The hold lit up in places, and from memory where the smudged infrared signatures had been, now sat familiar sacs. She dismissed those for now, assuming, or hoping, they were as dead as those in the corridor. Arin swept right, towards the back of the hold and the huge mechanical doors that led out into space. Something moved there, scurrying from side to side, trying to dodge the light.

"It can see the UV," she said. "Whatever's out there knows we're looking, that it's been found. Take it down, Arin."

"Kill assigned, action code Breakers," he responded. The shot rang out, followed by two controlled bursts. "We have a hit, target down. I say again, target down. Cannot confirm kill."

Her HUD pinged; the map tagged where Arin assumed the target to be. "Savvo, flank left," Rebekah ordered. Bent low, she headed right, moving as swiftly as the boots would allow between the rows until she came across the first of the glowing sacs. It lay still, attached to the deck and apparently lifeless.

"Savvo, be aware. We have sacs everywhere," she said into her comms.

"Bypassing where I can," he came back.

Good enough, he needed to think on his feet. Her thoughts briefly wandered to his stim addiction, trying to recall a moment in the last few days when she'd seen that whirl in his eyes – and none came to mind. A good sign. Boredom was dangerous, more so for those that were used to constant battle or the rigour of training.

Rebekah sidled past the glowing sac, half an eye on it and relieved as she began to move away. A quick glance back showed no movement. Another came into view, and she dodged into a cross row, and then took the next gap between the myriad stores to keep heading in the same direction. A quick check of the map, and she paused next to a scarred collection of barrels, one of which had been torn from its restraint and hovered across her path. The gentle sway of its movement caught her eye, the markings on its side glowing in the UV light.

"The *Scourge*," she whispered. "It's General Ashma's old flagship. Oh shit."

Focus. Target.

She moved on swiftly to the next cross row, her HUD flagging Savvo just a few metres away to her left. Between them sat the potential target. "Cover me," she said. Savvo affirmed, and Rebekah crept to the edge of some plasteel girders, her carbine up, synced with the HUD's UV imagery. A splash of black pooled outwards, and as she rounded the corner, a form lay stricken upon the deck, its legs kicking. The voice whined, the sound striking at Rebekah's heart. She eye-clicked her HUD, keeping the carbine locked onto the bundle on the floor. In the strange light, a naked human appeared, eyes suddenly shining back. He half-scrabbled at the deck, pushing himself away, one leg shattered by Arin's bullets.

She so nearly lowered her weapon and went to help the wretched man, until Savvo's voice cut in.

"Careful," he warned. "Bustan 8, remember."

Yeah, she remembered. The booby-trapped wounded. It had only been one town of the many they had broken, but it had been enough.

The man whined again, dragging himself away, and she raised her gun, depressing the trigger until it clicked once. If infected, *it* couldn't be touched. If not, the man would bleed out.

Her HUD pinged, a message dropping in marked urgent.

"Captain?" said Savvo.

"A second. The *Sunstar*." She raised her hand, signalling wait and read the message. Parts of it were gibberish, others nonsensical. Toms attacking the ship? Cutting in?

She spun away from the sight of the injured man, making sure Arin watched on with her HUD auto-adjusting for the glare of his UV beam. She blinked, thoughts railing in. The time stamp on the message, if correct, was several hours ago.

Shit.

With her chest tightening, thoughts seeped in of the twins, deathly blue and spinning about an airless ship, while the vacuum sucked them dry. Hendricks, Davina. Her crew.

She opened her comms, but the words wouldn't come. Her lips moved, but what to say?

"Captain?" Savvo raised his weapon, the barrel pointing towards the hapless man. "Am I to …?"

Her comms crackled, then cleared. A link request dropping into her HUD. It was the *Maverick*. The fucking *Maverick*, ready to gloat. Perhaps offer an exchange, and likely leave them as dead as their crewmates. As the children.

"Wait," she whispered. "Scan him. Get ZZ3 ..." was all she managed, then walked away. "Arin, cover me."

She found a space and leant against a cargo box, both hands inside her gloves whitening as she pressed them onto its metal edge. She accepted the link.

"*Maverick*, this is Captain Kahn. Go ahead." Rebekah closed her eyes, trying to blot the imagery that pervaded her mind.

"Rebekah, it's me, Tremil." The monotone voice cracked, tears flooding the comms.

"Tremil? What?" Relief swept her words away. She sucked in a breath. "Where are you Tremil? My HUD has tagged this as coming from the *Maverick*. Are you okay? And Heki?"

Her words came out in a rush. The discipline of a Marine and ship's captain lost for a moment as fear for the twins took hold.

"We are uninjured. Davina says it is too long to explain, but we must let you know we are safe. We have the *Maverick*, the *Sunstar* is holed and a mess. The engines are down. We are on the way to rescue Dricks and her." Tremil's voice rose and fell, the emotions high and rarely flat as it usually was.

Rebekah pushed herself off the box, squeezing her gloved hands together. Safe, when a moment ago they were lost to her. And Davina had insisted on the contact, understood what effect the garbled message would have.

"Stay safe. Do as Hendricks and ... and Davina suggest. Understand? And keep this channel monitored. I'll be in touch."

"Yes, Captain."

Rebekah smiled, the seriousness of the response striking home.

Fuck. How the hell did I get into this?

"Captain Khan out," she said, and turned back as Savvo's carbine barked. ZZ3 loomed further down the row, its lights fully red as it approached at speed.

"I ordered you to analy…" she began, but the mess on the floor writhed, tendrils splurging from its open chest. The hybrid floated away from the floor, dead tentacles releasing their hold upon the deck. "Shit. Naked. No magboots. Get your head together."

Savvo nodded. "Naked, yeah. Took me a moment. This fucking ship is insane – demons, monsters, whatever the hell they are."

Rebekah could do nothing but agree. "Arin, are we clear?"

She waited, noting the sweep of his UV beam from above as it danced over the cargo bay.

"Clear," he said. "You all okay down there?"

"Yeah," she said. "But you need to hear this. Both of you, and we need that thruster fuel ASAP." She glanced over to ZZ3. "This mission is turning as sour as Savvo's farts."

"On my way, and nothing can be that bad," replied Arin, and the clunk of his boots echoed across the bay.

"Want to bet?" she responded.

Savvo glanced over. There was a flint to his eyes that her HUD view captured perfectly, and he flexed his neck. "We could do with the 'throwers," he said. "You know, they have their uses." He eyed the dead hybrid, its tentacles floating, seeping blood globules. "For when things get messy."

"We have ZZ3."

"Yeah, we do. Exactly my point – weapons. By my count, there is a helluva lot more of these bloody things out there."

Chapter 27

"Pinion release in 5-4-3-2-1 and firing," Heki said, her voice steady over the comms.

Davina noted the puff of smoke billowing from beneath the *Maverick*, then the long javelin-like spike that speared across the void, the thick synth-rope trailing behind. This the third attempt, the two others having glanced off and now lost somewhere in the black. For all the computing power aboard the salvager's ship, even a slight miscalculation led to a missed opportunity. The javelin slammed into the *Sunstar*'s hull, striking a few metres from the ruined airlock. An explosion shook the ship, Davina feeling it through her feet. She desperately wanted to check its success, and despite her misgivings after last time, approached the airlock. With the power gone, it was eyes on only. Ensuring her magboots were locked, and the tether she had come to rely on was in place, she gripped the inner handhold and peered out. The metal spike had dug in, and the puff of dust and smoke indicative that the explosion had sunk it deeper as the tip splayed wide to grip on. A salvager's tool. Rough, ready and effective when dealing with wrecks. Smaller objects got the joys of a magno-lock.

"*Maverick*, this is Davina. We have a hit. It appears set."

"Testing," said Heki.

Davina knew she had to be patient, but a glance towards her scrubber gauge and the battery icon wasn't helping her mood. Hendricks' suit wasn't much better, but at least the woman had given in to the meds and slept the pain – and more importantly, the stress – away.

"Clear, we are in the green, Davina. Ready for this?" said Heki.

"I would be lying if I said yes," she replied. "Fetching Hendricks now." She clomped through to the medbay and undid the engineer's straps, letting her float before grabbing the tether and attaching it to her belt. The synth-rope, already shortened after Hendricks had cut it, had a new karabiner. She checked it again, and with a grimace, led the space-suited woman out of the door, guiding her down to the airlock. There, she tested her own lifeline. With that, she hefted the jetpack she'd readied earlier, and eased it out past the ladder rungs and felt it clamp to the hull. She thanked the girls who'd watched a hundred times or more how Savvo and Arin worked.

"I may swear a lot, Heki," she said. "Apologies in advance. Its PYP time."

The girl giggled in response. "Just don't SYP, okay?"

"That may be difficult. I make no guarantees." Davina unclicked her right boot, and with her hand upon the inner rail, swept her leg out to rest against one of the ladder rungs. Next came a hand, and she gripped hold, pulling herself out as the second boot click-released. She breathed heavily, heart racing and not daring to check her HUD. With a shudder, she pulled one leg beneath her, and felt the *click,* and far too slowly, the *clamp,* onto the hull.

"Fuck me," she said, and repositioned the other boot with a click. With one hand still on the rung, she pressed it down and as it attached, let go of the hull, her thighs and ankles screaming at her for the unnatural movement. "Shit, shit," she repeated, letting the complaints ease as she focused on the jetpack – denying her brain the chance to process where she stood.

Davina reached for the jetpack, and then caught herself, remembering Hendricks' tether. They had planned for it to be attached to her as she collected the pack, but now, as the reality of what she was doing hit, she worried it was far too risky. Better, perhaps, to do what she feared twice, than fail.

She turned to face the pinion, and with eyes only for the ship's hull, strode across.

Do not look. Focus.

Within five strides, she reached the javelin, Hendricks floating behind but momentum bringing her closer. Trusting her boots, she untethered the engineer, and attached the clamp around the synth-rope with a prayer. They'd had enough shit-luck to be where they were, and she feared facing any more.

She tested it, and then slowly backed away, moving awkwardly without risking turning about. Her body complained, its tiredness obvious. But she didn't want to die, especially out in the starkness of space. On the fifth step, she looked back, and took another to collect the jetpack. Nervous fingers lifted it from the deck, and she sat it on her back in a seemingly awkward position. The girls had been scant on detail about how it attached, but she felt the magclip lock on and something brushed her thigh. The belt buckle, and with a little more searching, she found the other end.

"Can't trust everything," she said to herself, and tightened the strap. With that she walked back to the pinion, Hendricks floating oblivious on the far side. She stared at it, sure there was something she should do next. Her analytical mind fogged, and a sliver of dread crept in. Her eyes flicked to the HUD, the display showing the scrubber on the verge of entering the red zone.

Davina pushed down the panic and ran through her mental checklist. Finally, her eyes alighted on Hendricks, and then her tether.

Relieved, she slid her hand onto the engineer's lifeline and attached it to her belt. In her head, she'd walked through every part of what was expected, breaking it down step by step. But theory doesn't always play out when oxygen depletion starts.

She coughed, and a little blood splattered on the inside of her helmet. Refusing to accept what it meant, she attached her lifeline to the *Maverick*'s synth-rope, and disconnected the tether attached to the *Sunstar*. Numb, ignoring the consequences of what she was about to do, Davina placed both hands on the jetpack handles. With her fingers on the controls, she pressed the buttons for both gas thrusters. She rose, and stuttered, adjusting her fingers to the upper buttons. These pushed her forward, and finally she began to slide along the synth-rope and towards the *Maverick*.

Elation flooded her thoughts, and Davina attempted to calm her body, slow her breathing – and ignore the wetness congregating upon her lips. She tried not to, but the tip of her tongue dipped into blood, the metallic tang dampening her brief celebration.

She let go of the controls, feeling the momentum slow a little with the friction between karabiner and rope. The pack seemed to balance well enough, and she reached down for the emergency oxygen bottle attached to her thigh. To her horror, it wasn't there, the clamp empty. She whirled about, eyes roaming behind. The stupidity of this soon dawned as the synth-rope bounced with her jerky movements. Even if she could see it, what could she do?

She coughed again, using the pain in her chest to suppress thoughts of her situation – of the vast expanse of *nothing* she floated so precariously within.

"Fuck, fuck."

"Davina?" said Heki. "Are you okay? The coughing?"

The tears flowed, and the scrubber clicked over into the red.

"No. Heki. I'm not." The warning light flashed. "The suit ... there's no time ..."

Tremil cut in. "Davina, listen. You need to do as I say. You hear me? Come back."

Davina's mind felt like sludge. "Yes," she responded.

"I need you to cut the line. You understand? Cut the line, and attach it to yourself. We'll reel you in."

Davina blinked, her thoughts wading through a swamp. A gloved hand fumbled with her pouch, and she extricated the hooked knife. Numb fingers held the grip, and she placed it against the rope. But if she cut, it could slip away. Lost.

She looked at her own lifeline, and then Hendricks. The temptation to cut her loose, use her line to tie herself on, made her hands shake. She reached towards where the tether pressed against her lower chest, fingers stumbling over Hendricks' karabiner to grab her jetpack belt. She heaved a loop of the *Maverick*'s line underneath, sliding her arm through and gripping the end. With an ungainly stroke, she sliced at the rope trailing at her side, blanking out what she was doing, focusing on the motion. Twice she sliced, nearly scraping her own gloves, almost unaware of the consequences as she tried to concentrate on the task. The third stroke cut through, and she coughed, blood splashing against the plexiglass.

As the abyss began to drag her in, her fight to survive almost depleted, she let the knife go and pulled the fistful of rope through the loop, yanking it tight.

"Heki ... pull."

Heki sat by the medtable, following the stream of data on the medbot screen. Fingers danced over the keyboard – selecting and deselecting options – until she sat back. Eyes sunken, and with lips dry, her tongue worked along the back of her teeth, keeping a sharp mind off the multitude of problems the medical assessment was throwing out and dealing with the bare facts.

Tremil slid through the door, pressing herself against the wall in the small medbay. Hendricks, still in her suit with the helmet removed and locked to the floor, lay on the main table. The engineer's eyes were closed, breathing laboured but steady – for now.

"What does it say?" asked Tremil. Each word was forced, as if her throat was constricted. The tone flat.

Heki glanced to the engineer. "The hip is crushed, her vertebrae a mess." A catch in her voice threatened to break the monotone, while an inner pain narrowed her eyes. "If we remove the suit, I think she'll die. At least, that's the medbot's assessment."

"Then we don't remove it. Or at least we wait until Rebekah returns," said Tremil stiffly. "I can't … we shouldn't make that choice. We're not in charge."

Heki nodded, and in a rare moment, her hand fell upon Tremil's forearm and squeezed. Their shared trauma temporarily locked away after waking up to a nightmare they had caused, only to face a potentially fatal injury to one of their family. "Rebekah told us to listen to Davina. I take that as an order, as a crew member. We stabilise Dricks, keep her alive and …" Heki pursed her lips as Tremil slid her hand away, making Heki flinch.

"We can't wake her up. The assessment says she needs to be on the ventilator, and slow her bodily functions down. There could be brain damage if we don't do this right. It falls on us. They have been there for us for the last four years, and now it is our turn." Tremil eased behind Heki's chair, taking her place beside the Incini. She pressed her hand against the woman's brow, feeling the life inside. When they had reeled them in, she had sensed the woman's urge to survive permeating even through space, penetrating her mind. It was perhaps the first time that her own emotions had been pierced, rather than letting someone in. No, that wasn't true. The second. Rebekah had shattered their walls with a simple hug.

Heki grimaced, quickly adjusting her face back to the stoic one she had frequently practised in the mirror. "I know we discussed this, but I don't know if I trust her, Trem. She spins us a tale we knew was a lie, put us to sleep, then we wake up on this ship. And ... then that ..." she waved her hands towards the doorway and what lay beyond.

"But we are alive, Hek, and both Davina and Dricks could have died. She could have lied to us again, or tried to, and left Hendricks behind. Left her for dead and taken her filters. And as you said, Rebekah wanted us to trust her." Tremil ran her hand down the woman's sallow cheek. The blue tinge had receded, but she was pale and the assessment of her lungs, poor. "We should do our best for them both. It's up to us to keep them alive."

"*And* we need to be ready for the crew when they return." Heki tapped at the screen, and the medbot rumbled, the tubes entering Hendricks' suit filling with a liquid that gathered, squeezing out the air, then flowed into the suit and subsequently the engineer. "Okay. I'll stabilise Davina. Follow the assessment and the med programme." Heki glanced at the blood-covered gloves, half hanging over the waste disposal slot in the wall. "I did the first half; you get to clean up the rest."

Chapter 28

Rebekah swept the area in front of the armoury with her ultraviolet light. Still clear, just the glow of the sacs in among the cargo that reflected off some of the shinier surfaces. Satisfied, she approached the armoury door with some trepidation. The captain of the *Scourge* and relevant officers would have maintained an entry code. Any ship under fire would release that code depending on circumstances, and in the ultra rare case of being boarded, would actually lock the armoury down if the enemy closed in. And why? Because some of the weaponry in there could blow a hole in the hull if you tried hard enough. Their method of entry a case in point. The inner skin blown wide open to, in her opinion, purge the corridor.

However, an emergency shutdown would leave it deadlocked and under restricted minimal power, with only the door pad providing access as per the bulkheads. It would still require the code, or worse, a retina scan from the relevant officers. And where the hell were they? Decomposing in a sac somewhere, or worse, reforming into something horrific.

"Captain," came Arin's voice over the comms. "The third warbot is absent. I can't find any sign of it. Nor can I access any kind of manifest either, so whether it has, you know, been taken by one of these hybrid bastards or not, it is likely somewhere else in the ship."

"Fuel?" she replied, mentally crossing her fingers. "Please tell me we have the thruster fuel."

"Absent, but I may have a solution. The bot ZZ3 took out … I'll see if I can drain any from the … the carcass."

"You could have chosen a better word," she said, shaking her head.

"I could … but it kinda fits. Arin out."

Rebekah sighed, mind running over the possibilities. She glanced at the armoury door, and then spun, a noise out in the cargo bay setting her on edge – metal clinking against metal. They'd checked the filthy chains that had taken out the drone, their links thick with mucus and now floating awkwardly above the bay itself. Logic said they *were* just chains, probably used by the hybrid for whatever reason to get about. The hooks on their ends all scarred and pitted when viewed through their HUDs.

"Savvo? Checking in," she said.

"Nothing's changed," he replied. "All still clear."

"Set ZZ3 on guard and come help with the armoury door," she instructed, and approached it, eyes scanning the pad. It was as dirty as the chains, with imprints of fingers – she hoped they were fingers – where they had tapped at the screen. She rubbed the dried gloop with the back of her glove and brushed the remainder away. With her fingertips, she pressed the pad, and to her relief, it activated.

"I'm here," Savvo said, a faint click of the comms setting her at ease before he spoke. "Anything?"

Rebekah eyed the flickering screen, the expected shimmer of a green-tinged menu replaced by the red of lockdown. "Shit," she said.

"Let me have a look."

Rebekah stepped aside, letting Savvo work. It didn't take long.

"Locked out. And I mean, tight. As if they were being boarded, or an internal threat going by the shit we've seen. But nothing suggests these hybrids use weapons."

"They may not have known." She peered at ZZ3 who stood in the shadowed edge of her lights. "Maybe it was the hybrid warbot? Allowing that access to what's in there would have been suicide."

Savvo stepped away from the pad, and he looked behind Rebekah, scanning the murk of the bay. "There's still got to be, what, at least a hundred and possibly a lot bloody more of these things." He returned his gaze to her. "We're not tooled up for this, Captain. Not without getting in there."

Rebekah had to agree, mulling over what they had already found out about the ship. "You thinking what I am? That the contract is null? Take the thruster fuel and retreat? But that fucker Duboit will just release what he knows about us. We can't go back, we deserted, Savvo, and with a war prize to boot. Once the deets are released, Countess Sigfer will get wind – even one inkling it's us and she'll send the fucking Inquisitors."

"We could run," cut in Arin. "Bribe those pillars of the solar community, the Senti, and run for another system. I have some recent horrific memories in my chip I don't want. They'd be worth a fortune to those dream-sucking bastards."

"You got the fuel?" she asked, unable to keep the eagerness out of her voice.

"Draining this beautiful combo of bot and monster as we speak. Give me ten and ZZ3 can make like a starship and fly us out of here."

The silence hung heavy, followed by a click on the comms as if Arin wanted to add more. As the *Sunstar*'s sub-engineer, she knew he would have. But as a Marine, and a Breaker, he followed orders having already said more than he should. But here, there was no commanding officer. No oversight. They were without that noble who gave less than a shit if they lived or died, as long as they *won*.

Right now, living was a win. And she had others to think about. To care about.

"And you, Savvo? You wanted out. If we run, you're stuck with me – with us – for a while longer," said Rebekah.

"Can think of worse places to be. Like stuck to a bloody wall inside a sac made of my own skin. Kind of changes your view on things." The comms clicked, leaving a pause as if he was thinking. "This is fun in a screwed-up type of way. Like being alive again. And I would get to travel ... see other systems. I mean, what's not to like?"

"Looking over your shoulder all the time."

"The moment we stopped doing that, we would already be dead. We just get to do it somewhere new," added Savvo.

"Then, Breaker, take ZZ3. I want a sit rep on the way we came in. Check the watchtower on the stairwell, and report back. Now, Marine," ordered Rebekah.

"Aye, Captain." Savvo left, speaking to ZZ3 as he passed, and clomped his way towards the exit corridor.

Rebekah took a last glance at the armoury door, then headed off to find Arin inside the warbot room. He stood on top of the hybrid bot, a tube strung across his elbow that plunged into the bot's back, an electronic hand pump he'd recovered from the debris in the other. She took guard.

Savvo reached the corner of the right dog-leg that led onto the collection of human hybrid remains. He eased his carbine around the corner, checking his HUD as the weapon's sight synced and displayed the viscous mess. Where ZZ3 had cleared a path, the remains had seeped back to float along the passageway. As dreadful as it looked, it was at least how he had expected it to be. He flicked over to his UV lights, pleased to see the same minimal presence as in the bay itself. Whatever they had encountered before, these were dead. He didn't care why, only that they weren't doing something weird and alien-like and reforming ready to ambush him. He turned the UV off, returning to the natural light his brain felt most comfortable with.

"ZZ3, clear a path," he said.

The bot strode into the foul remains, arms spread and gathered the flaps of skin and bone, shoving those that batted off his body out of the way. Savvo followed, daring to glance at the hanging flesh. In his time, he had shot, blown up and killed soldiers and unfortunate innocents alike. On the inside, they had all looked the same, until the twins had taken the veils off his eyes and opened his mind. He shuddered, noting the odd joints and distended bones, the flesh like rubber. The uniforms the only sign they had once been the crew of the *Scourge*. If they abandoned the mission, they would never know what happened and why. And for that, he was grateful. Some things were just too big to know. Beyond a simple Marine.

A clang of robot limb upon door announced they had reached the end of the corridor. On its own, and under the Breaker protocols, the warbot would have spun the handle and entered, following its programming to the letter. Attack and destroy, preserve those targets on its database assigned to live, and eviscerate all others. A killing machine. One, by rights, they should have spaced when they first had the chance. It marked them as Marines. But ZZ3 had saved each one of them ten times and more. Yes, they were sentimental over a machine. That, and the bot was another layer of protection for the twins.

"Enter and evaluate protocol. Action code, Breakers," he said.

ZZ3's limbs heaved, and refusing to step sideways into the visceral chaos that hung nearby, Savvo chose to follow behind.

ZZ3 pulled the door towards them, and Savvo's HUD flashed, identifying trace chemicals it recognised as the air mingled – residue from the watchtower's guns. The warbot stepped inside, and the air was thick with shattered, twisted bodies. The bot lashed out; a sickening wrench followed. Then a second, and a third. Savvo needed information, and spun out from behind, carbine up. The dead and the dying filled his vision. Soulless eyes milled with spinning limbs and foul tentacles as ZZ3 stood down. The watchtower lay twisted on its side and covered in mucus. Its barrels smoked, and Savvo laid a bet with himself it was spent. He eyed the lifts, but they appeared sealed, and he kept his back to them as he approached the open stairwell.

Shots rang out, and he threw himself to the side, the bullets pinging off the deck near his boots as they disengaged. Another burst, short, controlled – so odd among the chaos – ricocheted from where he had been. ZZ3 grasped his flailing leg, and gently reattached him to the deck.

"Shit," he said, spinning about, carbine up and waiting for the pounding of boots down the stairs. They never came.

He took a glance at the downward steps, and then at what he could see of those leading above.

"ZZ3, threat assessment," he said.

"Indicators are we have a dual threat," it replied. "Unknown, further data required."

"Collect the watchtower. Access camera," he said, sighting along the carbine as the warbot complied. It took two steps towards the guard unit, bullets bouncing from its tough armour as it came into view of whoever, or whatever, was on the level above. When ZZ3's third limb stretched for the watchtower, Savvo heard a distant click in his helmet speaker.

"Enemy grenade," he shouted down the comms, and ZZ3 turned its back, exposing the thickest of its armour. The grenade erupted, the light blinding with Savvo's HUD a step behind. He staggered back, his training kicking in as he kept the carbine high and finger on the trigger. With his eyesight filled with blind spots, he activated his chip, the warmth spreading through his brain. The tingle rolled in waves along his nerves, his old addiction raising its ugly head as the chemicals eased his stressed body and mind. Even the dead splattering against his back raised little fear, now just another obstacle to overcome.

And then his HUD died, and he was plunged into utter darkness.

Rebekah reached the dog-leg, the explosion rattling down the corridor, carrying with it the bodies and remaining shreds of their sacs. She waited, and then her HUD lit up, its threat detection systems blaring.

"Back," she shouted, and slammed flat against the wall. Though she couldn't see it, her HUD detailed a wave of electromagnetic radiation spewing along the passage, weakening as it spread from the epicentre. Somewhere near that would be Savvo. His suit was protected like hers, and with time to adjust, would have closed down if the EMP had threatened to overwhelm its system. It all came down to what type of grenade had been used.

"Clear," she said as her HUD flashed. She spun back to look down the corridor. The emergency LEDs were out, and only her lights caught the swirl of bodies that drifted her way. She ignored them. "Arin."

He passed her, carbine up and moving as swiftly as the magboots would allow. Once at the edge of the bulkhead, his suit a mess of red, he signalled her on. Rebekah copied his movements, entering the doorway as boots pounded down the steps. Magboots. She fired, the carbine spitting bullets that peppered the legs where they emerged from the magnetic footwear. Screams echoed down the stairwell, and she fired again, the second burst missing as more boots retreated. Weapons fire echoed, bullets pinging. A grenade bounced down the first step. Handheld, powerful.

"Enemy grenade!" she bellowed

"I have Savvo!" shouted Arin, his breath heavy in the comms. Rebekah registered an inactive ZZ3 in her HUD, at the same time as a pull on her suit. With a prayer, she unclicked her boots, and Arin yanked her back into the corridor.

The eruption filled the stairwell, fire and flame turning whatever it touched to ash. Rebekah barely caught a glimpse as the shockwave rippled through the air, sending her spinning back along the corridor, wrapped about Savvo and his dead suit until they crashed into the far wall.

The light and noise cut off. A clang of the door and a spin of the wheel setting the deadlocks.

"Rebekah, I need something to hold the lock," panted Arin.

Rebekah used the wall to right herself and forced her feet to the deck. When the magboots locked, she took a brief moment to re-orientate her mind and body, then pounded to the warbot room. She collected metal bars and cable, returning through the red and globule-filled corridor to Arin. His strain was obvious, and she slotted the bars home, her suit's motor providing enough juice to bend them into place.

"That do it?" she said.

Arin checked the door pad. "For now. I didn't see any motorised suits like ours, but I make no guarantees it'll do more than delay."

She nodded and turned to stomp down the corridor to where Savvo bobbed. His eyes were open, his face twitched. Disorientated, she decided, ignoring the annoying voice in her head. Had he activated his chip?

She grabbed his boot, and with Arin helping, hauled him to the deck and kicked the front button to activate them. Once stationary, she tried to catch his attention, but he was distant, lost. Amid whatever he had seen and done; he had dipped into old ways. Exactly what a Breaker should do, survive. But at what cost to an addict? Arin started the suit's system reboot.

"ZZ3 is on the other side of the door," she said, stating the obvious despite the pain it would cause Arin. She eye-clicked her HUD, briefly playing through the recorded scene. The bot was stricken, eyes dead. Behind it she had a partial image of whoever had been on the steps. They were in a uniform, but the type and colour were lost in the play of lights and gunfire. She sent it to Arin, knowing it would pain him. "Can you see it?"

He nodded in reply, one hand pressed against his helmet. There was fear in his eyes, adding to the weight she already felt.

"What can do that, Arin? ZZ3 has been at our side for years, and not once did the Bustans manage to shut one down. They tried, bloody hell did they try. It would have turned the war."

"A tailored EMP bomb – has to be. Only we know they don't work. Unless you have inside knowledge of a warbot's systems. We carried out one or two recovery missions when they got into trouble, just so that couldn't happen." He fiddled with Savvo's suit, slipping open a lower chest plate. He nodded at what he saw and pressed a couple of buttons. The whirr of motors was a welcome sound, and the lights in Savvo's HUD began to gleam.

"We're on an Almaarian ship. Whoever fired on us, are likely to be from the original crew. Marines even. Fuck me, Arin. It can only be them, and you're saying it was targeted? A planned attack to take down ZZ3."

"I can't see it any other way. This fucking ship is giving me the creeps. Monsters *and* Marines."

Chapter 29

Rebekah scanned through her HUD, checking her suit's systems as Arin talked Savvo through the events post his shut down. Her battery stood at twenty percent, and she swapped it over for her spare. The suit had been sucking air from the ship and stripping it of anything untoward. Once that filter gave out, she would be down to just the scrubber with its constant recycling of oxygen. A glance told her the external filter sat at thirty percent, perhaps two more hours with the strains of combat, while the scrubber was well within parameters, and they all should have one spare.

"Arin, Savvo. Status check. Filter and battery."

To her relief, they both returned with similar numbers.

"And ammo." She retained three clips and just two grenades, the others four clips and four of the barrel grenades. Not exactly war ready, but they had their suit's weaponry if need be. Though not a way off the ship, or for that matter, out of the asteroid field. They had come to rely on the bot, and just how much was hitting home.

"Okay, Breakers. We need a plan. Without ZZ3, we're screwed as far as I can see. No way off this ship, or this rock, without the sync system," she said, eyes on Arin.

"The probabilities are extremely low, but not impossible. We minimised the use of the jetpacks, so odds are we would have enough juice, and the HUDs have the field's projected movements loaded." He glanced towards Savvo, who showed no response. "I'd give us a twenty percent chance."

"Of dying?" said Savvo, his voice harsh. "Or surviving?"

"Surviving," said Arin. "Each of us."

"Then we need ZZ3 back." She glanced at the two small cans of thruster fuel Arin had recovered. "And as soon as possible. The chances of the Jetpacks being where we left them are next to zero. And when our filters are done, including the scrubbers, we're sucking whatever shit is in the air." She shuddered. They had no clue how the hybrids came about, and the thought of an airborne contagion horrified her.

Savvo stood up from the remains of the cargo box he leant on, and tapped at his helmet. "Then we go back, take the fuckers on and get our bot back. What other way out of this is there? Even if we want our packs, we have to go that way."

"It'll be a deathtrap now. Without ZZ3, they'll just lay in wait and party on our arses. We need to go another way." She brought up the map on her HUD, tracing the presumed passages and corridors. The cargo bay connected to a second entry point parallel with the first, which also had a linked cargo lift down to the next level. They already knew the bulkhead down there was open, and likely the source of the hybrids that had swamped the watchtower, and the Marines who followed. She sent the info direct to Savvo, whose pale face had begun to get some colour back, and Arin, whose eyes skimmed over the detail.

"It's likely to be hell down there," Savvo stated. "And they'll have the stairs guarded at least. And the lift is a huge risk. Exiting will pose the same dangers, narrow space, one field of fire. A suicide run."

Rebekah nodded. The assessment not only accurate, but damning.

"Captain," Arin said, and he flagged up a section of the map. "This wall divides the bay from the lower galley and the rec. The one with the red shit across the inner skin."

"And?"

"We're stood in a warbot repair centre," he said, letting that sink in. "We spent four years learning how to salvage autobots and mining ships. This is what we do."

The plasma torch lit the corner of the bay as Savvo etched the first scar into the metal. Rebekah adjusted the makeshift shield she had constructed from broken boxes, and secured it with a nail gun recovered from the repair table. The flare of the torch started again as Savvo marked out an upper line.

Satisfied the light could be barely seen from her side of the shield, she gave him a thumbs up. There had been no stirrings from the many sacs in the bay, and hopefully they were all as dead as the ones in the corridor, but she was taking no chances.

The torch flared brighter, and Savvo focused on the wall, slowing his movements as he began to cut through. The molten metal sloughed from the scar, and it wasn't long before she could see through to the far edge of the wall. The occasional glow from the plasma lit the room beyond. Clearly a rec area, she could make out tables and chairs bolted to the deck in the immediate vicinity. Bringing up the schematics, they showed a small bar, and a secondary access to the galley. If anybody, or thing, arrived to defend the space, it was going to be tough. Speed was of the essence.

"Nearly through," said Savvo. "Nice torch this, maybe we should bring with."

"I wish," she said, eyeing the trailer they had used to transport it. Arin had mooted the idea of opening the armoury with it until they'd checked the plate thickness, and the likely defensive systems that may or may not be operational. "We can bring the hand cutter. Not as quick, but useful. Better than our basic kit."

"One tap," said Savvo, switching the torch off, "and we're in." He stood and attached the torch to its clip on the power unit with a wistful look.

"Good work. Arin, you ready?"

"As I'll ever be. Check this out." He clanked along the deck, an odd contraption strapped to his spacesuit that Rebekah took to be some form of oxygen tank at first. He unhooked an awkward-looking machine gun, one she recognised. Nicknamed the *Hammer*, because nothing got up after it was hit.

"Is that …?"

"Dangerous shit, yeah, but it's not exactly as if we have a lot of options. Besides, that warbot wasn't using it, so why not? Found it underneath all that crap in there, and the belt feed." Arin tapped the bottom of the tank behind him. "Counter says I have about two hundred rounds."

"And no grav, remember? Might find you back on M2 by the time you're done," said Savvo with a grin. "Possibly even Almaar."

"Okay. We move. Savvo, you knock it down. Arin, I want the last drone to sweep the room, then bring it back. We can't lose it just yet." Rebekah unshouldered her carbine, checking it over and nodding to her second-in-command. He kicked the plate, which careered into the rec room. The drone whizzed through, spinning and scanning the room quickly before flying out in a wide spiral.

"We got sacs," said Arin. "Three." He flagged them up on their HUDs and ordered the drone back.

"We take no chances. Targets assigned, use UV lights and take them down," said Rebekah, eye-clicking the sacs. "Savvo in first, Arin last. And save the *Hammer* for when I'm not in a fucking room with you."

Savvo paused, then went in, carbine up and moved left and towards the outer hull, with Rebekah sweeping right. She focused on her own target, the bulbous sac glowing far brighter under her harsh light than in the cargo bay. She squeezed the trigger, a short burst aimed for the central mass. The membrane split, and the contents flopped out. Tentacles and teeth, it mirrored the ones they had first encountered. A second burst drilled into its malformed head, the cut-off scream confirming it had been alive. More rifle fire cracked from behind and to her left. Rebekah turned in time to watch Arin's target spill out. The tentacles scraped along the deck, hooks dragging the monstrous thing towards Arin. His carbine spat again, a controlled burst that raked the skull and down to the vestige of a spine.

"Rebekah, come see," requested Savvo over comms, and she passed behind Arin as he nudged at the mass of once-human flesh. Savvo's sac was clearly dead, the membrane shrivelled and hard.

"Switch to standard lights," she said, and clicked through to take a better look. The sac was stuck to the inner skin of the hull, one section of it stretched out and forming a double thick barrier along the hole Arin had spotted on his external survey. The hardened shell itself had cracked where Savvo's rounds struck, the crimson pieces shattered and milling in the air. She tracked up, wishing she hadn't as the abhorrent, twisted features of a man stared eyeless back at her. The shoulders were just visible, the uniform clearly Almaarian Navy, and emerging from the sleeves was a parody of an arm that ended in five hardened tentacles where the fingers should have been.

Savvo tapped the muzzle of his carbine on the hybrid's skull. It had split where a bullet struck, leaving the atrophied brain exposed – and its wetware.

"Chipped, like we all are. How the fuck else could they pay the dream-stealers for the transport?" Rebekah said, the words sour on her tongue.

"And trackable," Savvo said with a brief smile, eyes on the dead hybrid. "If we can link the frequency to the HUDs, we should get a heads up. The ship's main systems are down, so we're not going to get a full view, but even localised it gives us an edge."

"You could have thought of that sooner," said Arin. "It's not like we've been busy or anything."

"Do it," ordered Rebekah. "Arin watch the corridor entrance; I'll sweep the galley."

Savvo grimaced at the task he had given himself, drawing the suit's knife from its forearm sheath. As the blade approached the hybrid's brain, Rebekah moved away, slapping Arin's shoulder and gesturing for him to do the same. By the time she'd reached the galley door, Savvo's curses had begun.

The door swung open with a nudge of a shoulder, and she eased the carbine ahead, checking the sight. With the limited light, she gained an idea of the initial layout and then switched over to UV. On pushing the door fully open, the room seemed empty, devoid of life – human or hybrid. She began to turn back, when her HUD pinged. Glancing up, the room map showed a signature in the far corner her eyes had missed. With an eye-click, the lights switched to infrared, and a small warm glow appeared on her HUD. She lifted her carbine, syncing the sight and slowly edged around the food preparation table. As she reached the corner, the glow shifted, turning around. She could make out its shape, reminding her of a cuttlefish with a cone-shaped torso and small tentacles at the front. Yet eyeless. You didn't need eyes when you were a symbiote.

She whispered into her comms. "Savvo, Arin, I have a fucking Senti symbiote in my sights. I kid you not."

"A memory sucker. Bloody hell, Rebekah. They don't leave their partners, or at least I don't think they do. Is it alive?" said Savvo.

"Check your HUD," she replied, and sent the image.

The symbiote, no bigger than her hand, appeared to sense her eye-movement, the small tentacles at the front rippling as it skittered forward, almost swimming through the air. Rebekah took a step back, only to bump into the prep table. The creature kept moving, sending a shiver down her spine. She had been subject to those tentacles in the past, their dryness a surprise until they secreted a mucus that slid over your shaved skull. The rest, of course, a little hazy as the symbiote drew upon her chip, salivating as it tasted the memories held inside. A Marine's battles, loves, banter and drunken nights sucked away as payment to feed the Senti addiction. That was until, according to the officer-nobles, it became too much for them and their society began to crack, and they put an end to the war. Forced the cessation by denying access to their faster-than-light transports, all paid for in memories of blood.

What do I do?

Rebekah backed away around the table, the symbiote following her, skin wavering in a multitude of complex coloured patterns. It was trying to talk, to communicate, but she had no clue what it was saying. If she allowed the symbiote to touch her skull, then whispers would get through. Images and pictures she knew the more astute could interpret, but that was all. And at a risk they would draw upon their memories. Without wetware in your skull, payment left you bereft of what it took.

Her elbow struck the cupboard units at her back, and with one eye remaining on the alien, slid gloved fingers into the magnetic catch. Yanking the door open, the usual collection of space galley equipment sat maglocked inside, including a lidded pan. This she fished out, and turned back to the encroaching symbiote. Rebekah shouldered her carbine into its magclip and tore the pan lid off. Feeling less than confident, the alternative was to abandon a sentient being, and having seen what lay in wait about the rest of the ship, that she could not do.

Not anymore.

The alien symbiote paid no heed to the pan. She doubted it even knew what it was, and with a deft swing, scooped the creature out of the air, and clicked the lid in place. A twist locked it home, and she popped open the steam release. Rebekah had never thought about it before, but the Senti appeared to be oxygen breathers, and she wasn't prepared to take a risk. A tentacle tip slid through the hole, its end glowing blue, but she ignored it and took her prize back into the rec room.

Savvo was fiddling with a set of wires protruding from his suit's hip, and with a grin snapped them into the ball of fibrous wires and boxes that made up the wetware they all had wrapped about their brains. Some Marine somewhere had nicknamed it *chip*, because they had to chip open your skull to attach the bloody thing. Har bloody har, as Arin would say.

Savvo glanced towards the top of his HUD, eyes blinking, and Rebekah suddenly had a map on her screen. It flashed, indicating Savvo and Arin's presence on their standard frequency. A tweak, and two blue dots representing the recently dead hybrids flickered into place.

"I'm in," he said. "If it lives and breathes, tentacles or not, it'll show up within ten metres if shielded by an internal wall. Triple that in an open space. Remember, that's in *all* directions, including on the vertical bloody axis."

"And the dead don't show?" said Arin over the comms.

"Not after forty-eight hours," said Rebekah. "If it works the same way for the hybrids as us. Did you access any of the recordings?"

"There's no way I'm watching what disgusting things happen inside one of those pulse-filled cocoons. I looked for any data stored, but it's been cleaned," replied Savvo, and he pointed at the pan she held. "I'm guessing your new pet may have something to do with that."

Chapter 30

"Sit rep, Arin. What you got?" asked Rebekah, eyeing the Marine as he paused at the corridor junction. They'd followed the passageway for the last five minutes, with no contact visually or via Savvo's feed. Somehow it put her more on edge. That, and leaving numerous closed doors to their rear they had no time to reconnoitre.

"Stairs to the right and left," came back. "Looks like this is the main thoroughfare."

Rebekah rechecked her map. "It's the lifeboats. From the map, they run all the way down both sides. Hold up." She joined Arin and glanced over to the left-hand side before checking the right and making her choice. "Keep that bastard gun pointing to the left. If it moves …"

"Hammer it," he replied, his voice full of gleeful malice.

"Savvo, with me." She headed down to the right, the passage opening out onto a row of the escape capsules the cruisers carried. Six berth, one pilot station and enough scrubbed air for twelve hours. They had done two dummy runs in the damn things, only coming out alive after Angel had threatened Arin with a gag.

Angel. Shit.

She shoved the horrific memory down. One she would be happy to trade with the Senti.

With the carbine up and ready, she swept the space. Empty. "Savvo, the stairs," she ordered, keeping her weapon levelled at the top three steps as he passed.

Savvo peered down the stairwell and switched to UV then infrared. "Clear," he said. "Except for the stains. A lot of blood."

"Hang there," she replied, and turned back to the lifeboats. There were none missing, which galled her, and she walked over to check on their status. Her lights gave no indication there was anything inside, and a tap at a couple of the screens showed them to be fully operational, despite the batteries being a little low after the engines went cold. A waste. Things must have happened fast … No. She tapped at the menu again.

"Savvo, they locked the 'boats down."

"Say that again, Captain. I'm sure you said the lifeboats were locked down." Savvo's voice sounded strained, disbelieving. Exactly how she felt.

She opened a different lifeboat's screen, and the red 'piss off and leave me alone' sign bleeped back. "They were locked out. Denied fucking access."

Stepping back, a kernel of disgust wrapped itself into a ball and settled in her stomach. Everything they had seen spoke of desperate people trying to survive. Yet amid all that fear and loathing, someone had prevented their escape. An act of murder on a mass scale.

With a final glance at the escape pods, she walked over and surveyed the bottom of the stairwell. Savvo was right, it was caked in old blood. "Cover me," she said, and began to descend, keeping low. She should have sent the drone, but her patience was wearing thin, time getting ever shorter. Nobody fired at her vulnerable legs as she emerged onto the next level, and her lights highlighted why.

"Fuck. Savvo, Arin, check my feed." She took the last few steps, scanning the corridor whose position matched the one above. It was filled with the dead, more along the walls. Some with hands outstretched, reaching for the escape pods, while others held loved ones in their final moments. They were all in a state of decay. Only their magboots held any lustre.

"Murdered," she said. The Breakers had all seen enough death to recognise a massacre.

Her HUD pinged.

"We have incoming," said Savvo over the comms.

"Where?" she replied, scanning the map. It didn't help her mood. The enemy were approaching from the lower stairwell and the corridor. A pincer. Either they made a stand here, or retreat and lose precious time.

Fuck it.

"Arin. I need that gun. Savvo, get down here. We ain't running."

"Copy that, Captain," came the dual reply.

She dropped to one knee, carbine covering both entry points as Savvo pounded down the stairs. He took up station aiming down the last stairwell, and she switched to the corridor. A noise echoed, dulled by the carpet of death, but she knew it well enough – magboots clicking their way along a metal deck at pace. Lots of them.

"Arin! Hurry!"

Savvo fired, backing away from the stairs to minimise his potential as a target. Another burst gained a response, bullets ricocheting off his chest armour.

"Careful," she said, spying the first shadow along the passageway.

"Always," Savvo replied. "Grenade!" And with that, the *thunk* of his grenade launcher echoed in the room.

Rebekah fired a quick burst, encouraging whatever the shadow was to stay there. She was out of luck, and what was obviously a very human Marine dropped into sight. His rifle flared, but she had already clicked and sidestepped. The corner of the corridor now cut off her view, but she didn't really need it. Arin's boots had hit the last step, and the room roared with sheer power.

His boots quivered and suit vibrated. The strain on his face obvious even from the short burst of metal he poured down the passageway. Aiming was clearly tricky, as puffs rose from the already dead.

"Savvo, sit rep?" Rebekah asked, risking a peek down the dust-filled corridor. There were no shadows, but two bloodied Marines rocked back and forth, still attached to the deck by their magboots. She stared at the uniforms, there was something about them she couldn't place.

"Map's telling me I have six down there. At least three of those are out of action."

"Okay, hold your position. Arin, on point, I'll follow." Rebekah ducked behind, allowing Arin free range ahead. He began to walk forwards, noticeably slow, his boots locking down tight after each stride. A hand popped out from the junction, the one she'd been waiting for. The sight auto-locked and the single shot struck the wrist. She swore, she had lost their free pass by missing the grenade. The soldier cried out in pain, and the explosive left his hand to float slowly down the corridor. She took it out with a second shot, filling the space with curved flame and shrapnel. A couple of pieces pinged off Arin's armoured suit, about the same time he opened up the *Hammer* again. It tore through the smoke in a short burst, his entire body shaking at the huge recoil.

The return fire was short-lived, and as the fireball burnt itself out, Arin took the chance to advance further. Now four steps from the junction, Rebekah heard the click of his trigger.

What the hell?

In the hubbub she was mistaken, it wasn't his weapon – he had unclipped his magboots. He leapt forward, spinning to the side and let loose with the machine gun as he flew past the corner. The recoil slammed him backwards into the wall, where he reattached, keeping the trigger depressed and rounds spewing into whatever and whoever was around the corner. The noise was deafening.

After a few seconds the gunfire spluttered and died, the weapon spent. Rebekah checked Arin's feed, seeing the passageway fogged with globules of blood and gore. Nothing stood, only shattered bodies wafted back and forth. A bloodbath, and most likely thoroughly deserved.

"You're insane," she said, turning away and heading for Savvo.

"Hey, I work in space for a living. Firstly, being insane is a prerequisite. Secondly, you learn there's more than one *up*."

Rebekah dropped in beside Savvo, his shoulder plate now bearing another scar where a bullet had struck. "How goes it?"

"Two retreated back as soon as hammer time started. The other four haven't moved. Reckon the grenade took them out." He glanced at his shoulder, a wary look on his face. "I miss our old armour."

"I'm just glad we have some. Cover me." Rebekah stood, keeping low. She grabbed a bag from the pile of human debris and launched it down the stairs where it hit the bottom step with a *clunk* before flying away. Nothing. She proceeded down the steps, carbine low, surveying each of the four blips in turn. Their twisted and bloodied bodies were a good sign, but she put a bullet in each. She'd had enough shit for one day.

Reaching the bottom, Rebekah backed away, eyes always on the passageway until she knelt to check one of the bodies. "You see this, Savvo? Arin."

"I see it, but what's it telling me? I can't remember every emblem," replied Arin. "Now if it was a whisky label, I'm your man."

"It's General Asham's, the Scourge's personal guard," came back Savvo. "Am I right?"

"I reckon." Rebekah turned the woman over to expose the scar that ran across the back of her skull. "But that is something new. And it's not Senti workmanship. They leave your bald-ass head as neat as a pin. But I'm thinking that scar is exactly where the wetware sits."

"What the fuck is all this?" said Arin.

"Wish I knew. Too many pieces, not enough brain. Okay, junk the *Hammer* and get your arses down here." She scanned the bodies, and their weapons. Four carbines, and a couple of handguns. With one eye on the corridor, she retrieved the clips. There were no grenades, but she wasn't surprised. If they had, she doubted they would have made it through the last few minutes as easily as they had – despite the heavy machine gun and its gleeful wielder.

Boots clunked down the stairs, the sub-engineer bringing six more clips, and to her relief, scavenged grenades for their carbines. If nothing else, they had a little more firepower.

Rebekah stood by the passageway, eyeing the corridor with her hands on her hips. "We follow their trail as best we can. It's the only thing I can think of." It was an obvious thing to say, what else could they do? They needed ZZ3, or her crew – her squad – were condemned to die on that rock, or worse. "Savvo ..."

"On point, yeah, I know. It's safer there, already told you that. Trouble follows Arin wherever he goes. Like a puppy."

"That's because you're usually hiding behind me." Arin tapped the bag at his hip. "To drone or not to drone, Captain?" he asked.

"Save it for now. I'll tell you when." She nodded to them both. Proud of who they were, and sucked in by how good it felt to be a unified squad again. If only it hadn't taken a massacre to achieve, one she wanted to exact a little payback for. "Let's get our warbot back and perhaps break a few more heads on the way."

Chapter 31

"Baron Stimpson, you're 3 o'clock is here. A *Mr* Erikson?" The voice annoyed him more than he could put into words. Davina may have been an Incini and expert negotiator, but she was also a superb personal assistant. Always striking the right tone, her insight into his clientele only matched by her ability to be at ease within his social circle. Never missed a beat when working with his holo presence as the mysterious Mr Duboit on Karal. Fine qualities that he missed, leaving those floating on the asteroid family unaware of who they were truly dealing with. After all, it was important one retained your status and your anonymity when dealing with the degenerates of the lower classes. Such qualities were unmatched by the PA he had been forced to promote after sending Davina out to Karal, and now into the black. It was time to try someone else. Someone with a little better breeding. Perhaps he could afford another Incini? One to work alongside him here, while Davina maintained his presence where the money was.

He sighed. "I am unaware of this *Mr* Erikson," he said impatiently. He prided himself on his preparation, aided by Davina's thoroughness. It was most unseemly. "Have you not prepared properly for this?"

"I'm sorry, Baron Stimpson, but you added Mr Erikson to the diary personally. Do you not remember? At ..." he could hear the rummaging over the comms. The dreadful woman wrote things on paper, of all things. Memory aides, she called them. "10:31am."

"I definitely did not." He pulled up the diary on his desk slate, finding the addended entry with the time stamp and facial ID. His heart sank. The system had been infiltrated. The intended fear and stress the entry was designed to cause throbbing in his chest. It may have had his name on the ID, but the face wasn't his. The dark green uniform, characterised by the stiff collar and golden undershirt, threatened to send him into apoplexy. The Emperor's Enforcers.

"I'm done," he said through gritted teeth.

"Sorry, Baron? I didn't quite catch that?" replied the PA.

The palm of his hand sat against his forehead as he stared at the sparkling eyes on the ID picture. However hard he stared, he could not recall seeing this man before, despite his familiarity with the higher echelons. Conceivably, this was one of lower rank, trying their luck against a baron. A visit to set their stall. Implant their presence. A chance, perhaps, to wiggle free. He had nearly convinced himself when the PA spoke up.

"Am I sending them through, Baron Stimpson?"

"Yes, yes," he replied, and pulled out a drawer. He withdrew a beautifully woven towel that he ran over his perfect face, followed by a quick check to make sure every strand of hair was in place, and rings situated where anyone of breeding would recognise his status. The Emperor's Favour positioned on his thumb where any handshake would alight upon it.

By the time he had finished, a gentle tap at the door announced their arrival. The handle turned as he let out a calming breath, trying to still the thunder echoing in his chest. He had decided to remain seated. For anyone of equal status or, may the Emperor be blessed, higher standing, he would of course have met them as they entered. He prayed the choice wouldn't damn him.

The man stood at two metres tall, lithe, exquisitely manicured and wearing a beautifully cut suit that flowed with his movements. It smacked of status and importance, yet the baron recognised instantly how easily it would be mistaken as plain by someone without his eye for detail. He cursed himself, rolling his worry back a little when he eyed the man's hand. Just the two rings, unadorned.

"Mr Erikson," said the PA, and with a smile, pulled the door closed.

His visitor approached the ornate, oak desk, his eyes only for the baron. The man, at least, not indulging in the rude behaviour of the uncouth who would be admiring the office, and not the noble who awaited their attention.

"Sit, ah, Mr Erikson." The baron's hand extended to indicate the chair, though not offered in a handshake. The rings spoke all, Mr Erikson's fingers bereft of a commander's signet band.

"Thank you, Baron Stimpson." He gracefully approached the chair, and eased himself in, all the while ensuring he kept his gaze upon the baron.

"Would you like to explain the intrusion, err, Mr Erikson? I assume you have a rank I should address you by?" Stimpson waited as the man's lips pursed, and his eyes dropped as if contemplating an answer.

"None that I can share with you, Baron," he eventually replied, though there was no accompanying smile or smirk. Just the steely eyes of someone who was used to being in control. "May I?" He indicated to the inside of his jacket.

Taken aback by the response, the baron nodded. Erikson delved inside his jacket, eventually pulling out a sealed envelope no bigger than two fingers width. It had the green and gold edging of the Enforcers, and the baron reached for it. Before he knew what was happening, Erikson grabbed his arm at the wrist and pulled him forward, while forcing the hand back.

Something snapped inside, but before he could scream, the other hand had smothered his mouth and pressed his head against the desk.

Erikson whispered in his ear. "I have *no* rank, *think* on that, Baron. I have dispensation to act as I see fit from the Emperor's Court. With a snap of my fingers, I can order your death, or worse, your titles publicly stripped and have you and your family cast into the slums." He bent closer, lips brushing his ear. "Would you like that, *Baron*? Exiled to live among the unwashed masses?"

Unable to make himself heard under the clamp of the man's hand, the baron shook his head.

"Do you think I could make that happen? Do you *believe*?"

The baron nodded, his squeals beneath the man's strong fingers desperate.

"I think you might be telling me the truth. Might. But if you scream, whimper, or generally disgrace yourself, *Baron*, I will snap my fingers. Am I understood?" As the baron nodded again, Erikson released his grip on his wrist and mouth, patting Stimpson's quivering cheek before sitting back in the chair. With his legs crossed, fingers steepled beneath his chin, Erikson eyed the baron who cradled his wrist, biting back the pain.

"Now we understand each other, let me explain why I am here. And, when I ask a question, I expect a truthful answer or," he pressed a finger and thumb together with a malevolent smile, "snap."

The baron nodded.

"I can't hear you?" Mr Erikson replied, cupping his ear, smile still in place.

"Y-yes," replied the baron, wincing, his chest tight, bile in his throat.

"Good. You bought information from a Teel Richarlison."

It was a statement, not a question, and the name forced the bile a little higher. He nodded.

"Who, I understand, used to be a Navy officer. Lower rank, as befitted her social status. Family poor. But also bright. A thinker, and I might add, dangerous as far as I am concerned. Is that a good description, Baron?"

Stimpson nodded a reply. The Enforcer leaned in, smile gone, eyes narrowed.

"What did she sell you? What snippet was worth … ah, let me see. A million creds? No, that wasn't it. One point three million creds that left your supposedly masked account a month ago. Need the date, or is that good enough?"

"Sh-she told me she had a location." He closed his eyes, lips moving fervently in silent prayer.

Erikson nodded, his chin running along his steepled fingers. "Of?" he said.

"A … ship. Ex-military, abandoned. But she claimed there was valuable *tech* aboard because of the protections they put in place. Of Bustan origin." The baron looked the man in the eye for the first time since his wrist had been snapped. "She had a whisper from one of the team about where they were working."

"Ah. *Illegal* tech. That explains the additional point three million. Transport to the Senti facility, for a memory wipe. I had wondered why she didn't crack under the torture." The smile returned, and the baron's bladder made itself known. "And you have the location? The coordinates?"

The baron shuddered, then nodded. He leaned over to his desk slate, and through a combination of security checks and passcodes only retained in his memory wetware, he ascertained the information. He turned the slate towards the Enforcer. The man did no more than peer at the screen, an eye-blink an indicator of his own chipped status. It struck the baron that the Enforcer had no idea what they meant or where they led, he'd simply been following a trail that ended at his door.

"You have been most helpful, Baron. This information may save you yet. Now, what did you do with these coordinates, hmmm? Sit on them? I do hope so."

What was the point in lying? A few simple checks would bring up his offices in Karal, despite the pseudonym and Davina's presence. Even with the famous interference from the lowlifes who dirtied their fingers profiting from mining asteroids, they would eventually find the truth. Well, most if it. Not the sabotage of an automining ship using stolen nanotech.

"I sent a team out there, to have a look. To see if it was true."

"A team? You mean miners? Salvagers?" Erikson replied. "To an ex-military ship?"

"They are a repair and rescue crew, well-proven. It seemed prudent." He eased back into his chair, the throb of his wrist lessening as his wetware dulled the pain.

"Prudent? A crew like that would have no clue what they were looking for. None, so don't try to play me for a complete fool. They must have a target? Something you have tasked them to return. What are you not telling me?" Erikson raised his hand, ready to snap his fingers.

The symbology was not lost on the baron, who sighed. "Teel said there was a containment box. The whispers were they had locked away all the Bustan research in there, just in case they wanted to return for it. Some of it too dangerous to release right now." He leant in to tap at the screen and showed the Emperor's Enforcer the image he had.

"So that's the target. Finally. Now send me the details on this crew, and we're done here." Erikson stood, not deigning to gaze upon him, affirming his status as beyond the noble's. He brushed down his suit, and set his face hard. "I will have to consider whether you have told me the complete truth, Baron Stimpson. Only then will I decide what happens next. Until then, you and your family live on a knife's edge, and at the Court's whim. As the saying goes, I would keep your nose clean."

He let himself out.

As the door shut, Baron Stimpson thumped his desk with his good hand, letting out a scream of anger and restrained anxiety.

"Denee," he said over comms. "Cancel any other meetings and send my apologies to Countess Bryce. I won't be attending her soiree tonight. And Denee," he swallowed, "get Dr Twyre on comms, ASAP."

The baron sat back, eyeing the chair the Enforcer had left, the image of the man's finger and thumb pressed together foremost in his mind. For perhaps the first time in his life, he was at the mercy of someone of far lower birth, and far greater power. He hated every nanosecond of that feeling.

Chapter 32

Rebekah took a position next to Savvo, Arin on cover behind. Ahead of them were the large airlock doors to the main hangar bay of the cruiser. They were fully operational, access pads glowing with far more juice than they had witnessed anywhere else on the stricken ship.

"Got any thoughts?" she said over comms.

A few assumptions had been made as they hunted down the Scourge's guards. Taking corridors and passageways their HUDs identified as having residual movement, or scrapes along walls or deck. Those that look well-used. Emptiness was the overriding pattern, with no membrane sacs to hinder progress. A few organic patches remained, hints that they had once been there. But the trigger for the emergence of the hybrids had been light, and it seemed sensible that anyone travelling the corridors would want them gone to ease their way.

What worried her was the lack of monsters. Where were they? The watchtower had killed quite a few, and the odd sac they had encountered during a few wrong turns had been quickly destroyed. But the crew were far from all accounted for.

"It would seem logical that they use those airlocks regularly. But why? If the hangar doors are open, and exposed to the cold and vacuum, then yeah. But why keep going back in there? Maintaining heat and air in such a space, well it's impossible without the drives working." Savvo's eyes went distant as he began to click through his HUD. "But I have no signatures, no blips."

"But this is the way. It has to be. We need those doors open." Rebekah glanced back to Arin who was on the half-turn, watching three access corridors to the large entrance area as best he could. "Try and get us in, I'll be on watch with Arin."

She stood and took station looking towards the bow of the spaceship. The corridor was stark, but switching to UV, she could make out a sac fifteen metres down, and behind it likely another. The *Scourge* was a big ship, not in the same league as the battleships whose crew nudged nearer a thousand, but large enough. She clicked through the mapped areas, overlaying the schematic. Living quarters were dotted all over the cruiser. Most in areas exposed to space, and the evidence suggested hybrids died as quickly as humans, bodies stripped of moisture after – she assumed – emerging from the protective sac. Not a theory she wanted to test. Even if the sac membrane kept them alive, they were dead to her. Lost to whatever the hell this was.

She reached behind and disengaged the pan attached to her pack. The symbiote stirred, tentacles rippling and poking a multicoloured tip through the air hole. If they were about to enter an airless space, she would need to block that up if she was right about its need to breathe. And then there was the warmth. How long would it survive? The Senti biology, by definition, was completely alien to her. She flipped the air hole closed.

"Yeeha!" echoed in her comms. "Woo-hoo. The bot is back."

"Come back, Arin," she said. "What are you telling me?"

"ZZ3. I have had its tracker flagged since they took it. The idiots have just booted up our lovely bot," replied Arin.

Rebekah's mind whirled, hope creeping in. "Where? You got a bead?"

"Running it now ... come on ... come on. Bingo! Whoa. You're not going to like this," said Arin.

Rebekah's HUD pinged, and she eye-clicked the flag. "That's from underneath. How far? That's about forty metres down. That can't be true. We're at the base of the cruiser."

Arin tutted. "There's a lot of interference, but yeah. *In* the asteroid, Captain. You know what I mean?"

"It's hollowed out?" The implication hit home. The docking clamps hadn't really made sense until now. Some asteroids had them. Those that were heavily mined but too small for a docking bay, or it proved too costly. But they were spinning. Hollow and gravity? You were talking a lot of creds to make that happen, and an odd place for a prison ship ... unless that had been a complete lie. "Have we been played?" she said.

"Undoubtedly," replied Arin. "From the moment we first encountered the nanotech. Mr Duboit is an utter bastard, so my bet he's a noble to boot. This is General Asham's ship ..."

"With his personal bodyguard on board. Fuck, Arin. Is this place his lab? The Bustan called him the Butcher because they claimed prisoners of war went missing. That wherever he went death followed, bloody and raw."

"Welcome to hell," replied Arin. "Don't like his choice in housemates much."

The comms clicked. "I can get us in, but no guarantee it'll work on the other side," said Savvo. "This might be a one-way trip."

"We're the Breakers. We do what's needed. Whatever happens, we're screwed without ZZ3." Rebekah strode over to Savvo as he fiddled with the pad, a pair of wires from under his lower chest plate taped to the screen. He nodded as she reached him.

"We clear, Arin? Take our six."

"Aye," he replied. "On my way."

Savvo pressed the pad, quickly extracting the wire kit and sliding it back into his suit. Rebekah was already at the outer airlock door, waiting as it spun open. A rush of air jetted outwards, and the inner controls blazed red.

"Move, Arin!" shouted Savvo. "It's detected my interference. Thinks there's a bloody system error and is shutting down." He pushed Rebekah forward, making enough room for Arin to force his way in with their bulky suits. The red alarm flashed again, and the door spun shut. All three raised their carbines, eyes on where the exit was about to appear.

The opening slid round, and with a flash of green, the doors aligned. Shots rang out, the first slamming into Rebekah's shoulder, jerking her back. Savvo shoved her aside and fired a short burst with a follow-up grenade. He ran through, the bursts repeated in patterns of three and aimed towards a welded barricade twelve metres back.

Rebekah's shins hurt, forcing her to disengage the magboots after Savvo had clattered into her. As she floated to the side, Arin grabbed her arm, and dragged her behind while pounding through the exit. More bullets clattered into her armour, until she fell, hitting the deck. Her instincts were to push herself to her feet, get up and fire. And they were wrong. She clicked her boots, a brief glance to her HUD letting her know the suit wasn't compromised, but another hit on the shoulder plate would mean serious trouble. She checked around, and rose to her haunches, repositioning herself towards the threat.

The HUD indicated four soldiers hidden behind the welded metal, with another two flanking either side. Savvo had a bead on the barricade, his short bursts keeping their heads down. Arin took the odd shot, trying to strike those helmets that popped above the edge.

"These are in full fucking suits," said Arin, eyes aligned with his carbine's sight. "Marine-issue. Tough."

"Keep them pinned," she said, and ran from behind the flatbed Arin had dragged her to. Checking her HUD as she went, she guessed the flanking guard's plan, and knelt to wait. He emerged from behind a crate, the suit patched and of an older design, but sturdy. Reliable. He caught sight of Rebekah as she released the grenade, his single shot ringing off the metal box by her helmet. The guard, however, flew backwards as the explosion shattered his stomach plate at the hip joint – the force of impact enough to dislodge his magboots. She followed up with a few rounds, but as blood congregated into globules around him, she knew he was done. Vacuum took no prisoners, and those suits didn't self-seal.

"Know your enemy," she whispered. "Left flank clear. Come back, Savvo."

"I'm in trouble," he replied. "Pinned."

Her eyes flicked up to the HUD, her squad's positions contrasted against the guards. They had relied on overwhelming them in the airlock, a mistake, but they were tough.

"Arin, go help. I'll cover." Rebekah ran towards the flatbed, drawing fire that clattered off the deck and pinged from her boots. On reaching her previous position she raised her carbine, ignoring shots that flew her way. She pressed the trigger. Bullets swept the top edge of the barricade, chipping away at the metal, Rebekah aware it wouldn't keep their heads down forever. At some point they would split, probably in pairs.

An explosion hit the low-loader, domed fire rising and spreading out in a ball. The flatbed jerked forward, slamming into her chest and pushing against her boots. Set low, they disengaged, and she flew backwards, firing through the sphere of flames. With the HUD tracking her enemy's wetware, she thanked Savvo for the innovation in as many languages as she could muster, while keeping her enemies fearful of her aim. Bullets sped her way in return, and she clattered into the side of a large metal container. Engaging her boots, she took aim again, and released another grenade, targeting the top of the barrier where two of the guards huddled. The barrier erupted. Shards shattering helmets and shredding their shoulder plates.

Rebekah, captain of the remaining Breakers, and now the Wrecking Crew with their talent for working in zero-g, clomped down the side of the container, and righted herself on the deck.

"Enemy flanker down, come back," said Savvo, his breath heavy on the comms. "You okay, Captain?"

"Just peachy," she replied, and checked her HUD. "Savvo return the favour, flank around to the right, Arin keep them as occupied as you can. There's only two left; I want one alive if you can but do not – I repeat – *do not* risk yourselves."

"Affir-ma-tive," said Arin, and the barricade erupted as his grenade smashed into the twisted metal. "Low risk, you said."

She shook her head, and began to flank out to the right, her legs complaining and she activated her chip. The wetware soothed her nerves, dulled her brain's responses to the pain. She could hurt later.

By the time she had rounded the clutter in the hangar, and had eyes on the inside of the barricade, Savvo had already downed one of the remaining guards. The other was ducked behind her compatriot, gun bursts keeping Savvo back.

Rebekah flicked through the comms frequencies, speaking on each until she got a heavy breathed response.

"Go to hell," was all that was said. In horror, Rebekah understood what the General's guard was doing a little too late. The soldier's handgun shattered the plexiglass of her own helmet, with the second bullet ramming between both eyes and on into her skull.

"Fuuuuck," said Arin. "Did she ...?"

"Yeah," said Savvo. "There's loyalty and fucking loyalty. Madness."

Rebekah stared at the mess, her mind already struggling to put all the pieces together, now filled with utter shock. What would drive someone to such an act? Was it the wetware? Perhaps the botch job she had found on the other guard was the issue?

Faulty maybe.

Or even scarier, not faulty at all.

"Check for any ammunition, or whatever we can make use of," she ordered. They scoured the dead for clips, finding only a single grenade amid the carnage which Rebekah took. Sticking together, they moved past the barricade, and on into the middle of the bay. Several small craft were docked there, each burnt out, their hulls compromised. Only one stood whole, a light frigate. A little bigger than the *Sunstar* and in one piece, its engine warm but not fired up. By its side, the deck had been torn open, and mechanical machinery placed around it. Regular, well kept, and clearly servicing a lift of some kind.

"Pay dirt," said Arin. "ZZ3 is straight down."

Savvo looked into the hole, engaging his light on full beam. "Hell's mouth," he said, voice rasping over the comms. "Maybe they're demons, after all."

"The only demon I want to think about is the dead kind." She pointed to the frigate. "Not keen on leaving that behind me without checking it first. Any idea how we get in?"

"Knock," said Arin, but her growl shut him up.

"If we're lucky, their suits will be programmed with an entry protocol," said Savvo, still gazing down the hole. "Of course, we can count the amount of luck we've had so far on … err … no hands at all."

Chapter 33

The dead guard slumped between Savvo and Arin. The suits were programmed to maintain motor drives and life support until the occupant was proven deceased. Then they auto shut down unnecessary systems ready to be salvaged, repaired and reused. They were damn expensive, and if the truth be told, of more value to both the Bustan and the Almaarian army than the grunts who wore them. At least, that's how the officer-nobles portrayed it when they were sending them out into whatever meat grinder they had chosen that morning. They conserved power, a necessity in case the attempted salvager was of a different army, in which case it used the preserved energy to burn out its systems.

"Do the dirty," said Savvo.

"Me? I'm sure it's your turn," replied Arin, who turned away, looking anywhere but at Savvo.

Savvo tapped the wetware he had plugged into his helmet. "I paid my dues, now pay yours."

"I scavenged a hybrid sewn into a bloody warbot. I think that trumps all," replied Arin, glancing over his shoulder. Rebekah's HUD painted his wide grin perfectly.

"You stole its gun, and it wasn't even attached." Savvo shook his head, and slid his hand inside the shattered helmet to engage the comms protocol. His gauntlet withdrew, fingers covered in blood. The comms unit blinked once and the connection in his HUD flashed up. He sent the engagement code built into the dead guard's suit while Rebekah prayed it wouldn't check for bio signs. That might be a bit tricky with a bullet lodged in the brain.

The airlock lights flashed above the door, cycling through a sequence of greens, and a pained growl rose from the seal. Metal and synth-rubber separated to reveal an unclean airlock. It was filthy, whatever detritus floated about the bay clearly getting in every time it was used, but never cleaned – and about as far from ship protocol as you could get.

Savvo and Arin dropped the dead guard, and entered the airlock, weapons in hand. As expected, a tight squeeze for two, so three was out of the question.

Rebekah waited impatiently.

Her comms clicked after thirty seconds. "It's a bloody mess," grumbled Savvo. "To be clear, its like there were twenty Arin's leaving here picking their noses and farting all the time. My HUD wants to designate it a biohazard."

"Is it clear?" she asked. "As the HUD shows."

"It's a big ship," he replied. Which was true. She scanned the bay, half an eye constantly on the lift and the potential threat that lay at its bottom. The longer they were up here, the more time whatever was down there had to prepare. It galled her, but if the frigate was clear, at least they would feel safer going down. Her only bugbear was not having enough Marines to leave a guard on the lift mechanism.

"Clear," said Arin.

"Clear here, too," chirped in Savvo. "Opening airlock."

The door rotated open, and Rebekah had an urge to crack both her thumbs with the mess it contained. When the system cycled through, the sheer filth inside the frigate nearly forced her back out again. Eventually she gave in and clicked a thumb, swapping her weapon over and repeating the habit. Everywhere lay in disarray and the dirt was overwhelming. As if unseen by those who lived amongst it. She entered the bridge with a grimace.

"What the hell?" she muttered. "Is the rest of the ship like this?"

"Aye," said Arin. "Worse in some places. Captain, the engines are dead. Sabotaged. The main console's been blown and a chemical attack of some form on the transference cables. Someone knew what they were doing."

Savvo clomped along the corridor to join her, his head shaking inside his helmet. "A shithole next to a hellhole. Kind of ironic. There are no suits, not even basic survival kit. The galley is the cleanest place here. They've been living off ration packs and scavenged food from the main ship. Any clothes I came across, looked like they stank. It just doesn't make sense."

"Nor does this." Rebekah picked up a discarded slate left on one side of the navcom station. Dusty, stained, she doubted it would even switch on. She flipped it over, showing Savvo the ID strip. "This is the *Moonstrip*. You remember them? They carried the Skyriders, full-on Space Marines. The bad asses who raided ships in orbit. The Emperor's pride and joy."

"These are not them. No fucking way. They ride non-grav better than we do, certainly fight in it better than us. We'd have been chop suey out there." Savvo sat down at the navcom with an umph. "Talk to me, Captain. Tell me what the hell we've stepped in."

Rebekah walked over to the ship's command chair and console. The light frigate's bridge crew included a pilot, co-pilot-cum-navigator, and a designated weapons and sensor oversight officer. The captain was exactly that, commanding the team.

"We have residual power," she stated. "Check and see if the encryption's been enabled, and if not drag me up the ship's logs. We won't get access to any classified orders, but captains do like to talk."

"Not all of them," said Arin, his comms in her ear overriding the clomp of his magboots. He sat down in the pilot's chair, dropping a triple set of bagged rations on the console. "Hungry?"

"I'm not eating their shit," said Savvo, glancing around at the mess.

Arin grinned. "It's our shit. And I found the jetpacks, as well as a half-empty watchtower with a broken leg. I suspect they have been shooting at us with our spare ammo." Arin squashed the bottom of the rations, cracking open the inner lining. He proceeded to flip open a panel on his neckline and attached the bag's spigot. The contents sucked into the suit, and with one eye on Rebekah, squeezed the empty bag into a ball and threw it into the corner. He sucked at the tube, patently ignoring the glare from his captain.

Savvo collected the remaining rations, handing one over to Rebekah. They mimicked Arin, except the empty bags found a better home. While Rebekah ingested the much-needed food, she glanced around the bridge. Dishevelled and a mess, but safe. The frigate sat amid an airless hold, the best defence against the hybrids, and the barrier they constructed hinted at a rough-and-ready guard post. Constantly on duty, but protecting what?

"Now you can make yourself useful, and help me search the systems for the logs," said Savvo between sucks on his tube. "We seem to have power."

"They've spliced into the *Scourge*, or possibly whatever is inside the asteroid," replied Arin. He began tapping at the console, somehow managing to light up the screen. He showed Savvo, and between them they began to work side by side, running through the menus while Rebekah contemplated the assault on the lift system.

"No captain's log," reported Savvo after a few minutes. "They've been encrypted. But I have several entries from the navigation officer." Savvo tapped a few more times and swept the information over to the command console which immediately lit up. Rebekah leant forward. All text. A Transcript.

"So, they were sent here directly. Not on the *Scourge* at all." She checked the dates. Two months after the cessation was declared, nearly four years ago. "They rendezvoused here … seen this Savvo?" She highlighted a section and sent it back.

"Six hours?"

"That's a long wait before allowing them on board. Check the weapons log. Arin, see if the Skyriders have their own section of the system, yank up the same date, check what orders have been registered." Arin didn't respond, but leaned in and started skipping through menus.

"You know what's missing?" said Savvo, and he looked over to Rebekah. "There's no mention of the asteroid family. Just the main navigation orbit to bring them into the *Scourge* itself. Look, there was only one other rock out there back then, and about twice as big as it is now."

Rebekah stared at the data, pieces slotting in. "Not stopping us getting in."

"Yeah, to stop whatever's in here *getting out*. But no one knows fields like the miners, or those that ride them. Things collide you don't expect, holes appear. Ways in to be exploited."

"Captain," said Arin, his face intent on the information laid before him. "The weapons system was switched over from high alert, to point defences on entry. That normal?"

"No. All weapon systems should be securely locked down. Anything designed to shoot debris and micrometeoroids needs to be sensitive, and so are too high risk." She tapped at the screen where Arin had sent over the new log. They hadn't been used, just ready and on a human-led trigger. She had no idea how the *Moonstrip* carried out any boarding ops, but it certainly set the thought in her head. This wasn't a friendly meetup, at least from their side. "I'm betting the Skyriders were armoured up," she said. "Weaponised and ready to engage."

"I'm in," stated Savvo. "And you're not wrong. Two squads, full battle armour. No mention of orders or target, but the logs show armed weapons release. This was a boarding, or at least, a squad expecting a hot reception."

"So where are they?" said Rebekah. "And why were they here? Unless they were sent to rescue ..." She shook her head. "Maybe the *Scourge* sent out an SOS when all this shit went down, and they were the nearest?"

"A biohazard," said Arin, "even worse than this ship. You don't rescue it, you destroy it. Burn the weird crap and blow it out into space before it spreads. It fits the facts."

Rebekah sat back in the command chair, eyes running over the slate's ID. The Skyriders were an assault squad, pure and simple. Board, negate, control or destroy. If you wanted a dirty job done in space, that's who got sent. The Breakers had been out of the loop and on the run when this crap aboard the *Scourge* had gone down. A loss of the Space Marines would have reverberated through the army back then, unless it was utterly silenced. A hush hush op they didn't want anyone to know about, and then you cover up the shit with an asteroid field. But why not blow it up, destroy the hazard and evidence of failure?

"They're coming back," she said. "Not now, not tomorrow. But eventually. Whatever happened to the crew of the *Scourge*, they'll want it. The Court and the Emperor will see some potential, and what a waste it would be. Weaponise it."

Both Arin and Savvo looked her way, the consoles forgotten.

"That's why they were tooled up. A takeover, and it went wrong somehow," she finished.

"That's a big leap, and a bloody scary one," replied Savvo. "But where does General Ashma fit into this?"

"The Butcher ..." whispered Arin, his voice low and hard. "I think maybe we find out when we descend into the Hellmouth."

The drone dropped, motors purring as it descended into the abyss-like hole. The ship's shadow kept a vast amount of light out, just a circular sliver they could make out after the first ten metres. Here the machine whizzed about, the pictures identifying what they assumed to be a new hole was in fact a precise modification of the ship. An additional docking area added to enable access from below, and one that showed scars and the signs of battle. Two of the six hinges had been completely melted, and the electronic door mechanism showed similar signs of sabotage to the light frigate. None of the systems held power. Dead.

Arin sent the drone deeper once everyone was satisfied with what they saw. It entered the brief light streaking in below the ship, before passing into a void of precision cut rock that ended at another huge hatchway five metres down – the asteroid's outer airlock. A large, ragged hole gaped in its centre, with scorch marks either side. The wires for the lift plunged through this, and into the darkness beyond. Arin guided the drone in, and after some debate, switched over to the meagre light. The tunnel continued downwards for another five metres before ending at a scorched but intact hatchway of a similar size. The lift sat at the bottom, a simple flat disc with rope netting and a barrier around it, its winding mechanism punched into the steel door. The drone hovered above, flying in a loop.

"I think those are a lot newer," Arin said, eye-clicking a flag onto a double width hatchway inset into the cylindrical tunnel. "See the scorch mark? It crosses from side to side, but nothing on the hatchway. A new entrance."

"Assuming we can't just open the hatch, it'll take the hand cutter a few hours to get through, maybe a little less. But any soldiers worth their salt would have us pinned on entry and it would be death or glory, without the glory," said Savvo. "Can you get us closer."

"We're assuming they know we're coming," said Arin, and brought the drone nearer to the hatch. "After all, we've been quiet as mice so far. Every chance they don't know we're here."

"We need a solution, and fast." Rebekah eyed her HUD, running through her scrubbers and battery gauges. "There is no way I'm living out my days on that shit heap." She nodded towards the *Moonstrip*, and cracked her thumbs. "No way at all."

Chapter 34

The shuttle settled into its flight, the main engines cutting out as it emerged from Almaar's atmosphere. The screen set into the opposite seat regarded the beauty of their blue-green planet, and above it, the glint of Erikson's destination. The way station that orbited the planet, ready to transfer those with much further to travel to their waiting spaceships.

"The asteroid belt? Me?" said Erikson, his nostrils flared wide to match his eyes. He allowed himself that element of emotional body language – the call he was on being voice only – and even that, he doubted, resembled anything like his handler's real modulation. He briefly wondered just how many synthetics had been added.

The deep voice continued to emanate from the slate. "Yes, Mr Erikson. You."

"Did I go too far with that pompous git, Stimpson?" he replied. "You said whatever it took, and I decided violence was the only language he wasn't well-versed in." The memory of the bone cracking sent a shiver down his spine, cheering him up. The fact the noble swine probably had it fixed, bonded and manicured before he'd exited his palatial offices was neither here nor there. He had, however briefly, suffered.

"Your methods were effective. We now have a handle on his double dealings along the belt. All that bragging about his *potential* status at least had some substance to it." The voice rumbled; the distaste evident, though Erikson had little faith it was meant. Nobles played games, be it those on the periphery of the Court, or those with the Emperor's favour as it ebbed and flowed. The Enforcers were a tool, a task force to weed out the traitors and those who double-dealed too much. That might well be true, but he, and the inner Court, knew that the role more often involved intimidating those nobles considering straying from the Emperor's path. Another piece in the game.

Except this didn't feel like a game. Rare was it that the asteroid belt had any role.

"So, what are my orders? Are those coordinates real?" He pushed – aware he did so.

"They are ... inconsequential. A ruse to entrap Stimpson, that's all you need to know. However, it has brought up something of interest. And that will be where you come in. Take a look."

His slate blinked, messages dropping in. He opened the first.

"A grunt? What the hell is this?" he said, annoyed as the cropped hair and sharp eyes of a female dropship pilot stared back.

"That is Rebecca Kanista, now operating as Rebekah Khan. A pilot-sergeant with the specialist Marine Unit, the Breakers. Heard of them?" The voice sounded almost interested in his reply. Almost.

Erikson shook his head, annoyed on so many levels now. Was this a test? This was not a role for an up-and-coming Enforcer. "No, should I?"

"If you didn't have your head up your ass, then yes, you would know. They started out as the vanguard, smashing through enemy lines. They would force a gap, destroy the comms and wave the rest of the army in. Later, they were sent on black ops when it needed a little more *force*."

"And what's this got to do with me? I'm an Enforcer, these are army grunts." He sighed, feeling the years of hard work and grovelling seeping away. Of noble birth, just, he had clawed his way up the ladder. Not that you got to see the ladder, or know where you were on it, only that there were rungs above, and a long fall below.

More pictures pinged open. Each more annoying than the last. "A gaggle of them." The stony silence made him break out in a sweat. He needed to shut up. "A Captain Kendrich, Corporal Savotini, Private Enterman ... not enough for a whole squad."

"They operated in small units. Drop in, smash through, evac out. On their last mission, they went MIA. We found four of their squad with seriously messed-up bodies, and their dropship was returned to us by the Bustans after the cessation, but they were not among the POWs. We assumed they'd found out who they were and quietly executed them. And this is where you come in." The voice changed pitch, marking the importance of the last statement. "It turns out they are not Missing in Action after all, or unreturned POWs. They were alive and well when Baron Stimpson employed them."

"Aha. The salvagers he mentioned." He had an urge to divulge what he thought the mission was, but he'd pushed things enough already, so Erikson waited for the voice to elaborate. It still felt significantly beneath him, but he had to suck it up.

"That's right."

"And my role in this?"

"You are going to be their handler." The seriousness in the voice nearly made him choke.

"Handler," he said, cautiously. "I'm an Enforcer, why would we need grunts?"

"Isn't it obvious? They are MIA, off the board. A piece in the game we can play a little more freely. And you would be surprised what uses we can put a team like this to. It's a rare opportunity to find an unaffiliated squad still alive."

Erikson let that sink in. There were definite benefits, the addition of the unknown in the employ of the Enforcers. The more distant they were, the less likely any of their investigations could get corrupted or sidetracked. It would need someone with talent, however, to keep them that way. He could feel the sun break out from behind the dark clouds in his mind.

He knew enough of what happened post the Senti forcing the cessation to be aware that going MIA had been common enough among units whose officer-nobles switched the blame to their soldiers. That had to be the angle.

"Who was their commanding officer?" he asked.

"Countess Segfi."

"Ouch. The warmonger herself. And that's my lever?"

"You're getting it now. That's the way to recruit them. Keep them quiet. But they'll need payment, resources. A base of operations. Apparently, Baron Stimpson was most forthcoming after your visit, in return for you *not* snapping your fingers."

With some effort, he contained a laugh. Memories of the baron's stricken face seeping in. "Okay, I'm warming to this now. But you can't be serious about living my time out here? What are holo comms for but dealing with such … lowlifes from a distance?"

"Face to face will hammer home how serious it is. Gain some respect. After that, it won't matter so much."

The shuttle rumbled as the docking thrusters shifted it aside. Erikson glanced up as they rapidly approached the way station and its collection of docked and parked ships awaiting their next journey. He hated space, and those who revelled in its danger. He liked to be in control, and not at the mercy of anyone but himself, including the complex equipment that sat between him and certain death. But there was more opportunity here than he first thought.

"I assume you expect them to come back from this mission Duboit sent them on?" he said.

"I do. We fed Duboit a line of bullshit to pull him in. Its just a rock and a crashed ship. If they claim anything else, shut them down. Tell them they have encroached on a restricted war grave owned by the Emperor's Navy, and another reason they don't want us revealing who they are. Understand?"

"And if they don't comply ... a word in Countess Segfi's ear?"

"Kill them, skin them and send the lovely Countess their bodies with your compliments. They're just grunts, after all."

The shuttle clanged as the docking clamp took hold.

"That they are."

Chapter 35

Rebekah ducked. The flat bed trailer scraped across the top of her helmet – causing a moment of heart-in-mouth panic – until it bounced safely away, She swore loudly.

"Careful," said Savvo, and took hold of the restraining chain on his side of the transport.

"I'll second that, Arin. That nearly cracked into my helmet." She dropped further down the stairwell, pulling the straps about her shoulder with each magboot step she took. Eventually she reached the next level where a hundred empty eye sockets stared her way. To her left, the corridor remained awash with the blood Arin and the *Hammer* had eviscerated from the guards' bodies.

She clanged slowly out into the middle of the landing, eyes falling upon the lift doors. They had opened one set above, to be greeted by a multitude of sacs bulging from the lift below. Infrared and UV had shown them as being very much alive, the thought of using the lift shaft sickening despite the advantages of a straight drop. They had opted against wasting ammo and had shut the doors.

They were doing this the hard way.

Arin joined her, his own straps angled away to stay the momentum of the trailer should the forces at play prove perilous. Savvo walked at the rear, his eyes on the plasma torch and the block unit it was attached to. There was more than one way to cut open a hatch.

Rebekah approached the next step when a scream echoed in the lift by her side. Horror-filled, mournful, it doubled up as a second voice joined, then a third. A glance over caused a rawness to her nerves. Mucus slipped from between the lift doors, forced out by the pressure from behind – mixed with pieces of the scarlet membrane she loathed.

"Captain?" said Arin.

"We woke them up. Take our rear," she responded, and headed towards the stairwell. "No heroics, if they get out, delay and run. Understand?"

"Aye," he said, and undid the straps around his shoulders. Arin took his carbine in hand. The shift in movement unbalanced the flatbed, but they were out of options. Rebekah upped the juice to her suit, and the motors whirred as she started down the first step.

Savvo trailed behind and guided the plasma unit carefully under the ceiling of the next level down. It bumped and scraped, and with a bounce dipped beneath, allowing Rebekah to clank down the next steps. More cries echoed from the lift, eliciting a response from the one next door – a single voice – high pitched and in pain.

Rebekah finally clamped onto the lower deck and dragged the flatbed a little too quickly towards the corridor that would eventually lead them to the hangar. She glanced at her suit's battery level, and one check with Savvo told the same story. The risks were increasing with all the additional stress they were putting on themselves and the suits.

"Slow it down, Savvo," she cautioned, and the pressure on the straps shifted. "Wait here." She unclipped, and took hold of her carbine, heading back upstairs.

Savvo's eyes followed her. "Captain?"

"If we rush, we'll push the suits too far." Rebekah stomped up the stairs, meeting Arin who was plainly intent on going down them. As her head became level with the deck floor, the sticky mess had reached the top step.

"The lift," she said, pointing. "Open it."

"What?" Arin replied, though he walked cautiously towards the door controls.

"Now, Private." She reached the top of the deck, with Arin's finger poised over the pad. "Open it."

The doors separated, with a sea of green and red slopping to the floor.

"Grenade!" Rebekah shouted, Arin already on the run.

The explosive smashed into the back of the lift, piercing tentacled flesh on the way and exploding. Rebekah ignored the screams, and with two bursts cut through the hybrids that had begun to rise from the obscene deck. Short, accurate, she turned away, not allowing herself to be sickened by what she was forced to do. They were already dead, no longer human in her eyes. She needed it to feel like she was putting down a sick animal, not taking the soul of a human.

"Arin, you're up," she said, wading through the gory mess to wait by the next lift. He took his position, carbine ready and the glow indicating it had synced with his HUD.

"Now," he said.

Rebekah dinged the pad. The door stuttered open, and Arin's finger squeezed the trigger. No bullets flew, Rebekah capturing the look of sheer horror upon his face. Lifting her own weapon, she sidestepped with difficulty to his side. In the centre of the lift was a partially open sac, with a perfectly formed human emerging from the top – his uniform adorned with a lieutenant's band. Below the waist, tentacles writhed, sharp spines along their edges. The man stared at them, eyes swimming with blood.

Arin fired, a single bullet crashing between the man's eyes. Rebekah, relieved he had acted without prompt, dropped in a few more rounds to be sure. The half-man collapsed.

"Come on." She grabbed Arin's arm. "We've got to go. Savvo is on his own." Rebekah half-dragged him to the first step, but he soon followed, and they re-joined Savvo, taking their previous positions. Twenty minutes later, and they were back at the *Moonstrip*. After another ten – including a detour to collect their recharged spare batteries from the frigate – they had the plasma cutter positioned near the asteroid's docking doors.

The torch kicked into life, and Savvo began to work. With Arin using the hand cutter on the newer airlock, he focused on the much larger and scorched docking bay door. Rebekah had hoped such a two-pronged approach would unsettle whoever awaited them inside, splitting their forces perhaps. What other choice did they have?

"Arin, any change of ZZ3's status?" she asked as he worked, her carbine in hand.

His eyes flicked up to his HUD, mindful of the heat as the cutter sliced through the hinges of the hatch. "Still the same. Got the location, can't raise the comms. Either they dug it out, switched it off or they're blocking it somehow."

She chewed a little on that. Blocking the tracker was difficult, but not impossible – the very low frequencies, however, were rarely tracked, their pattern intermittent. Generally, it would need to be deliberately caged somehow, but it still gave her the feeling they were being led to ZZ3, rather than them chasing the warbot down. However, they had killed to get this far, so if that was the case, whoever led them there was willing to make sacrifices of others. Certainly, most nobles wouldn't blink for a second before sending lowlifes to die for them.

Nothing added up.

When they discovered the Skyriders, she thought they were possibly a rescue party, sent in as the *Scourge* descended into chaos to extract General Asham. It still fit. But for them to fail, and subsequently the asteroid family being realigned, hinted that whatever infection had entered the crew was seen as a potential weapon. Otherwise, blow it up from orbit and let it suck vacuum.

And then there were the surgical alterations of the wetware.

"Aaaah," she said, Arin eyeing her as he finally cut through the first external hinge.

"That a medium grade outburst, or the beginning of a breakdown?" he said.

"Both. Too many unanswered questions," she replied, her mouth twisting as more thoughts intruded.

"I say we keep it simple. Just find out where the bad guys are, and kill them. Like the old days." The cutter switched to the next hinge, its glow lighting up Arin's helmet.

"In the old days we didn't get to think, or make choices. Or count how many innocents we took down in the name of Almaar and its Court." She checked on Savvo, suddenly aware he was two-thirds done. The plasma torch was top of the range, and now on her wish list should they get out alive.

"Yeah, you had to go spoil my best ideas." He pointed his free hand towards Savvo's work. "I think we have our in. Want me to keep going?"

She eyed the cut hinges, well aware that the inner door mechanism would likely still keep it sealed. The hope was they could start work on that, but the hand cutter was clearly not up to the job with the time they had. "Stop."

He switched the cutter off, letting it cool and walked over to Savvo who was absorbed in attacking the main door. He was a few minutes from completion. By the time the cutter had cooled, and Arin had stowed it and prepared his carbine, Savvo had stood away and tuned the torch down.

"How are we doing this, Captain?" he said. "Apart from carefully?" The grin told her he was thinking of the complete opposite. Breakers until the end. Except, they were uninformed. They had no knowledge of what lay below them.

"Spin the drone up," she replied. "Let's at least get a glimpse."

Arin prepped the machine, saying a final goodbye to the last drone as Savvo melted a section of one corner. As soon as it was wide enough, the drone dropped in, wafting with the heat and the sudden suck of air that blew outwards. The machine tumbled, buffeted, until it righted itself and spun quickly around, lighting the space and filming as it went. Something rang out, a shot perhaps, or the clang of metal on metal, and the feed ended abruptly. Bullets slammed into the edge of the hole. A few ricocheted through, causing Savvo to dodge aside after realising he was in the firing line.

"Quick analysis," ordered Rebekah.

Arin watched the feed over, eyes blinking while his brain tried to process. He slowed it down, flagging the relevant parts and sending it across.

Rebekah ran over the update. The inner was curved as she had expected, with the furniture set on the outward plain, as it would be if the asteroid spun fast enough to create a modicum of gravity. It didn't, and that irked her. This was an offloading area, with a dual airlock, one human-proportioned, the other clearly for much larger cargo. Both were closed, and four autobot guards were stationed about the room. Spherical, levelled by gyroscope and usually carrying dual weaponry – a stun whip and a small machine gun. They operated in grav, low-grav and in non-grav with equal proficiency. And not a human or hybrid in sight, her HUD confirming no one utilising the enemy's wetware frequency was present.

"Assessment?" she asked.

Savvo seemed agitated, then glanced her way. A rueful smile appearing. "I have a really stupid idea. We'd need someone reckless and possibly a little insane to do it."

"Why are you both looking at me?" said Arin.

Rebekah thought about contacting the twins. But what would she say? *'We're just off on a reckless and ridiculous mission that we may not come back from. Be safe. Speak soon?'*

Arin and Savvo had reached the shaft bottom, sliding along the lift wires with a guard's body each. She shook her head, trying to clear it. As a captain of the Wrecking Crew, and the Breakers, she had made decision after decision. But as a … a what? A carer? Nothing made any sense. So instead, that's what she did. Nothing, hoping it was the right choice and knowing there really wasn't one.

"Ready?" she said.

"Ready? Oh yes. You know when I am wild, and *out there* with my decisions? It's because *I* decided to be like that. No one else. And, I might add, *I* get to choose the plan. Not Mr Safety First, oops, changed my mind if Arin's the one doing it."

"I'll take that as a yes. Get to it, Savvo." The hand cutter sliced through the last two sections left in place, and Savvo stepped back. He slammed his boot down once, twice, and the piece gave, slowly spiralling inwards. Rebekah fired, the bullets sprayed across the inner room, not aimed at any target, and she stepped aside as machine gun fire whistled overhead. Savvo shoved the corpse into the room, the guard flying straight while bullets smashed into the suit. A second guard went next with Rebekah and Savvo working in tandem. Distractions to confuse the targeting systems.

The autobots kept firing at the second body, petering out as a third sailed in with Arin and the plasma torch attached – aimed by Rebekah with an almighty push after adjusting for the autobots' positions. She made sure the torch's power line was clear then picked up her weapon and opened fire, keeping moving, as Savvo dropped in next, using the fourth body as a temporary shield.

Arin whipped the torch at his selected opponent, the lance slicing the bot through the middle after it ignored the cadaver. A second bot took aim, recognising the threat and bullets slammed into the body he was using as protection. Rebekah's bullets struck it in reply, the bot adjusting only to be pierced by the torch as Arin bounced from the ceiling to drive it home.

On the other side, Savvo dug his hand cutter into the third bot, but the fourth had spun around, realising something lived behind the corpse. Two bullets struck his arm, and dread washed over Rebekah.

"Grenade!" she yelled over comms, and not waiting, fired. There was no time, if Savvo had survived the first two rounds, he wouldn't another. The grenade struck, the explosion ramming the spherical guard backwards. Cracks appeared along its hull, and Rebekah emptied her magazine directly at those. Burst after burst, the autobot stuttering under the attack until an electrical fire sparked inside. It spun haphazardly, lights flickering out.

"Savvo?" she said, eyes flicking up to her HUD. Life signs pinged from his suit, but she couldn't trust the data until she saw him. A scream of metal on metal squealed over comms, then gunfire. It wasn't Arin, he had righted himself, and shoved away from the wall to sail towards where she thought Savvo might be. A second round of gunfire followed.

"Let go, Savvo!" shouted Arin.

Smoke rolled out from the corner. Rebekah desperately wanted to drop in, but knew she would just confuse matters. Her role was as cover and distraction.

"Die, you bastard, die," said Arin as even more ash swirled about the room. "Yes, like that."

"Savvo?" she repeated, again checking the HUD. An alert flagged on his suit, much like her own. The arm plate was completely shattered but the inner lining had held. If the room had been sealed before, it was certainly exposed to space now and any leak was a death knell if not quickly patched.

"I think Arin is right," came back Savvo, his breath heavy. "Far too sensible a plan. They shot the guards when they shouldn't have yet their wetware was still active. I don't get it."

"They could have seen through the ruse. Maybe they have our chip frequency, knew you and I were there. Or the bots analysed mass and volume, deciding there was more of a target," said Arin with a shrug.

"You could have mentioned that before," Rebekah said.

"Yeah. Except he only just thought of it."

"Too right," Arin said with a grin as he floated into her eyeline, the plasma torch still operational but set low. "Want me to slice and dice anything else?"

"The airlock," she said. "If it breathes, let's fuck it up."

Chapter 36

With Savvo at the rear, his suit's integrity a worry, Rebekah had Arin on point allowing her time to visualise the tunnels as they moved. For those unused to the vagaries of space, the asteroid would have been disorientating, brains struggling with the switch in perception. The change from a top-down perspective on the outside of the asteroid, to now walking on what such a viewpoint would label as the ceiling, could send them off-kilter and a liability going into battle. Adding to the strangeness was the asteroid's meagre spin, far from that required to produce a viable gravity. Whoever designed the tunnels had clearly expected the asteroid to be spun up, requiring the *Scourge* to dock with its topmost hull facing towards the asteroid to ensure the grav effect pushed the crew out and towards the deck. Another anomaly.

The second issue was that the asteroid was smaller than most hollowed out for long-term living, more akin to the mining communities who swapped in and out for short stays. Drugs and exercise could only do so much for the body in low-g or experiencing a high rpm, and anyone who had been here for an extended period would be suffering mentally and physically. That could explain the General's guard detail, and the state of the ship. She had never checked their muscle mass, why would she?

Arin had stopped at a junction. So far, the tunnel had been wide, around four metres across and three metres high, and completely straight with no rooms off it. The HUD showed they had walked fifty metres inside its outer rim. They had shot out a pair of cameras at the outer doors of the tunnel, though the HUD had shown no electrical discharge from them. Arin had stopped as he'd found more.

"There." He flagged another set of cameras to the right, five metres in where a metal door stood at the end of a short corridor. Rebekah checked his feed, then peered to the left. It was no surprise to find a similar set up. Again, it spoke of the intention to have the asteroid spun up and pseudo gravity in place, each camera positioned on high. Her HUD was blank, the cameras likely inert. Possibly due to exposing the asteroid's tunnels to cold, airless space. It wasn't as if whoever was here didn't know they were coming.

"Take them out," she said, and with two short bursts, destroyed the right-hand cameras. "These could be dummies, with more covert ones embedded in the walls. Make no assumptions," she said.

"Aye," came back Arin.

"As ever," replied Savvo.

There were no room plates above the doors, just a number. Seven for hers, eight for Arin's. Simple, neat and no clues. "I'll take cover at the junction, you two see if you can open up room eight."

Her lights illuminated the passageway, overriding the strip of red emergency lights that barely reached a glow. They reflected off a second junction, no guesses what lay at the end of those. It was clean, well-scrubbed and very unlike what they had witnessed above.

"I'm in," said Savvo. "Nothing fancy like the outer doors, just a vacuum deadlock and a standard bio scan."

"Take my place, Savvo," she said, and as he arrived, left him wearing a grimace. He wasn't happy, she knew, but the state of his arm plate was on her mind.

Arin waited until she was in position against the wall, then tapped the pad. The door opened inwards just a crack, the air inside hissing out and spreading into the corridor with a fine mist forming. It quickly dissipated, and no shots rung their way. Wishing for a lost drone wasn't going to help, and she crept in low, easing the carbine around the door and its synth seal. The sight connected to her HUD and showed no signs of life. She flicked over to UV, the resultant glow familiar, and finally to infrared. With the rapid heat loss after opening the door, she had expected little to show up, but the red glow towards the back of the room told a different story.

She sent Arin the images, then stepped fully into the room and a weak ceiling light sprang to life. The UV had shown six sacs, but to her surprise they weren't scattered about the room. They were contained inside transparent tubes, the outer membrane pierced by a multitude of wires and probes. She eyed the light, assuming it wasn't strong enough to trigger the sac to split open.

"Arin," she said quietly over comms, and signalled for the far corner. He passed her by, his magboots barely gripping the floor as he eased around the last two vertical tubes.

"Bot," he said, and Rebekah checked his feed. It sat in the exact spot the infrared had glowed. Arin's camera swept the rest of the space, and by a collection of monitors and equipment, it typified a lab. One a little different from the last they had entered, there weren't two terrified girls for a start. Nor the carnage that followed. At least, not yet.

She joined Arin, eyeing the humanoid looking robot that sat inert but very much operational in the corner. It was not a design she recognised, and it didn't make any move to intercept. Probably some form of automated laboratory drone, carrying out tasks in replacement of fallible humans.

"Come on," she said, and backed away. Rebekah had no doubt the bot relayed their image to whoever was at the end of the corridor, so she threw in a curve ball and left it operational.

"The sacs?" queried Arin.

"You created a vacuum, remember," she replied. She had been tempted to destroy them, curious, to a degree, as to what lay inside. The pale-skinned versions of the cargo bay, or the tentacled monstrosities that had been most common. It could wait; they weren't going anywhere.

They repeated their efforts on room seven, to be greeted by the exact same scenario, right down to the bot sat in the corner. They moved on and approached five and six. The door security remained the same, and it sprung open on Arin's tap. Rebekah instantly knew the layout was different even before she eased the carbine around the door. When the icy mist cleared, there were no vertical containers – just two rows of four metal tubes, like coffins or medical scanners. She sent Arin around the far side, hunting out the warm glow in the far corner and the expected lab-bot while she approached the eight metal cylinders. The closer she got, the more the HUD flashed up their rapid temperature drop, the outer metal glistening as ice leeched away.

Closing in, her skin crawled, itching. A sense of dread hung heavy over the containers, compounded as lights began to flicker along their sides. Green at first, one by one they switched to yellow and finally red as the exposure to cold space took its toll. Her mind told her to run, that the cylinders would crack open like coffins and a horror emerge from each seeking her blood.

I'm a Breaker. Nothing breaks me.

Her gauntlet alighted on the first metal hull, and slid along to the window that ran the full length of the tube, scraping away the last of the ice. Inside, a liquid bubbled, green and thick. Crystals formed within the fluid, spreading outwards and illuminated by a red warning light. They slid over the torso of a man, his chin chiselled, hair cut close and well-built. On his chest was a tattoo depicting a bursting sunrise behind paired wings. A Skyrider.

Fuck.

No eyes flicked open, no rising of the chest nor twitch of a finger. The crystals spread rapidly, encasing the body. In her mind she heard an audible crackle as the body froze solid. The last thing she saw were familiar scars about his skull, marking, she expected, a new set of wetware.

"Captain?" said Arin.

"Skyriders," she replied, removing her gauntlet from the icy coffin. "Do you remember how many they had in each squad?"

"Eight," he said, as his eyes swept the cylinders. "The log stated they had two squads on board. Shiiit."

"The bot?"

Arin grimaced and eyed the doorway with Savvo on guard beyond. "Same set up. Why is nothing stopping us? Where are the guards?"

"We assume waiting for us, so stay sharp. Make no assumptions, get no surprises," Rebekah glanced over Arin's shoulder towards the lab-bot. It remained still, unresponsive, but it gave her a sense of being watched and judged. "ZZ3?"

"Dead ahead."

"Great choice of words," she replied.

Savvo's comms clicked in. "They're waiting for us, Rebekah. Like mice and cheese."

"I prefer chocolate," she said. "With a side order of kick ass. Let's get this done."

The huge bulkhead door hummed, and swung back, Savvo rescuing his wires just in time. Rebekah and Arin's sweep through UV and infrared showed nothing untoward as the air rushed out, misted, then cleared from the corridor ahead. Room five had proven empty of any life. A manufactory filled with automated lathes, chem baths and forges as well as a set of industrial 3D printers. Three bots were stationed in their recharge corners, built from a strange mishmash of parts that they had likely made for themselves. A fourth bot, however, had taken her by surprise. A warbot, thankfully not ZZ3. Thoroughly dissected with each piece carefully separated and labelled. This time, Rebekah had taken no chances and allowed five minutes of Savvo's hand cutter to seal the door shut.

"Just the four more rooms. We could end this shit and choose room number one. I'm betting I know what's behind that door," said Arin, tapping his helmet. "One very lonely warbot."

Rebekah ignored him and positioned herself so she could see down the remaining corridor. Ten metres further along was a T-Junction – they were nearly done. The two pools of darkness either side promised answers, or perhaps, something worse.

"Knock, knock," said Savvo. "Room number four is ready for inspection."

"Stow it, Savvo," she bit back. "It's been too easy, focus."

"Yes, Captain," he replied, his voice hard and emotions held back. He was soon by her side, but didn't look at Rebekah. That was fine with her.

She entered the room cautiously, her mind on the task ahead. The UV was negative, the infrared doubly so, and when she rounded the door, Rebekah was greeted by a stark corridor. On one side were a set of hatches, along the other, cells. They couldn't be anything else. Metal bars and locked doors. She clicked her lights up brighter, and entered, the clunk of her boots on low setting still reverberating amid the multitude of metal. The first cell, at three metres square with a low-grav toilet and wash bowl, lay empty and clean. The rest similarly so, though as she turned away from the last something caught her eye. She closed in on the bars, peering closer, moving her light from side to side to catch etch marks in the cell wall.

"You seeing this?" she said over comms. "Arin, Savvo?"

They were clearly letters, and next to them scratches that she assumed marked time.

"Bustan," came back Savvo, his voice clear and steady. "It's a Bustan name, Minta. Female."

She didn't ask how he knew, but proceeded back down the cells, spotting more words and rough pictures similarly etched now she knew where to look. Some Savvo recounted as names, others simple cries for help or peace in their next life.

"The Butcher," she said, "after all. Why else would they be here?"

Silence filled her comms.

She checked the hatches which proved empty of all but a water tap and a food processing unit that hadn't been used for a while. The bare necessities for survival, or to keep prisoners and, dare she say it, test subjects, alive.

Another piece slotted home, the shape of the puzzle disturbing her more and more. The Breakers had been lethal, and violent, but had never killed indiscriminately. There had often been prisoners along the way. How many had ended up here to be experimented on? To end up like those crew who had been infected on the *Scourge*?

By the time she stood at the corner, Savvo and Arin at her side, she had pushed all that down. Locked it away. Emotions would only weaken her resolve. Be it anger at what she assumed had happened here, or feigned ignorance. Placed in a cell like the ones she left behind, and deal with whatever came next.

It sounded good. What a Breaker would do.

Chapter 37

Their eyes ran over the multitude of samples glinting inside jars and sealed dishes along the wall. Each neatly divided, a code number beneath, and displayed like a giant vending machine across three of the four walls. In the centre lay four low medtables, sparklingly clean, and above them a wealth of machinery that put Rebekah in mind of a medbot, yet with far more complexity of instruments and limbs. Its purpose was obvious, and it rattled against the bars she had placed in her mind. Two of the metal cylinder coffins were pressed against the fourth wall, and one, on closer inspection, had her head reeling.

The black eyes and blue-green skin of a Senti stared upwards, clearly in some form of coma or preserved death. The lights on its side already flashing a fateful red only a few seconds after they had opened the sealed door. Rebekah reached behind to find her clip empty, remembering, to her relief, that she had left the symbiote back on the Skyrider frigate and its supply of air. Was this its partner?

She swallowed, and glanced at the second, reeling back from the dreadful sight inside. It had the same shape and form of a Senti. The elongated head, narrow shoulders that led to the unusual, flexible arms of their kind.

Except, there were sections of its torso and skull cut away, and probably stored somewhere amid the freakshow behind her. She sent enough of her feed to inform Savvo and Arin, then backed away.

"Fuuuuck," said Arin, she assumed he had seen the second metal container. "Are you …" he choked over comms.

"It's not an infection, is it?" said Savvo, anger spilling over into his voice. "It's deliberate. Whatever happened to the crew was a made thing. The Skyriders, do you think they were here to rescue or destroy?"

"I can't answer that. I wish I could. Maybe both, but rescue what? What was created here? Or the one who made it?" she replied. None of the possibilities brought any comfort.

The lights dimmed, then crackled. No … no, that was impossible, they were in a vacuum now. Her heart thudded against her chest, beating in her ears.

"Did you hear that?" Rebekah said.

"Hear what?" replied Arin. "Other than a clunk on our suits, we ain't going to hear shit in a vacuum, Rebekah."

"I know," she whispered. Was it the room giving her the creeps? The sheer sterile atmosphere of pre-programmed death?

She walked towards the exit. "Arin leave," she said. "If I had enough grenades, I'd blow this fucking place to hell. Seal it, Savvo. There's nothing alive in there. Or at least, nothing I want to allow out into the world."

Her comms crackled, or was it a faint voice? A mechanical laughter, or breathing?

Savvo engaged the cutter, the small plasma blade melting and sealing the door, eventually giving out before he could run it along the bottom, its power dead. Her second stowed the tool on his pack, a rueful look upon his face.

"Are we finishing this in order?" asked Arin.

She knew the answer: of course they were. She cracked her thumbs, then sent Savvo ahead. Two more rooms. Two more puzzle pieces.

Savvo reached the T-junction, letting Rebekah know it was all clear but a change to the pattern they had been used to. The room to the right had the usual door, marked with a number two, the one to the left was much larger, double width. It didn't take much to work out where ZZ3 would be – in the mouse trap behind door number one.

"Let me guess," said Arin, and he clomped slowly towards the smaller door. "This one?"

Rebekah glared his way, but signalled yes. "Savvo, the watchtower please. Then the door."

She collected the robot weapon, one leg taped with a metal spur Savvo had found aboard the *Moonstrip*. Rebekah handed it to Arin, and she indicated towards door one before joining Savvo.

He was working at the door, his face twisted in concentration. The beeps and flashes from the room's entry pad more complex than she had previously seen. He let slip a few swear words, and ran down a secondary menu until eventually, the pad glowed green.

"Tougher," he said. "The coding is from our time. Older, maybe."

"But you got us in." She glanced at the door, then back towards the double set. He followed her gaze. "Savvo, if I don't get out. The twins ... I know you want out, but they need to be safe."

"Out?" he replied. "That feels like a lifetime ago. This is an easy one, El Capitaine. If you don't get out, it's because we all fell first. Now open the bloody door."

The sliver of a smile on her lips faded away as she turned to face the entrance. Savvo moved back, finishing the watchtower's set up as Arin joined her. She slapped the panel, backing to the wall as the air seeped out and the resultant mist dissipated. With her carbine in hand, she eased the barrel around the door, flicking through the light modes. It was empty of the life they had encountered so far, and she slid in to be greeted by a bedroom and kitchen unit.

Just the one bedroom. One set of quarters.

One human.

It was perfectly presented. Everything in its place. The bed sharply made, unruffled. The kitchen sparkling under her light.

Unused. At least for quite a while.

Arin shuffled in behind her, his weapon held high but lowering it as he took in the room. He said nothing, and she could sense him just staring into the blank space.

Empty.

Devoid of life.

Her comms crackled. A distant voice echoing. "Rescue? No …" Laughter ensued, fading into silence. She spun to face Arin, but his gaze was for the stark room, not her. He hadn't heard it; she wasn't even sure that she had.

"Door one," she said, and shoved past him. "We finish this now."

Savvo had prepped the watchtower, positioning it at the corner down from the double doors so it wouldn't engage a target and fire immediately. A tactical delay should they need to draw out an enemy, or retreat at speed. "Target?" he said.

"Anything that's not us – the Breakers," she replied. "And saddle up, you follow us in. But watch that fucking arm plate."

She felt him stare at her shoulder, eyes on the shattered armour, but brushed it off. Needs must. He sighed and walked over to the panel and repeated the digilock opening process.

"Same code as previous," he replied. "Self-adapted, but I got this." Rebekah watched him work, clearing her mind of anything other than what lay beyond those doors. After a couple of minutes he stepped back, snapping the wires back under his armour.

The pad flashed.

"Arin, with me," she said. "You go right, no quarter, understand? Savvo? It's us, or them."

"Yes, Captain," they both replied, checking over their weapons.

She thought of the twins, of Hendricks. Davina. Orbiting outside of the asteroid field, still with a good chance to survive. Their only hope lay in ZZ3. She knew she had delayed, perhaps should have gone straight to the target. But the fate of the Skyriders and the *Scourge* crew sat heavy. She had needed to know. The puzzle was nearly complete, but what was the cost of the final piece?

"Nothing breaks ..."

"A Breaker!"

"I say again, Arin, flank right, I go left. Savvo, adapt as you see fit." She leant over, hand hovering above the door pad. Images flooded in, memories of a hundred missions or more. From drones to meat and bone, they had fought them all.

"Rescue ..." crackled over the comms, a tinkle of laughter.

She hit the pad and went in – low and swift.

Bullets rained in – somehow unexpected after how they had arrived – an autobot tracking her across the room. Rounds glanced off her armour, and she dived behind some form of console. The stream of metal cut off, and she eye-clicked her HUD to get a concept of the room. A square, about twenty metres each side. Data banks strewn along one wall, the ceiling filled with wires and robotic limbs. More bullets echoed from the doorway, these the familiar bark of a Marine carbine. A glance told her Savvo was inside.

She kept low, sidling around the console when a streak of light slammed into the deck by her feet. The heat set her suit alarm off, and Rebekah peered up to catch a drone whizzing to get her back into view. Whatever weapon was slung below it, glowed again, and she was forced to leap sideways, the weak magboots releasing as she flew aside. Heat traced across her boot, scoring the metal and reigniting the alarms. Rebekah hit a set of data banks, spinning about, clamping one boot on while spraying bullets towards the darting drone. She missed, but had delayed any retaliation. The carbine's sight synced, and Rebekah fired again, letting the HUD guide the shot. One half of the drone shattered, the pieces spreading wide.

The suit's threat alarm activated, and Rebekah swung the carbine about to come face to face with an autobot. Its gun spun, but no bullets flew. The bot tracked her, and not wanting to lose the advantage, she fired while diving, utilising the zero-g to fly back behind the consoles. As her boot disengaged, the bot fired, bullets striking her arm, cracking the plate. Again, the bot stopped firing as she landed behind the console.

The console.

A data bank.

"They're avoiding the hardware, I repeat they will not fire on the computer systems."

"Copy that. One bot down," came back Savvo. "Three more in operation. What the fuck." Savvo's comms died. Rebekah eye-clicked her HUD, the blink indicating Savvo still lived but was now much deeper in the room. She rose, bringing the carbine up and spraying over the top of the console.

"What happened to Savvo?" said Arin, the chatter of his gun firing off as he spoke.

Rebekah simply eye-clicked and flagged his position, sending it across before sidling to the console's edge. She pushed the carbine around the corner, firing off a burst but checking her HUD for what was happening in the centre of the room. ZZ3 stood there, eyes glowing red, its limbs extended. There was something about the posture that didn't feel right. It wasn't in standby; their warbot was active.

"Oh shit." More gunfire echoed from Arin, and something sizzled in the air, the heat splashing across her HUD.

Three bots, and whatever drones remained. And an unknown in ZZ3.

"Rescue ... me?" The taunt caught her breath, but didn't numb her mind. If it was real, it was designed to be off-putting. A tactic used by the powerful, to imbalance the weak.

She wasn't weak.

"Arin, I want you to run," she ordered, and clicked the comms twice, "back to the bay. I need you to live."

"What the hell?" came back, and too long a pause ensued. Rebekah counted the seconds and prayed, before a responding double click calmed her thoughts. "It was a pleasure to serve."

"Now," she said. Arin moved, heading for the exit, pounding out of the room as she rose and sprayed the area before ducking back down. She ejected the clip, eyeing her HUD. Arin had made the corner, and his glance around showed two of the bots and a drone in pursuit. She allowed herself a brief smile, widening as the watchtower opened up at the three targets appearing in its sights. She hoped half an ammo box would be enough.

Letting out a breath, she activated her chip. The warmth spread through her brain, dampening the adrenaline where it wasn't needed, heightening everything else where it was. She toe-clicked, and exploded upwards, her HUD seeking a target. The remaining autobot tracked her movement, wary of the data banks, and the grenade she released caught it just below the weapon as it spun up. The shrapnel peppered the console, tearing into the metal casing and shredding whatever was inside. A third drone swept by, angling its slung weapon, looking for a safe shot.

Rebekah didn't give it time to cook her, the rifle burst peppering the ceiling and raking across the drone with abandon. Its outer shell cracked, wires and electronics spilling out as the machine spun crazily away to crash into something on the far side of ZZ3. It lit up, and as Rebekah slammed into the tangle of wires and limbs slung across the ceiling, she recognised the containment box Duboit had sent them for. Their target.

A limb snapped about her shoulder, metal teeth grinding into her suit. Pain sent her nerves into overdrive, and the carbine slipped from her grasp, spiralling away. She looked up in fear, and was greeted by glowing lights and a second of the strange limbs sweeping from the ceiling. Rebekah raised her arm, the strength of her elbow motors blocking the blow as it crashed in. She screamed, wrenching her bad shoulder round and activating the suit's forearm weapons. With the chip dampening her nerves, she aimed towards the second limb's motor, bullets smashing into the metal and pinging off her plate. Fire spurted, and the limb collapsed. More pain erupted in her shoulder as the jaws pressed in, and she fired again – this time from her other arm – and the grenade slapped into the limb's joint. The force of the explosion drove her downwards, forcing her towards the floor. Shrapnel scored and cracked her suit, but it was lost amid the alarm going off. A breach. The jaws had crushed the remainder of her shoulder plate and nicked the inner skin – she was leaking precious air.

Chapter 38

Rebekah groaned as her back slammed into the deck, bouncing up as momentum demanded. The spinning disorientated her, coupled with the alarm's blare. Short on time, she desperately tried to eye-click the HUD and give herself space to think. The second click shut it down, and as she flew towards the ceiling and whatever threats it held, checked the suit's safety protocol. Right now, she needed something, and prayed it had been set to self-heal. The ceiling got nearer, and a limb whipped out, long and glowing red. If she had been in a factory, she'd have called it a soldering iron. Fuck it, it *was* a soldering iron, and spearing towards her. Shots echoed from below, but she was either dead from the hot metal lashing her way, the autobot's bullets or the leak in her suit.

Take your pick, life as a Breaker was always full of surprises.

Her boot arced out and caught the limb with a sideways blow that gave a little hope. Her second boot struck just below the tip, and she shoved the soldering iron into the ceiling. The hot tip burned through whatever it hit, and she braced her legs before pushing away. Her spin was gentle, and though misjudged, she managed to bring one bent leg down onto the floor and activated her boot. With a twist that pained her hip and shoulder, Rebekah managed to engage the second. A quick glance at her HUD showed the alert had downgraded to yellow, and cold at her hip declared the suit was doing the expected – auto-sealing the hole. It was, after all, a spacesuit whereas the Breakers fought in powered armour of varying degrees. Relieved, she took a moment to assess the room, with Arin having returned and pumping bullets into the last of the spherical autobots. Further into the corner, Savvo hung upside down, and though his life signs were green, he was out cold.

Rebekah eyed the passive warbot, and headed for her second-in-command, calling out his name. With the lack of response, she overrode his suit under emergency protocol, and activated a stim. He wouldn't forgive her. It had been clear from the moment he had first donned the suit that the old Savvo was back, and drug-free.

"Savvo," she said. "Come back. Do you hear me? I need you awake, Marine." She considered a second stim, but the urgency of her suit's leak was playing on her mind. She eye-clicked the HUD flag, and read the message. It had used a reserve bottle – no – *the* reserve bottle, and plugged the hole with a self-hardening gel. Just the news you wanted when they faced a jetpack flight out through a chaotic asteroid whirlwind.

"Captain ..." said Savvo, and she noticed him wince inside his helmet. "Captain, ZZ3 ... it threw me."

She felt a presence at her back, as if something malevolent waited there, watching, looming over her shoulder. Breathing. Except warbot's don't breathe. Savvo's eyes were wide. Rebekah threw herself to the left, pushing off her right boot and praying the other would unclick. A thick, powerful limb smashed into the floor behind her, sending shockwaves through her lodged boot. It disengaged, and she careered on, grasping the console and thrusting herself towards the double doors.

"Rescue me?" echoed in her ears. "They came to imprison me. To put me in virtual hell at the whim of the Bustans. A gift to seal the cessation, those traitorous bastards." Rebekah gripped the edge of the doorway and yanked herself through. A clatter of gunfire behind rattled off something hard, the bullets pinging around her hardly slowing with the lack of grav. A shout in her comms, and a crunch had her fervently checking her HUD. Both Savvo and Arin's markers had them in the far side of the room. Both were in the yellow, and her stomach flipped.

"Survive, regroup," she shouted in the comms, and gripped the corner of the T-junction, throwing herself forward to bounce off the wall. "Come on you bastard. The Butcher, is it? That's what they call you. A hacker of bodies. No hero of ours."

Her comms roared in response, and without glancing behind, she activated her boots, running, desperate to give her squad time. The deck reverberated as ZZ3 pounded after, each step getting closer.

"Arin, come back. Arin!"

She ran on, eyeing the bulkhead door. It was unwieldy in her mind and would take too long to swing about. And even if she managed it, what then? Abandon Savvo? Arin?

"Come back, Arin. Come back!" she bellowed again. Her chest strained. She engaged more of the chip, consciously eradicating the pain from her nerves and boosting the adrenaline. It was her last play, and useless against a warbot. With the extra biochemical impetus, she dived again, angling for the ceiling. ZZ3's limbs sailed by, swiping at her legs and missing. A clang against the wall cheered her, perhaps it slowed the metal beast down.

Who was she kidding?

"Rebekah," came a voice, barely a whisper over the comms. "What's happening?"

"ZZ3 on my tail, I'm about to be mush. Stop it."

"Uh?"

Silence followed, filled only by her heavy breathing, when something slapped at her ankle, sending her into a spin. ZZ3 was no more than three metres back, four limbs thundering into the deck, the other two lashing out for her. Behind those, she saw the glow of a plasma torch igniting on its back.

"How many fucking ways do you want to kill me?" she said, knowing the adrenaline kick was beginning to affect her thoughts. ZZ3's lunge for her had knocked her off course, sending her away from the primary exit to the lift shaft that now whizzed by.

"Comms are blocked," said Arin. "Rebekah, there's no way I can get in."

She hit the junction, dragging her legs underneath to shove herself up the roughly built diagonal deck. ZZ3 slammed into the wall behind, its speed barely blunted, the plasma torch searing a hole into the metal wall. Her hands hit the deck, and she shoved off again. A limb lashed at her wrist, slicing the plate in two and scraping against the inner skin. She left it to the suit, hoping once enabled, the safety protocols remained active.

"Arin, it spoke to me. Just me, in *my* comms. Trace that." she shouted, eyeing the hatch that lay ahead. Her momentum carried her on, and she hit the curved metal door with a thump. ZZ3 barrelled after, its limbs shoving the warbot hard to ram into her. Rebekah smashed against the hatch. The spacesuit compressed. Her breath erupted. Alerts sprung everywhere as the seals began to give.

The hatch burst open – the hinges Arin had hand cut giving way – and she flew backwards into the tunnel, gasping for air. ZZ3 batted the spinning hatch out of the way, red eyes glaring, and only for her.

"They didn't come to rescue me ... they liberated me. Made me see that humanity is weak-willed." The plasma torch lashed.

"ZZ3, pacifist program ZZ, action code Breakers. I say again," Arin's voice seeped into her ears while the plasma tip speared towards her vulnerable helmet, "pacifist program ZZ, action code Breakers. Night, night, buddy."

"ZZ3 comply. Night, night." The words filled her mind, the plasma burning hot mere centimetres from her helmet. "Captain," said the bot, and it pulled the torch away. A pair of outstretched limbs gently grasped her arms, and ZZ3 spun about, its back taking the impact as they hit the tunnel wall.

Rebekah felt the jolt, but her eyes were for the bot. Five seconds ago it had marked her for innumerable deaths, and now cradled her like a baby. The image wouldn't leave her mind, and the world came crashing in as the adrenaline wore off.

"Ahhhhh," slipped from her lips, though by no means deliberately. "What the hell?"

Her eyes fluttered open, acutely aware a surge – like an intravenous hit of caffeine and pain relief – thrilled along her veins, but ten times stronger.

"Sorry," said Savvo. "But we need to get out of here ASAP."

Rebekah blinked, then sat up, realising Savvo had one arm holding her down on the console. A glance over to Arin showed he was fine, though a graze and bruising lay across his cheek and eye, with a sombre look to his face.

"What a rush," he said, and a wide grin cut through his low mood. "Did you see that? Shit. That was sooo clossssse."

Rebekah thumped him on the shoulder, quickly regretting it as her mind spun, still out of kilter. "I saw every-fucking-thing," she replied. "From this far away." She held her thumb and forefinger a centimetre apart to make her point, and then eased herself off the table to engage her boots. ZZ3 loomed near the double doors, its posture passive. She shook her head, unable to quite process the complete switch from deathkill-robot-ten-thousand, to puppy dog. She collected the carbine Savvo handed her, and attached it to the magclip after checking the remaining ammo.

Savvo tapped the containment box, its lights flickering, two unattached, thick cables protruding from its base. "The box is attached to the floor."

"More embedded. Part of the whole system," added Arin, sweeping his hands around the room. "One big bastard computer, with this as its core. Not a truthful word from a noble's lips has been spoken."

"An AI?" she said.

"Big enough, but it's not talking. Unlike whatever was in your comms," said Arin. "And whatever that was, emanated from the box itself. At least the transmissions I could trace-match."

Savvo grimaced, tapping the back of his helmet. "We discussed it being the Bustan Battle AI, but who knows?"

"It spoke to me, afterwards. I accused it of being the Butcher. It didn't argue, just got angry. Told me they were here to imprison him, send him to the Bustans." She tapped the box. "We open it, screw Duboit. Open it and then we get out of this hellhole and leave its demons behind."

Arin nodded. "I agree. ZZ3, if you please. Protocol 'open the damned box', action code Wrecking Crew."

ZZ3 lumbered over, taking its place at the box's side while the rest stood away. A heave produced little movement, and the bot fired up the plasma torch, making Rebekah flinch. It only took a few seconds, and with the torch stowed, robotic limbs heaved. The lid shifted aside, appearing like an archaeologist sliding open a stone coffin. The bot stepped away, turning its body and returning to its station. Rebekah eyed ZZ3 warily, ice sliding down her spine. A bead of sweat perhaps, except it was cold.

They all stood around the box, lips parted, trying to process what lay inside. A broken, shrivelled cadaver. Clearly dead, but wearing the uniform of an Almaarian general. The tufted beard and moustache were familiar from the news clips. Asham, the Scourge. Or, as they would forever know him now—

"The Butcher," whispered Savvo. "In the dead flesh. I don't understand."

"Virtual hell," said Rebekah, gripping the sides of the containment box. "ZZ3 mentioned a virtual hell. Being traded to go to prison. It's brain patterning. Senti tech. They were going to copy his *self*, his *mind*, and give it to the Bustans."

"Except he didn't want to go. Threw a fit ... murdered and killed until there was no one left but the rewired personal guard." Arin stepped away from the containment box, peering back towards the exit. "The hybrids. That was the work here. The prisoners, just like the Bustans said, and it spread."

"Or a wider test, released when he knew the end was on the cards," said Savvo. "But where is he, *it*, now?"

Rebekah shrugged. "It had control of ZZ3. You think ...?" She glanced over to the bot.

"No way." Arin spread his arms wide, taking in the entire computerised room. "It's like copying all the world's books onto a thumbnail sketchpad. Not happening. Megalomaniacs tend to be just that, with a sprinkle of ego on the side. ZZ3 is just too small."

"So, we know, at the very least, he's not inside that body or that box?" asked Rebekah. They both agreed. "Then ZZ3, protocol extraction, target containment box." She flagged the image from her HUD. "Action code Wrecking Crew. Cut the bastard out, and you have permission to do it really, really badly." She eyed the rest of the room and flagged the lot. "All of this is in the way. Make sure it gets a little Wrecking Crew love."

ZZ3 stomped in, and the plasma torch flared once again.

"Come on. We have work to do."

Chapter 39

Tremil yawned, stretching as she pushed herself off the berth in her shared cabin. She checked the much-reduced collection of toys on the table, noting those that Heki had pocketed and taken with her – a signal to her mood and what comfort she needed. In the lab, she had made cloth dolls from her bedding, tying ragged material together and hiding them away from prying eyes. The hated scientists always found the dolls, delighting in demonstrating their investigative skills. Tremil was sure they thought it was a game, and not a desperate need to love something that gave unconditional love in return – to cuddle an inanimate object because it couldn't hurt you back. Now all they had were those toys they had rescued and buried in their survival kit before the salvagers had ripped them from their home, the *Sunstar*.

She adjusted a couple of the printed toys, a brief smile crossing her face as she thought of Arin and the care he took making them – and the sheer emotion he exuded when handing them over. They both knew when a new toy was on the way, he glowed all the way down the corridor, shedding love and fear around the ship. But that ship hung dead and lifeless out in the black, as empty as the void.

With a huff, she checked her skinsuit was perfectly aligned, and slipped on the uniform. The loose material chafed and annoyed, but it also spoke of belonging – of having a place. She was crew and loved. The skinsuit, with its pressure against her body, reminded Tremil all this was real and not a dream. A comfort to her senses, and that she wouldn't wake up back in the dreaded restraining mask chained to a laboratory wall. The combination of both sets of clothing helped make sense of the world.

Being on a different ship, however, did not.

She exited the cabin and headed for the medbay. Davina's monitor beeped merrily away, and Tremil quickly checked her stats. The Incini was stable, on the mend, and if they had the mind, could wake her up. At the moment, she let her sleep in a drug-induced state, agreeing with the medbot that the sedatives could slowly be reduced.

With a sigh, she stood by Hendricks, taking the woman's hand. They had stripped off what they could, and adapted the suit to make her sanitary needs more pleasant, but beyond that they dared not remove the beloved engineer from the spacesuit and its supportive pressure. Tremil hardened her thoughts, trying to pull them in as Hendricks twitched and mithered in her sleep. Her own fears for the woman, she knew, would send the ex-captain into hellish nightmares. It was a struggle, and she let go of her hand, forcing herself out of the room so as not to make things worse.

Tremil paused, immersed in a wave of pure joy rolling down the corridor from the cockpit.

"Tremil," echoed over the ship's comms. "They're on their way. They're safe."

Her own thoughts collided with Heki's, a relief then that no one was awake in the ship as there wasn't an earworm strong enough to have saved them from the tumult roaring through the corridors. She ran, her magboots clomping against the deck, to take her place in the co-pilot's chair. The trembling girl scanned the incoming message and played the audio back. The sound of Rebekah's voice made her weak at the knees. Heki's hand fell on hers, just briefly, a squeeze and it was gone – but enough. They were no longer alone again.

Heki had set up the responder beacon, and on checking ZZ3's trajectory, corrected the *Maverick*'s orbit. They had both filled their time learning, devouring what they could from the ship's computer. Occupying their minds lest the nightmares creep back in. She had no doubt Heki knew enough flight theory to have got them home, as long as nothing unexpected happened. And she had learned enough about spinal injuries to settle deep worries in her heart about Hendricks' prospects.

"There," announced Heki, tapping at the screen. The image enhanced and over the next few minutes the bot came into view. Savvo, Arin and Rebekah flew in sync around ZZ3, its massive limbs wrapped about a strange box whose ragged edges glowed with dying lights.

Tremil stared at the monitor, trying and failing to suppress the sheer joy. A gentle finger wiped away a tear streaming down her cheek, Heki's, and wide-eyed, her sister watched it form a rivulet along her skin while her own settled in the corner of her eyes. Such emotions were dangerous to others, to their friends – their family – but they would overwhelm the crew if they didn't release them soon. With a strange relief, the twins took each other in their arms, and wept until they were empty.

Rebekah strapped down the containment box in the hold. She felt completely out of place, not only in a ship that was not hers, but as its captain. Where was she, and for that matter, where were her crew in all of this now? They had, despite the trauma of events upon the asteroid, been at home with their identity. Together, they were the Breakers, and it had felt right. But what now?

"ZZ3, protocol silent guard, action code Wrecking Crew," she said.

The bot took two steps and settled by the containment box. It had flown them in perfect unison out of the *Scourge*, and subsequently the asteroid family. Had saved them during a few hairy moments as they came across new trajectories and shifts in orbit. But unease still sat on her shoulders as she remembered the events in the Butcher's lab.

She walked down the corridor, listening to the voice coming from the medbay. Arin, all sobs and verbalised pain as he held Hendricks in his arms. She made to pass by, to let him have his space, but she couldn't. With a tap on the door, she entered, finding Arin stripped from his spacesuit and smelling like he'd had a week in a sweatbox. Rebekah lay her hand on his shoulder, the man sprawled over Hendricks' prone body. He slid off and wrapped his arms about Rebekah's waist. She left him there, his head against her hip, her own hand upon the sleeping engineer. They said nothing, what was there to say? They both loved the woman fiercely, and she was in a mess. Alive though, and in life there was always hope. Unlike the ravaged bodies back on the *Scourge*, who had become the Butcher's vile experiments.

"We will get her the best help we can," she said, pushing back the tears, trying to sound confident. "Whatever it takes."

Arin ran his already wet sleeve over his face, nodding. Red eyes spoke of his pain, but he couldn't speak. She touched his cheek, a final reassurance, and left, sparing a glance to the Incini who slept on beside her. Whatever else had happened on the *Sunstar*, Davina had rescued Hendricks. Sacrificed her lungs and risked her own life to save the engineer. In Rebekah's eyes, these choices weighed heavily in the woman's favour.

Eventually she reached the galley area that, unlike on their ship, was off to one side. It was a little larger than their own and welcome for it. Savvo sat there, hands clasped about a flask of coffee with a second waiting for her. She pulled it free of the table and took a welcome sip.

Savvo's eyes were keen, focused. His gaze full of life. It took her by surprise, considering just how tired they all were.

He held up his hand. "No stims, before you ask. I know that look."

"Then what's on your mind?"

He tapped at the slate recovered from the cockpit, and held it over, taking a sip from his coffee with a smug smile. "That is an autodrive. Fully fuelled, and serviced, I have to say, regularly. Toms knew to keep his equipment in good order."

"You mean ...?"

"I do. With the *Sunstar*'s kit and this, we can get our baby back home. To M4, get her repaired or if that's not possible, we can sell her for parts."

"I'll be honest, Savvo. I have no idea what comes next. Toms, this crew ..." She sat by his side, cradling the coffee. Her hands shook a little, and Savvo squeezed her fingers.

"We splice the vid evidence, like we've done before. The *Sunstar*'s feed will be damning, their intent was clearly murder. And the black box on board the *Maverick* will corroborate their positions and manoeuvres – all the data Karal will cross reference. We just need to doctor the ships' recordings. The girls will be safe, we can do this." Savvo gave her fingers a reassuring squeeze, then backed off.

Rebekah cracked both her thumbs, one after the other, then took a sip of her drink. "The girls can't tell me what they did. I think the trauma is buried deep, but they hinted ... they hinted at what happened when we first found them. Every drop of fear came out all at once. *We* will need to splice the vids first, then let them have that to smooth out. We can't have the twins watch what happened all over again."

"On that, we most definitely agree."

Rebekah downed the indigestion tablet, her stomach roiling and joining the headache creeping across her brow. She discarded the slate, sitting back on the chair with a sigh and massaging her sore shoulder. There was an expected knock on the cabin door.

"Come in," she said, and adjusted the chair next to her, its base locking to the deck. Davina walked in, her face pale, lips as red as the rims about her eyes. Rebekah gestured towards the chair.

"I feel like I'm about to be interviewed," said the Incini. "Or questioned." Her voice was a rasp, and she took careful breaths between each sentence. But the prognosis was good. Better than could have been expected thanks to the girls' speedy intervention.

"I know what I saw on the cameras, and heard over the comms," said Rebekah. "All of it could be interpreted in different ways. You could have been selling the girls out to save your own skin, or doing so to save theirs." Rebekah shrugged. "I'm sure you'll have a story to back you up whichever way it falls."

Davina made to speak, but under Rebekah's stare, changed her mind.

"You saved Hendricks, and the twins. Whatever else happens, whatever sins against my crew you may or may not be guilty of, they are wiped clean. The only stain is what sits in the cargo hold." Rebekah waited for the Incini to speak, refusing to fill in the gap.

"I told them they were telepaths," Davina said quietly, as if to save the strain on her breathing. "You can check that. Not empaths."

"And you knew they'd be shit-scared ... You killed Toms and his crew as much as the girls did." Rebekah nodded, a smile slowly appearing. "Sneaky, conniving and a little evil. I like that. Fine traits in an Incini. Did you see what they did?"

"No, I was unconscious when they brought me on board." Her eyes met Rebekah's, narrowing.

Rebekah made a call at that moment; one she hoped wouldn't condemn her crew and the twins. But short of throwing the Incini out of the airlock, she had little choice. Her finger tapped the slate, and she slid it around. Fear-filled words spilled from the speakers, immersed in pure hate and self-loathing that cut off to the sound of gurgling blood. The Incini's hands rose to her mouth and Rebekah clicked it off.

"Two others spaced themselves. They found Toms ... never mind. They know what they are. Can you imagine how that makes them feel? The constant sword hanging above your head ... and over those you have learned to trust."

Davina pushed herself up from the chair and headed for the door. She paused there, turning back to face Rebekah.

"You have completed the mission under the terms of the contract. Nothing the girls did affected the outcome. If you can provide evidence to that fact, then Mr Duboit will have to follow through on those terms. That part is up to you." Davina coughed, a little blood splattering onto her hand as she covered her mouth.

"You'd better get yourself back to the medbay. But one last thing. Do you know what's in that box?"

"No," she replied, shaking her head slightly for emphasis. "It is not part of my role. I am here to affirm the contract is fulfilled. You have the box intact. You were to bring it to M1. Those were the terms."

Rebekah looked away and down at the table for a second. She decided against pushing any further. They had all been manipulated by Mr Duboit, and what she feared most was the man would continue to do so. Renege and threaten to reveal the truth in return for more favours. Their hope lay in Davina, her role as an Incini, and she needed the woman onside.

"Good," she said.

Chapter 40

Rebekah bounced from foot to foot, the feeling of gravity on M1 immensely satisfying after the past few weeks. Her body still ached, and the extra weight did not help, but it still felt good.

The lift pinged, and the doors slid open. There were no horrors inside, just ordinary people going about their everyday lives. Davina entered ahead of her, and Savvo followed in. Within a few minutes they were at Mr Duboit's stark door. There was no name plate to announce himself to the world, no ostentatious proclamation of his money and power. The irony made her smile when she thought of the Butcher and his lab.

Davina pressed the pad which lit up and the door swung open. The room was just as Rebekah remembered, except the doors to the Incini's office were open. Rebekah took a seat with Savvo sat by her side as they waited.

"This is odd, no?" whispered Savvo, his hand covering his mouth.

Rebekah knew if they wanted to know what he was saying, it wouldn't take much effort. On her last visit, the office had been packed with sensor arrays. A man of Mr Duboit's means would have the best surveillance money – and power – could buy. She simply nodded.

After a few minutes, Davina appeared at the door.

"Mr Duboit is ready to see you," she said. Her posture was stiff, and there was something about her eyes that was off-putting. She remained unwell, but had to confirm the terms in person as decreed by Duboit.

Rebekah rose and followed Davina into her office.

"I have confirmed the terms," she said as they reached the door. "He just wants to see you both." Davina was fiddling with an old-fashioned pen. She clicked it two times, eyeing Rebekah as she did so. "And not me."

Savvo tensed, but Rebekah laid her hand on his arm. If there was danger here, it wasn't physical. His office on the most important asteroid in the Karal domain was the last place for that.

"Thank you," she said. And meant it.

Davina knocked and opened the door.

The first thing to hit Rebekah was the scent in the room. The second, as she activated her chip, that Mr Duboit was apparently here in person, the flicker of the holo-mask confirming her suspicions. She used the wetware to calm her mind.

"Mr Duboit," she said, and approached the chair, hoping Savvo would play along if he had also noticed the change.

"Captain Kahn," Duboit responded. "Please sit."

He didn't even glance at Savvo, and the voice was the same, but the gestures merely similar. Not a bad facsimile, but not Duboit. She sat, hands resting on her lap and eyes only for the holo-mask. The door shut behind with a soft clunk.

Duboit's head tilted to the side, and his hands tapped at the table. It drew her attention, she assumed deliberately. The hand was bare except for two plain rings. She recognised them and understood his intent. A simple message. He knew he had been made, and that he was an Enforcer.

Or to put it less politely, they were in the shit.

"Savvo, stay quiet unless I ask you something," she said, and squeezed his arm. He turned to face her, nonplussed. "This *person* is not Duboit, if he ever existed at all. This is an Emperor's Enforcer, in the flesh. Stay silent."

"Very good, Captain. Or should I say, pilot-sergeant?"

Her skin crawled.

"And Mr Duboit does exist, I assure you. Though, of course, that isn't *their* name. I do know yours, however, and err, Savotini, is it?" The voice hadn't changed either. Still sounding much like she remembered of Duboit.

Savvo nodded.

Erikson continued, "And aboard the ... *Maverick*, we have Kendrich and Enterman of the famous Breakers. Am I right?"

Rebekah didn't respond, what was the point? And besides, there were others her words could betray.

"I'll take that as a yes, which is good. I am going to keep this simple, Captain. You were designated MIA, missing in action, and apparently thought dead under the care of our Bustan friends. Yet here you are, hale and hearty, and acting on behalf of Mr Duboit after eking out a living on the belt. What a surprise, one I am sure Countess Segfi would love to hear about."

Rebekah twitched at that name. Savvo grunted.

"Now you are getting the full picture. I would like to keep your existence out of that noble's ear. It would give me great pleasure to see you carry on living in anonymity." The holo-mask smiled; it was as false a look as she had ever seen. Behind it was a predator, toying with its prey and enjoying it.

"That would be good," she said, her lips dry, voice harsh.

"It would. So, I have a proposal. It's simple, you say yes, you get to live. No, and you won't have time to run. I understand the Countess has her eyes on many, many places. So here it is. You work for me. Maintain your place in Karal Mining, and when I need you to carry out a mission, I whistle, you come like a good dog."

"And the moment we don't, we're fucked," she replied.

"That's about it. However, I am not entirely without means. I understand your ship is damaged, and the *Maverick* maybe impounded further to an investigation. I – sorry – Mr Duboit, will have your ship repaired, and the investigation quashed. You will have to wave the salvage rights, however, to satisfy those lowlifes who have a stake in the *Maverick*. I don't want undue attention going your way. Agreeable?" He smiled again, and she felt powerless all of a sudden. But not hopeless.

"And a stipend? Resources?"

"Yes. Black ops pay grade, and whatever supplies are required for each mission of course."

Rebekah pursed her lips a second, then glanced at Savvo who was upright in his chair. She recognised the glare; he was going to blow any second.

"Agreed. On one more condition."

"Which is?"

And she told him, Savvo relaxing back in his chair, the fury still there but mingled with love, guilt and loyalty.

Erikson switched the infernal holo-mask off, thankful it was the one and only time he'd have to use such a tool around the lowlife Breaker crew. He fiddled with his slate for a moment, thinking over what he would say.

Should he inform his handler that they were soft? That this Rebekah Khan was astute, but emotionally frail? The Breakers were tough bastards by all accounts, remorseless. Yet she had sold her squad out for their ex-captain. Yes, he had guaranteed silence as far as Countess Segfi was concerned, but they both knew it wouldn't last forever. At some point their relationship would sour, their usefulness come to an end. And the Enforcers hated loose threads. They led to loose lips.

But emotions were leverage. Something he could use to squeeze more from his new operatives.

He liked that. He liked that a lot.

Erikson tapped at the slate, deciding to deal with their simple, but expensive, demand first. After all, he wasn't paying.

"Is that Dr Rusenski's department? Bodily rebuilds? Good. This is Mr Duboit. Yes, that one. I need to schedule a major body repair and upgrade."

Chapter 41

"This is Karal Mining Control, come back RCKN5QD. You listening Wrecking Squad? You there, Rebekah?"

Rebekah smiled, and tapped at her comms. "This is ..." She glanced over to Savvo, her eyes glistening. He nodded back, almost, but not quite, breaking out in a grin. "This is the Wrecking Squad, and you are coming in loud and clear, Pike. You got a new stick up your ass today?"

"Not last I checked. We have a rogue bot on K3. Want to go take a look? Apparently, it's been filling the holes back in." Pike sniggered over the comms.

"We got enough fuel to make the trip. We'll take it, Calc and all."

"For a mining bot? What's it gonna do, threaten you with a shovel? Pike out."

Rebekah dropped her comms unit onto the console, the magnet taking hold. "You okay to see us out?"

"Sure am, El Capitaine," Savvo replied, and spun his seat into position ready to tap at the screen. She squeezed him on the shoulder and left, heading for engineering. The twins were surprisingly in the galley, and her mind fed in an earworm as she passed them. They were engrossed in their slates, but even so, being out of their cabin was a step forwards. Rebekah didn't have to look to know what they were researching for – it would be the biology of a Senti symbiote – she had put them in charge of trying to keep the alien alive.

Arin's strained, berating voice, echoed from engineering. When she entered, he was halfway up the drive unit and strapped into a harness.

"You should be doing this. You're supposed to exercise the bloody implant, not lounge about all day," he said, a metal probe sliding into whatever part he was working on.

"You know that's not true," replied Hendricks, easing her back, and then swirling her hips in a circular motion. "Movement, yes. Exercise, no. They said I needed someone who loved me to look after my health."

"Know anyone?" replied Arin.

"Arin," cut in Rebekah, half wanting not to interrupt. "You had chance to run that diagnostic on ZZ3 yet?"

"No, Captain. Mardy pants here has had me running over all the patches the 'sloppy bastards from M4' have done." His broad smile lit up the room, and if Rebekah was honest, her heart.

She had done the right thing.

This moment, right now, was enough.

Rebekah felt Hendricks' eyes on her. The engineer, her ex-captain, knew exactly what she was thinking. Hendricks hadn't said anything to her since the operation. Rebekah had assumed she was fuming over their betrayal, and the lack of fight she had put up. But the gaze spoke much deeper than that. A thank you for her life back. The doctors had predicted complete paralysis, yet power talks, and now she had a rebuilt spine and hips. More metal and wire than was in their heads. And back, of course, to being the vital cog in the Wrecking Squad that she had informed the dubious Mr Duboit they couldn't function without.

With a wave, unable to put into words her feelings, she left engineering and entered the cargo hold. ZZ3 sat inert by the containment unit they had snuck onto the ship. A double-cross was a double-cross. Mr Duboit had obviously informed on them, whether under Enforcer duress or not, making the contract null and void. Right now, they needed whatever bargaining chips they could find, and what lay in the box had to be one. Though for the life of her, she had no idea how to use it. They had cleansed the lab and the *Scourge* as best they could before they left. Wired the drive on the frigate to blow, opened every bulkhead they had time for. Something would survive the inferno, she was sure. Partial evidence of the testing perhaps, enough samples for those who wanted to dig deep. But it wasn't going to be easy.

A funeral pyre for the crew of the *Scourge*. It still felt right.

"ZZ3, protocol alteration, action code Rebekah Khan."

"Affirmative, waiting on stipulations," the bot replied.

"Action code Wrecking Crew negated, replaced by action code Wrecking Squad. Confirm."

"Confirmed. Wrecking Squad action code agreed. Voice coding transferred."

"Good. Run protocol diagnostic, action code Wrecking Squad."

"Diagnostic protocol running." The bot's lights flashed. "Parameters?"

"Threat assessment, software viruses," she paused, "hardware and software compromises. Status report."

Four red eyes flickered.

"Hardware compromise evident, but negated. Software compromise evident, but negated. No viral presence. Threat assessment nil."

She stared at the bot, not understanding what her expectations were. But she couldn't get the concern out of her mind. She turned away, heading for the door to the corridor when it came to her.

No pause. No hitch in its response. Not once had it called Arin 'our glorious leader'.

She turned back to the bot. Was the Butcher still in there? Or was she reading too much into simple changes? Memories of their battle, perhaps, causing a chink of paranoia.

"ZZ3 status of pacifist protocol, action code Wrecking Squad," she said.

"ZZ3 unit is under pacification. Threat assessment nil."

And here ends The Wrecking Squad.
Watch out for the return of Rebekah and her crew in Butcher's Folly.

The Wrecking Squad Series

Thank you for choosing to spend your precious time reading The Wrecking Squad. To know that someone has considered a story worthy of reading to the end is the greatest honour an author can have.

This series has been stewing at the back of my mind for the last 12 months, so to get it onto the page has not only been a great relief, but also an opportunity to see something I have nurtured come to fruition.

And there is so much more to come! I have planned three more books in the series, with the potential for even more. I have so many stories to tell, and subscribing to my newsletter will keep you informed about any upcoming releases. It will also mean you can download Redemption Tour for FREE. This is the origin story for the Breakers, and explores what really happened when the Breakers first met the twins. Find it at:

www.nicksnape.com/subscribe

Redemption Tour - A Wrecking Squad Story

My new series, The Wrecking Squad, involves a squad of ex-Marines on the run. Their origin story is available in a FREE novella, Redemption Tour, which you can download by subscribing to my newsletter. Yes, absolutely free. Not only that but you get a second book.

The Lost Squad - A Weapons of Choice Novel

The Stratan Marines who we first meet within Hostile Contact have a surprise in store. A second squad followed them to Earth, those who appear later in the series in Book 7, Legion Earth. The Lost Squad, a FREE full-length novel, details their arrival soon after Yasuko's ship left the Solar System in Hostile Contact. The novel charts the alien Marines' action-packed experiences as countries and mercenaries vie for their technology and knowledge. They are a superb bunch of characters and were a real joy to write.

If you wish to learn more about their history on Earth, and I suggest you do as it's an excellent novel, then please subscribe to my newsletter via the link below:

www.nicksnape.com/subscribe

About the Author

Nick Snape has been steeped in Science Fiction and Fantasy since his friends first dragged him from his schoolwork and stuck a book under his nose. Lost to the world of imagination, he became a teacher by accident, though he thoroughly enjoyed developing the joy of reading and writing in his pupils. Having retired after thirty years, he thought it was high time to practise what he preached.

Nick's books feature everything from all out, heart-pounding, fast-paced action to thoughtful, character driven twists on the fantasy and sci-fi genres. Genetics to Artificial Intelligence, Artifice Dragons to Soul-Eating enemies, nothing is off the menu.

BOOKS BY NICK SNAPE

The Wrecking Squad

Butcher's Folly (The Wrecking Squad Book 2)
A court conspiracy, a rundown den of thieves, and the Bustan Space Navy on the way. What could possibly go wrong?
Recovering from the events aboard the Scourge, the Wrecking Squad return to Karal and their old job briefly before the Emperor's Enforcers come knocking. With no choice, they travel to the scum-laden Windward System and Benetai, a rundown space station full of the barrel-scrapings of humanity and the Senti. Tasked with recovering Marine wetware, they find their contact dead, the tech missing and the Bustan Navy on the way. Join Rebekah and her crew as they navigate conspiracies, in-fighting and battle tech, in their own inimitable style while keeping a deadly secret from the prying eyes of the Emperor's Court.

Warmonger's Wrath (The Wrecking Squad Book 3)
When the Warmonger steals something precious, how far will The Wrecking Squad go to get them back?
Like hounds on an Enforcer's leash, Rebekah and the crew of the *Sunstar* are bullied into a punishing schedule. Returning from an intense, sickening mission, they are immediately sent out to infiltrate the secret bases of

Court nobles hiding their intent as they play at war with real troops and weapons. But the Warmonger is stirring, Countess Segfi flexing her muscles as the truth about the *Scourge*'s secrets are exposed. The ex-Breakers have something she wants, and she'll stop at nothing to retrieve it. With Rebekah and The Wrecking Squad caught up in deadly Court politics, the Countess takes a step too far, and the dogs of war slip their leash. You may shatter a Breaker's heart, but they sure as hell won't stand around and let you do it twice.

Weapons of Choice Series

*'A truly epic saga of riveting sci-fi thrill*ers...'

It started with a failed military training exercise and an alien incursion, desperate and on the hunt. But survival was just the beginning...

After encountering a buried spaceship and its rogue AI on Earth, Finn, Zuri, and Corporal Smith (deceased) take refuge on an alien home world where they unravel the truth about the forced colonisation of Earth-like planets. With the ship's AI providing advanced nano-weaponry and evolving alien battle tech, Finn and Delta blaze a trail through the galaxy seeking a way home, walking a fine line between vengeance and redemption in this thought-provoking action sci-fi series.

Hostile Contact

Return Protocol

Zuri's War

Finn's War

Alien Rebirth

Invasive Species

Legion Earth

Nemesis Earth

The Scorching Standalone Series

The World in My Hands

"A deeply nuanced sci-fi standalone with slow-burn suspense, a diverse and unorthodox cast of characters and a spaceship straight out of your worst nightmares"

The world is heading towards global collapse as the Scorching takes full effect. Salvation vessels orbit the Earth, waiting to transport the chosen few away from danger and to start again; ten plantships grown by an alien species for the wealthiest and most powerful, or those lucky enough to be selected by lottery. Yet not all is well on board. Dark secrets lurk in the corridors and depths of their respective ships, dragging Jenna and Seth into a world of malice and violence they thought they had left far behind.

Just Press Play

"Staggeringly original and timely release from a masterful voice in modern sci-fi."

On a devastated Earth, the Drathken arrive with the promise of healing the planet. When anti-alien terrorists threaten the accord, Cop and Vlogger Josh Nkosi, and his MARC unit, chase terrorists into the Burnout Zone only to come face to face with humanity's stark future when the hunt takes a devastating twist. As a conspiracy emerges, Nkosi is forced on a dark path of discovery.

Warriors of Spirit and Bone

A Dragon of the Veil
"An INCREDIBLE start to anew, dark epic fantasy series."
In a realm no longer devoid of magic, the fate of a people rests with Laoch and Sura, and the Gods' weapons they bear – a thousand years of faith and lies reconciled in a single moment of hope and redemption. With whispers of an ancient evil's return, they are left reeling by their enemy's power, one even the Gods' weapons fear. For cast in iron and spiritfire - here be dragons.

A City of Ashes
"A work of coal-dark fantasy that is continually surprising, provocative, and compulsively entertaining."
With the Veil Dragon, Nathair, seemingly under the Spirit Captain's control, Laoch pushes away the grief of his first encounter with the metal beast and hunts for a weapon his new and distrusted ally insists they can use against the coming Constructor invasion. For an Emperor consumed by revenge has a new artifice, one that hungers to enslave.

A Queen in Blood
"A dark ambience largely unmatched by anything else I've read."
As the invasion of Brandshold begins, the realm is haunted by the Infected – devastated and spirit-poisoned townsfolk who hunger for flesh and souls to salve their pain. When the city of Jense falls to a wave of bloody teeth and foul claws, the Constructor's Emperor strikes, shattering city walls with his artifice dragon, and the dreaded *Kraken* soulship. For a queen bathed in the blood of her own people, hope lies in the alchemy of the meisters, a traitorous mechanical dragon, and loyal but broken soldiers.

Acknowledgements

As with all authors, this book would never have existed without the dedicated friends and family who were there by my side throughout the entire process. The least I can do is give them a mention for their patience with my obsession! My Beta readers, supporters and fiercest critics have been Pak, Paul Derwent, Martin Lejeune, Bryan Chaffin and TK Toppin. Amazing friends who have put that aside to make sure whatever I put out there was something they wanted to read

Julie, my wife, needs a special mention. Over the past few years she has kept me going, being there at every step through the dark and joyful times. I can't believe how lucky I am.

Finally, the New Year and Pub Night Crews. Wouldn't be here without you.

Thank you all.

Printed by Libri Plureos GmbH in Hamburg, Germany